For Joel, Jessica and Sarah,
my beacons of encouragement always.

ACKNOWLEDGEMENTS

I began this project in 2012 and to say the insurmountable (and valuable) lessons learned from then to now is truly an understatement.

My heart-felt thanks go out to Anne Bloomsburg, my editor during the creation of this book. She challenged me often and because of this, I have grown as a writer in many ways I never could have fathomed without her guidance.

To Sue-Anne Wilson and Christine Laudick—two exceptional women from Eagle Ridge Ranch in Gunnison, Colorado: on a cold (and snowy) day in May 2012, you welcomed this stranger to the splendor of this magnificent ranch which provided the inspiration for the backdrop of this story. I will hold the images of such majesty dearly in my memories always.

I am blessed and fortunate to continue to temper my pen by doing book reviews. It all started with Irene Watson of Reader Views. She is no longer with us, but her spirit lives on. To Ellen Feld of Feathered Quill Book Reviews. She keeps my war chest filled with enticing reads always and I am honored to be a member and contributor to this fantastic forum.

It is important for me to pause often and reflect on the incredible network of friends and family who continue to offer overwhelming support. Thank you to Joni Anderson whose spirit soars like an eagle, Dorothy Hanson for those girls' weekends filled with laughter and (sometimes) tears. Thank you to Betsy Miller: thank God for lunch hour chats and the girl who can still have fun in a box! Ebony Gore, my patient and witty sounding board; who, without a doubt, gets me. Thank you to Madame Ellis: Je vous aime mon ami. Thanks to Marty Bigley of Merry Point Farm for opening the gates of this spectacular place and allowing me to roam freely with my new four-legged friend Clover for some memorable photo ops. To my 'big sister', Linda Brice: I have the greatest love and respect for you and thank you for goading me into picking up my pen again... I love you.

Lastly, thank you to my husband Joel. Your love and true friendship rests in my heart always. To my beautiful 'baby girls':

Jessica Leigh and Sarah Rose; a mother could never want or hope for two more amazing children.

Part I

1

It was nearly seven o'clock when I stirred. The western skyline of the Denver city limits was behind us. I was happy that I had pushed through the previous night and made it to Evergreen. I wanted to wake up and see that we were a part of the mountains. I chose Evergreen because it was close to Red Rocks. I wanted to stop there before continuing our climb into the mountains so that Dani could see the park. I also wanted to see it again.

The sun was at work sweeping away the few remaining stars left behind from the receding night. We pulled out onto the service road and headed toward Morrison. I was excited to make our Red Rocks pit stop before we settled in for the remainder of our drive.

"Hey, Dani?"

"Yeah?"

"There's a place right up here that I'd like to stop for a few minutes to show you."

No response.

"Would you like to do that?" I asked.

"What is it?"

"It's called Red Rocks. It's an outdoor amphitheater where they hold a summer concert series each year."

"We're going to a concert? Seriously?" She was horrified.

"No, silly, it's barely seven o'clock in the morning and a weekday. We're not going to a concert. I just wanted you to see this place because it's pretty. I thought it would be a nice break since we're going to be in the car again all day. I also thought you might want to take a couple of photos. Maybe I could snap a few of you by some of the rock formations with your phone and you could twitter them to Chelsea," I offered.

Dani laughed. "Mom, you don't *twitter* stuff; you *tweet* it," she corrected me.

"Oh. Okay. Well, do you want to stop so we can get some photos for you to tweet?" I corrected myself.

"Sure. I mean, it sounds like we're gonna go anyway, so I don't know why you're asking me."

She dug into her pockets for her earbuds.

1

"Dani, can you please hold off on jamming those things into your ears until after we leave Red Rocks? I really want to enjoy the experience with you. We've driven nearly 2,000 miles together and have barely spoken a word to each other the entire way. I haven't asked you to do one thing this entire ride, and now I am. Can you please humor me just for now and not plug in? It's not like we're going to spend the day here. I just want to stop and walk around a bit, primarily to show it to you. That's all. Dani, can you do that for me?"

"Okay, Mom, whatever." She stuffed her earbuds back into her pocket and stared out the window.

As we drove around the next bend, to our left appeared Red Rocks Park in all her glory. Back up on the hillside were several walls and tables and sandstone formations of various sizes and shapes. The only man-made parts of the theater were the bleachers and the stage, hidden from view of the road. Everything else was the product of nature. There was a time when the park was considered to be one of the seven natural wonders of the world. Some of the most notable music royalty had graced its stage over the years: the Grateful Dead and the Beatles, for example, Dani, of course, would look at me like I had three heads if I shared that last bit of trivia with her. She knew who the Beatles were, but if I threw the Grateful Dead at her, she would probably roll her eyes and utter one of her profound "whatevers" in response.

We parked in the lower lot near the steps that led up to the amphitheater. We would be able to stand at the top and look down the bleachers onto the stage. It wasn't a very long climb, but it was definitely steep. About halfway up, I realized that I didn't have the lung capacity of a twenty-year-old anymore.

"Dani, you go ahead," I suggested, "I'm going to rest here for a minute and catch my breath."

She looked worried. "Are you okay?" she asked sincerely. "I mean, it's no big deal to me if you want to turn around."

"I'm fine," I insisted. "I'm just getting adjusted to the altitude. It's been a long time since I've been in this thin air. I just need to pace myself, and, yes, I'm fine. You go ahead. I'll catch up."

She spun around and continued to take the steps two at a time. I watched her finish the climb and round the corner underneath the huge

2

table rock that jutted out far above her head. I caught my breath and continued my climb. When I got to the top and rounded the same point Dani had moments before, I couldn't contain myself any longer. I looked across the park at the many walls and monoliths that surrounded the bevy of bleachers below me. The bleachers cascaded like a perfect waterfall and emptied into their riverbed of the stage. A slight breeze blew from one end of the arena to the other. The air felt cool and clear against my skin. Dani zigzagged her way down the bleachers to the stage. About midway, she stopped and looked up at me. She smiled, waved, and finished running down the remaining few bleachers to the stage.

I wanted to run after her but opted to pull up a seat on the higher bleachers and just watch her. The space was good for both of us. We'd been trapped together in the car for three days with another full day on the road ahead of us. For now, we both needed to get rid of some pent-up energy and do so in our own space. "This was a good idea, Lou," I whispered to myself. "Don't worry about assigning an educational tag to this place for her. Let her formulate her own opinion. Don't tell her about the concerts and the fun and the craziness you experienced here. She doesn't need to know about any of it. Someday, maybe one or two stories, but for now, just let her enjoy her first time at Red Rocks just like you did a long time ago. Let her make the memory she wants it to be for her."

A couple of hawks circled high above me. I leaned back to watch them. I'd been sitting there daydreaming for a while when Dani interrupted my escape.

"Hey, Mom?"

I sat up.

"Will you take my picture with those rocks in the background? This place is awesome. I wanna send a picture to Chelsea. She's not gonna believe this," she exclaimed.

"Sure, baby. After that we should think about getting back on the road. We still have a few hours to go before we get to the ranch. I'd like to get there before the sun goes down."

"Sure," she said. "I just want to get this picture before we go."

I snapped a few photos, and with the last click, Dani grabbed her phone and ran off ahead of me. I finished the climb to the top of the bleachers and stopped to take one last look behind me. The hawks had gone, but the breeze was still blowing. I looked down the bleachers to the stage below and let out a deep sigh. Being here was good. The gentle breeze provided a sense of reassurance, and the tranquility of the silence of the rocks comforted me. I felt right about this trip, right that it was a start in a direction towards renewal. I paused for one last glimpse of the majestic scene around me and headed back down the trail to the parking lot. Dani stood by the passenger door of our car, laughing and chattering away on her phone. No doubt she had already sent her photos to Chelsea, and a phone call was in order to critique them properly. Seeing that a slight crack had formed in Dani's formidable suit of anger was also good. I wasn't going to hope for miracles, but I would gratefully accept these baby steps encouraging me that we were headed in the right direction.

We drove through Morrison and got back on westbound I-70. Dani quickly resumed her copilot role, and that third passenger of silence settled in between us. I turned my attention toward the incredible scenery around us and concentrated on making the climb. Colorado seems to be the one place that, no matter what time of the year, is gorgeous. Winter storms could be formidable, but they were counterbalanced by equally beautiful summers. The wildflowers were in bloom along the roadside, and their patches scattered color across the meadows leading down to the river bank. The river level was still high from the spring runoff.

We drove on in silence. We made it through the Eisenhower Tunnel and were on the ascent toward Vail Pass. I needed to stop and stretch. I knew that we could stop at the scenic overlook at the top of the pass. Once we reached the summit of Vail Pass, I pulled off onto the scenic overlook. Dani pulled her earbuds out and looked over at me.

"Why are we stopping here?" she asked.

"I just need to stretch my legs a bit. This is such a pretty place; I thought you might enjoy the scenery and a break too. Wanna get out for a minute?" I asked, trying to encourage her.

"Sure."

We got out of the car, went around to the front end, and leaned against the hood. The day was stunning. The sky was endless blue, the temperature had to be in the midseventies, and the only sound was that of the infrequent occurrence of a car as it zoomed by on the highway behind us. I looked out across the valley below us and at the majestic mountains

4

in the distance. A slight breeze toyed with a clump of my hair, sweeping it across my forehead and dangling it in my eyes. Eventually, I gave into the challenge of constantly having to tuck it back behind my ear and just let it go. Dani had wandered away from the car and found a rock to sit on. She plugged back in and sat there with her chin resting in her hands, elbows planted in her knees. She looked content to just sit and watch nothing and everything at the same time.

I took a couple of deep breaths and thought about our road trip coming to an end. A part of me wanted to get on with summer, but an even bigger part wanted to relish these final hours because the past few days had been predictable. We drove. We stopped. We ate and drove some more. Monotonous, yes, but it was also a tangible routine. Come this time tomorrow, we would be in a new place with no set schedule. We would have no choice other than to open the door and walk into the unknown. One thing I understood was how very much I was looking forward to seeing Zack and Tessa again. I looked up to the heavens and breathed another silent prayer of thanks that we had such a place of refuge for the uncharted territory we would be traveling in the days to come.

Dani got up and dusted off her bottom. She grabbed a handful of rocks and began tossing them down into the valley. Her head was bopping to whatever she was listening to. Her expression was as clear and promising as the cloudless blue sky. She still held a chance of temper tantrum, but this hint of some sun was encouraging. I watched her toss the rocks over the side. I started making mental checklists: We'll stop in Glenwood Springs for lunch, and I'll call Zack and Tessa to give them an idea of when we should get there and call Jake when we get to the ranch. *Oh my god,* I thought, *I haven't talked with him in nearly two days.* I wondered suddenly what our approach would be with Dani. I felt terrified that we really hadn't thought this through or established a plan. *Stop it, Lou,* I chastised myself, *look around you. You don't have a schedule. Your schedule is Dani. Stop with the ridiculous control because you don't have any. Listen to your gut and follow its lead for a change.*

Dani tossed her remaining few rocks over the side, dusted her hands off on her pants, and looked my way. "This place is pretty, Mom," she said, smiling.

My heart melted. I don't know if I was more touched by being called Mom with tenderness behind the word instead of her usual contempt or the sweet smile that backed it up.

"It sure is, sweetheart," I agreed.

"Does the ranch look like this?" she asked.

"Well, there are definitely lots of mountains around it and some valleys. I suppose parts of it look like this. Yeah, a little bit," I said and smiled back at her.

Dani thought about that for a moment and asked, "Can we get going? I'm getting kinda hungry."

"Sure. I figured we'll stop someplace in Glenwood Springs. It's about an hour or so from here. It's a pretty cool town. I think you'll like it."

"Okay." She plugged back in and slid into the passenger seat.

When we got to the highway sign for the Dotsero exit, I knew we would be in the canyon soon.

I reached over and tapped her shoulder. "Look," I said. "There's the Glenwood Canyon entrance up ahead. You should sit up and check it out. It's pretty amazing."

"What's a Dotsero?" she nodded toward the highway sign as we passed it.

"It's the last town before we enter the canyon."

2

We continued snaking our way through the canyon. I was so happy and amazed at how much the roadway improvements really hadn't changed the canyon's pristine beauty. The tunnel that bore through the mountain at the Hanging Lake turnoff was a new addition since my last trip. Before, a turnoff for the trailhead had been off to the right, and now an actual exit through the tunnel led to it. I was glad to see they hadn't driven a demolition crew into the mountainside and destroyed the massive cliffs in the name of progress. Rather, portions of the roadway were built into double-decker highways. Not much of the natural habitat had been disturbed by the construction of the interstate. The Colorado River flowed in all its glory as though affirming the fact that it too had remained relatively unscathed. At points the white waters raged, churning and bubbling over the drop-offs and settling into intermittent swirling pools.

"This is amazing," I exclaimed.

"Oh my god!" Dani screamed and threw her cell phone to the floor.

I nearly ran my car off the road. "What? What happened?"

"Oh nothing much, Mom," Dani hissed. "It's just that I just got a text from Chelsea, and she's taking Alexandra and Alley to the beach with her and her family next week. That was supposed to be me!" she raged. "I can't believe you and Daddy did this to me. I can't believe you both hate me so much that you would take that away from me too. I mean, look at this place: a bunch of rocks and mountains and more rocks and mountains. What am I supposed to do with that?" she demanded.

"Dani—"

"Don't even, Mom," she said and held her hand up.

"Oh my God!" I shouted back. "You incredibly selfish little—do you have any idea what your father and I have sacrificed for you this summer?" I demanded. "Forget this summer! Do you have the smallest concept of what we have and continue to sacrifice for you?" I didn't even wait for a response. "I am so completely sick and tired of being sick and tired of the way you talk to me. And just when I think I can't get anymore sick and tired—I get more sick and tired!"

"Whatever, Mom! You just—"

"Shut up, Dani! Just *shut up*! You have pushed me too far once again. I just don't know what to do with you anymore," I said. "Do you think I wanted to put my life on hold again to try and make a difference in our lives? Do you think I look forward to walking on eggshells every waking moment and wondering what Dani I will be greeted by? Hmm. Let's see. Will it be happy Dani? Maybe it will be sullen Dani. Wait! I bet it'll be quiet Dani. Or possibly bitchy Dani. Better yet, it might be grateful Dani. Not a chance! There's no such Dani as grateful Dani," I said sarcastically, paused, then continued, "Nah. Grateful Dani doesn't live here anymore. She left a long time ago and left us with gotta-have-gimme-I-want Dani. That's the Dani we all know and love."

I couldn't believe I had allowed myself to get sucked into the dysfunctional vortex again. We had been to family counseling. We had tried individual counseling. I had worked with her school counselors. We had tried family game nights. We had tried giving her space, only to have her violate the privilege through poor choices or lies. Time and again she had stripped us of trust. I was still reeling from the fact I had told my child to *shut up*. I mean, I had gotten her attention, and she had shut up, but I was supposed to be the voice of reason. I was supposed to be the one who did not lose control. I was supposed to be the role model who was teaching Dani how to manage anger.

The ear-shattering, uncomfortable silence rolled back into the car like a thick, soupy fog to remind Dani and me that screaming at one another didn't work. I knew well this equation: We would stew and formulate our resentments and eventually sweep them into a closet, only to release them when the next rage blew up between us. I don't know how, but despite the battle, I had managed to drive out of the western end of the Canyon. We approached the first Glenwood Springs exit. I shook my head and slammed the signal on.

"Awww," Dani said and grabbed her nose. "What is that smell?" She looked at me in horror.

We were at the bottom of the exit for the Glenwood Hot Springs Pool, and to the right in the distance, I could see the steam rising from the public mineral pool in a constant stream toward the midday sun. I snapped out of my anger and started to laugh. I could see that my reaction immediately pissed her off, but in the next moment my laughter must have flipped a switch in her because she started to giggle. Her giggles morphed into uncontrollable laughter. I looked at her as she leaned forward, holding her stomach. She kept waving her hand in front of her nose in an effort to get rid of the nauseating smell that refused to subside.

"That's the..." I started to explain the smell but choked between fits of my own laughter.

"What? What is it? It's awful," she pleaded.

I was finally able to manage. "It's the hot springs. That smell is the sulfur from the natural hot springs."

"It's disgusting." She abruptly stopped, sat up, and looked at me in horror. "Do people swim in that stuff? I mean, it smells like one big, giant, gross fart," she exclaimed.

That did it for me. We both broke down into peals of laughter. We sat at the bottom of that exit ramp and just roared. The air between us had been so emotionally charged leading up to that moment that the abominable aroma of the sulfur pools intervened and opened the valve to release the pressure between us. We laughed so hard; we cried. I looked over at Dani, and my tears of laughter changed from laughter to uncontrollable tears of joy. To see the innocence of laughter with no boundaries spilling out of my child when minutes before there had been absolute rage seemed like an act of God.

That's right, Lou. That's what it is, I reassured myself. *There's your hope right there. If you just let it happen, it will, and it will continue to happen. You just have to quit forcing it to happen. Now snap out of it, dry those eyes, and get some lunch, damn it.* I followed my own instructions, hit the left turn signal, and headed toward downtown Glenwood Springs. I knew that I would set the tone for how lunch would go with whatever I said next and opted for silence. We pulled into a parking space in front of a quaint Mexican restaurant.

We got a booth near the back of the restaurant, and Dani continued on to the restroom. I browsed the menu and ordered some drinks for us. I already knew what I wanted and set the menu down to wait for Dani. I was anxious for Dani's return because even though our laughter broke the tension, there were some words exchanged that needed to be addressed, and I wasn't quite sure how to approach that.

9

"Here's an idea, Lou," I muttered to myself. "How about you don't—I don't mean don't talk about what happened—but how about you don't analyze the hell out of the situation? That's what you always do, and that's what she expects you to do. How about you let her bring it up and voice what's going on inside of her head and you follow her lead? Okay?"

"This place is ancient," she commented, interrupting my discussion on tactics I was having with my conscience as she slid into the booth.

We ordered, and after our waitress brought the food, we ate in silence. About halfway through our meal, Dani put her fork down, sat back in the booth, and looked at me.

"What? Is something wrong with your food?" I asked.

"No. It's good. I just—it's just that—well, I'm sorry," she said, obviously forcing out the words.

"Okay."

"Mom, I'm going to try this summer. I am. It's just that you never seem to listen to me, and when I do tell you something that bothers me, you just start talking over me. I—"

"Dani, I—"

"See," she said. "That's what I mean." She sat back and crossed her arms. "I was just trying to say I'm sorry and—"

"You're right," I interrupted again. "I promise I won't say another word and let you talk. Okay?"

"Believe me," she added, "I don't want to spend the next couple of months fighting with you. We could've just stayed home if that's what we're going to do. I just want you to stop smothering me. I know I make stupid decisions sometimes, and I even know they're stupid when I'm making them, but that doesn't stop me from doing it. I guess the reason I do it is to see if I can get away with it, and I can't. But, I also know that when you or Daddy find out, you'll do what you do: You lecture, Daddy yells, and that's how it always goes. I just—"

"Dani—"

"Mom, I'm not done," she insisted.

"Okay. Sorry."

10

"I guess the only other thing I want to say is that I'll try to be a better person this summer. I really will, but can you do something for me too?"

There's my little negotiator, I thought. "Well, it depends on what it is, Dani."

"Can you just relax and let me figure some stuff out and give me a chance to come to you if I screw up before you jump all over me?" she asked in what seemed a very sincere manner.

I thought about that last statement for a minute before I answered. "Is it my turn to speak now?" I asked.

"Sure."

"Okay. First of all, I'm sorry I told you to shut up. That was very wrong of me to say. There is no excuse other than the heat of the moment. As for the allowing you to screw up and come to me with your screwup before I find out on my own, that one is up to you. If you're really serious about owning your mistakes, I'm willing to give it a shot too. I will tell you, however, that your actions over this past year have stripped a lot of trust both your father and I had in you. Trust isn't something that magically appears overnight, Dani. It's something—"

"There you go again. Can you please not lecture me all the time?" she insisted.

"Okay. Fair enough. Lecture over right here, right now. This is officially our new beginning. Now let's get that check and get out of here. We've got about two more hours on the road and we'll be at the ranch. Wait until you see this place, Dani," I exclaimed. "I'm going to hit the restroom, and I should give Zack a quick call before we get back on the road. How about we walk over to that park across the street for a bit before we get back in the car? It'll give me a chance to call him and give us both a break from the drive."

We settled into a comfortable cruising speed, and I looked over at Dani. She hadn't plugged her ears against the world; instead, she was staring out the window, watching the scenery pass. We were coming up on Rifle, which meant we were just about halfway to the ranch. I was so excited to see Tessa and Zack, but was also a little nervous. Dani and I had been in a contained environment for the past few days. Once we got to the ranch, our road trip would end. We wouldn't have a schedule,

11

which also meant change. Summer working at the ranch had sounded like a great fix when I was two thousand miles away. Now that I was less than eighty miles from our destination, a slow panic was forming inside of me. Just exactly what was the grand scheme going to be, I wondered.

"Okay, Lou, Is this really necessary right now?" I scolded myself.

3

We took the interchange from I-70 onto highway 50 south at Grand Junction. Depending on traffic, of which there was none, we would have planned to be at the ranch by five or a little thereafter. I needed to stop for one final refuel in Montrose, then it occurred to me that Montrose would be our last stop before our road trip came to an end.

We pulled off into a small service station that had a country store attached to it. It was designed to look like an old log cabin. The sign above the entrance read Montrose Depot in big wooden letters. In front of the parking spaces that lined the front of the building, a split rail fence fronted a clapboard porch. A couple of old wooden rocking chairs sat along the front windows. At the far end of the building, a concrete slab with two picnic tables beckoned. Each had a colorful umbrella. The store and the highway in front of it, and two large meadows around either side and along the back, completed the extent of the scene. It felt like if we stayed long enough, we might see the afternoon stagecoach roll in. The building looked like it was the last man left standing after the American Indian War. The gas pumps were ancient. When I went to slide my credit card on the pump, I realized there was no place to do so. I looked up above the handle where a piece of cardboard taped to it read "Welcome. Please pay inside before you pump." I chuckled to myself, placed the nozzle back in its carriage, and followed Dani into the store.

Dani had already found a seat at one of the picnic tables. She had dumped all of her junk food she had bought in the store on the table and had torn into a couple of the bags of chips and snack mixes. There was no particular order to her smorgasbord. Periodically, she paused, sucked down some of her drink, brushed the stray hairs that danced across her forehead behind an ear, then returned to random snack choices.

"Here," I said, holding my phone out to her. "Why don't you call Daddy?"

She was about to stuff some pretzels in her mouth. "Why do I have to call him?"

"Because I thought you'd want to talk to him, silly," I said, laughing. "Don't you?"

13

"Yeah. Sure. It's just that I thought you were mad at me the way you told me to call him."

"I'm not mad at you. I just thought it would be a nice change if you called him and talked to him first and then I can talk to him," I said, reassuring her.

"Oh, okay." She grabbed the phone and dialed the number.

I sat down at the table across from her and let out a deep sigh. It was a gorgeous day. The sky was perfectly blue, and just enough breeze blew to temper the heat.

"Daddy?" Dani smiled into the phone.

"Hey, sweetheart! How are you?" I could hear Jake's voice come through the phone.

"Good. We're—"

She put her hand over the phone. "Mom, where are we?"

"Montrose," I answered.

"We're in Montrose," she told him.

"That's great! You're not too far from the ranch then. Are you?" I heard him ask.

"How far are we from the ranch?" she asked me.

"We're about an hour away," I said, laughing.

"Mom says we're about an hour away."

"Sure." She started to hand the phone over and snatched it back. "Hey, Daddy?"

"Yeah?" I heard Jake say.

"I miss you."

"I miss you too, baby. I love you lots and hope you have a great summer. Okay? We'll talk again soon."

"Okay. I love you too, Daddy." She passed the phone to me.

"Hey there," I said, smiling.

"Hey yourself," he said. "How's it going? Everything all right?"

"Everything is fine, Jake." I assured him. I glanced over at Dani. She motioned toward the field. I nodded to her and went back to my conversation. "It's going pretty good so far," I said tentatively.

"Well why don't you tell me about the part that isn't so good."

"We've had a few blowups since you and I last talked, but in fairness, I think some of them have been fueled by the fact that we've

14

been trapped in a car together for four days. I think we're both a little stir-crazy."

"Yeah, that makes sense," he conceded.

"I miss you and love you. Okay?" I said.

"Lou," he said, "I love you lots too. Big hugs to you and Dani."

"Oh, wait. How is Kylie doing?"

"She's great. As a matter of fact, I talked to her for a while last night. It sounds like she's having a ball. She was going on about how beautiful it was there and how she's already met some pretty cool people—you know. She gets started with the program on Monday. It sounds like she's been in a pretty intense orientation since she arrived, but she seems to be loving life. Now go! She's fine. You're fine. I'm fine, and it sounds like Dani is fine too. Get off the phone and drive safely. Okay? I love you, and talk to you soon."

"Okay. Love you too. Bye."

I motioned for Dani. She came back over to the table, grabbed the remnants of her junk food and stuffed it back into the bag, then took one last gulp of her Arnold Palmer, tossed it in the trash can, and walked back to the car.

The closer we got to Gunnison, the more I wondered what was in store for us. I wondered if I was truly capable of giving Dani the space she would need to do some serious growth. She was such a young fourteen. I caught glimpses of her turning into a young woman. Appearance-wise, she looked like she was nineteen.

"What?" Dani asked.

"Hmmm? I didn't say anything," I said.

"Well you look like you're mad about something," she said.

"Nah. I'm fine. I was just thinking."

"About what?"

"Nothing in particular. I was just thinking about the food we ate," I said.

Dani shook her head and put her earbuds back in.

Good lord, Lou, snap out of it, I thought, admonishing myself. *You're almost there, and it's a good thing, because I think your kid's starting to pick up on your thoughts.*

15

We were approaching the east end of Black Canyon in the Gunnison National Park. We were close. I also ached for at least one long summer day under the blanket of cobalt blue skies with nothing more than the wind in our faces, the sun on our backs, and the slow, steady climb up a canyon on the back of one of Zack's horses.

We came around that last bend on highway 50. Less than a mile ahead was the entrance to Echo Ranch. The thought of finally being at the ranch was overwhelming, and a perimeter of sweat broke out along my hair line and down the back of my neck. The pit of my stomach felt like a tight knot. I looked up and could see the entrance arch peaking above the small grove of aspens next to it. *Oh my god, we're here,* I thought. *We've made it, and now I don't know what to do.* I slowed down and hit my left turn signal. We turned off the highway and drove through the entrance. Once on the other side, I could feel my eyes filling with tears. I slowed the car, and somewhere in the distance I could hear my daughter calling me.

"Mom, are you okay?" She was visibly worried.

Disoriented, I looked over at her.

"Mom, you're scaring me. What's wrong? Why are you crying?"

I collected myself. "I'm okay. It's just—well, it's been so many years since I've been here—the memories. When I left, I was so sad to go."

"Oh, Mom," Dani said, obviously relieved; she reached over and gave me a hug. She was patting my back softly. I sat up and looked at her. I still had tears in my eyes. I looked at my brown-eyed girl and was struck by her tenderness. I hadn't seen this side of her in such a long time. I thought it had been lost forever. My emotional breakdown of returning to Echo Ranch showed me she wasn't gone, at least not completely. She looked around the fields on either side of the drive. "Wow!" she exclaimed. "So this is Echo Ranch, huh?" She continued to take in the countryside and asked, "Where are all the horses?"

Now there was the Dani I knew and loved: Enough about your moment, what's in this place for me? I threw my head back against the seat and began to laugh. As I laughed, she began to giggle. In the next instant, we were right back at that exit ramp in Glenwood Springs. We both just sat there laughing. I wiped the tears from my eyes and looked at her.

I shook off the rest of my moment and said, "Trust me, little lady. There are plenty of horses here. We've got about a quarter of a mile of road ahead of us before we get to the main house, and beyond that, you'll see horses and plenty of them." I smiled at her and put the car back into gear.

4

We made our way slowly up the incline to the main house. I was savoring every morsel of the majestic view that surrounded us. The valleys on either side of the hill were just as I remembered. I believe that it is true that places look smaller when revisited years later, but not Echo Ranch. The valleys stretched into infinity. Stands of pines covered the hillsides, and the creek snaked through them; all was just as I remembered. The late afternoon alpenglow had cast its spectacular rust across the mountains in the distance. I could see some of the trails that had been carved into the hillsides from many years of horses making their slow and steady trek up and down them. I looked ahead toward the tree line on the mountains and above them to the rocky cliffs that jutted up even higher to jagged peaks, which created an image of precise lines and formations against the twilight forming behind them.

"Wow!" I sighed. "I forgot how beautiful this place truly is."

Dani was plugged in, but I could tell by her expression of wonder she too was in awe. She was absorbing the panorama of glory and looked to be mentally snapping photos as fast as her mind's camera would allow her to do so. I knew the one thing she was in search of and determined to behold was the image of a horse. I smiled to myself and felt another wave of hope wash over me. The farther we drove into the unspoiled splendor, the more confidence I gained that Jake and I truly had made the right decision for our daughter. I refused to allow any doubts cloud what I felt right then and there.

She pulled out one of her plugs and pointed ahead. "Is that the house?"

I looked ahead to where she had pointed. What had been an arduous journey actually had an end in sight. The place we would call home for the next few months stood strong and sturdy in front of us. All we had to do was drive the next couple of hundred yards, put the car in park, cut the engine, and we'd be home.

"That's it! That's the main house at Echo Ranch," I said proudly.

"That place is huge!" She yanked her other earbud out.

The house sat on a large clearing of land with the San Juan Mountains serving as backdrop. The two-story structure was large, but

18

not pretentious. Rather, its design was humble, perfectly enhancing its rustic setting. The exterior was naturally stained, knotty pine logs. The roof was a dark hunter green with enough of a pitch to manage the winter snow. The many windows gave the house character and a feeling of warmth; especially in the evenings, when the lights from inside shone out, enhancing the beauty of the star-lit night sky. Meticulously groomed lawns surrounded the house and ran their course to a large fenced-in paddock with a couple of run-in sheds. Two horses grazed at the far end. They stopped and looked up as our car approached.

"Oh my god, Mom! Look!" Dani pointed at the horses. "Are those his horses?"

"Well, I think that's a fair assumption since this is his property," I said, laughing.

"Wow! Look at that chestnut. He's pretty. Oh! Look at that bay. He's gorgeous too. Oh my gosh! There's another one. She looks like a palomino," she squealed. "Let's get out. Let's go see them," she said, grabbing the door handle and flinging the car door open.

"Whoa, Dani," I said and grabbed her arm. "Those horses aren't going anywhere, I promise. I think the proper thing to do would be go inside first and see Zack and Tessa before we take over their property."

"Can't we just go over there real quick and see them? They won't mind," she pleaded.

"Absolutely not," I insisted. "This is Zack and Tessa's home, Dani, and the respectful thing to do—"

I looked up on the porch, and Tessa was standing there smiling. Time had been more than gracious to the elegant woman I remembered from years prior. Her hair was stylishly cropped just above her shoulders and the difference between then and now was a lovely shade of gray with a subtle hint of silver streaks. The color enhanced her brilliant gray eyes. She was meticulously fit and her outfit was further affirmation of her commitment to impeccable grooming—tailored jeans, a smart button-down white oxford, and her signature tall boots.

She ran down the steps to us. I jumped out of the car and met her halfway. We nearly knocked each other over as we embraced. We had been waiting for this moment for twenty years. I started to cry. I choked on my words. "Oh, Tessa, I can't believe we're here. I have thought about you so many times over the years. I can't believe we're here."

She held me tightly and stroked my head. "You're home, darling. It's so good to have you back home. We've missed you so much."

We gradually eased our embrace. I looked over at Dani. She stood awkwardly by the car and watched our reunion in silence.

I stepped back from Tessa and said, "Tessa, this is my daughter, Dani." I smiled and held my hand out toward Dani and motioned for her to come closer.

Tessa stood back and looked at her. She started to cry and looked back at me. "Oh my god, Louisa, she is a spitting image of you when you were younger," she exclaimed and looked back at Dani. "C'mon over here, darling. My name is Tessa. Come give me a big hug because we don't stand on formalities here." Tears ran down her face as Dani gave her a tentative hug.

"Stand back here and let me take a look at you," she said, beaming. "My god, Louisa. I cannot get over the resemblance. She is just as pretty as can be."

Dani continued to stand there, not knowing what she was supposed to do next. I'm sure she felt like some project that was being inspected and most likely was wondering what the outcome would be.

"She's dying to go over and meet some of your boarders," I said, gesturing toward the horses. With all the commotion on the porch, they had trotted up to the gate and were curiously watching our reunion.

"Oh my heavens! Of course, dear. Wait a minute. I'll be right back." She ran back up the stairs to a big wash bucket that was sitting on the porch by the front door. She bent down, grabbed a handful of carrots, and came back down.

"Here, dear." She handed Dani the carrots. "Before you go, let me tell you who those guys are." She pointed to the chestnut. "That big chestnut's name is Beau. He's a stingy fellow, so you have to give him his treat first so the other two have a fighting chance," she advised. "That dark bay is Black."

Dani looked at her and back at the horse and grinned.

"That palomino next to Black is Pearl. We called her Pearl because when she's in the sunlight, her coat sparkles like a silky pearl.

20

She's a little older than Beau and Black. She's almost nineteen. Don't let her age fool you though. No, sir." Tessa shook her head. "You better believe she doesn't take any grief from those other two. They know you have treats. They're not going to even think about leaving that fence line until you give them what you have."

Without hesitation, Dani grabbed the carrots and took off across the lawn toward the horses. We stood and watched her go then climbed back up the steps to the porch.

The house was just as I remembered. I admired the hanging baskets bursting with wildflower color along the length of the porch. Tessa had a discerning eye for design, as much as a commitment to hospitable comfort. As we made our way to the hanging swing, there were two conversation pits of outdoor furniture constructed in rustic pine with earth-toned, over-stuffed cushions. Next, we passed the welcoming touch I never forgot; two rocking chairs sat idly on either side of the bay window, patiently awaiting the arrival of their next visitor. We continued to the hanging swing and eased into our long overdue reunion.

"This place is even more spectacular than I remember," I said, looking out across the land. "You have no idea what this means for me and my family. I don't know that I'll ever be able to thank you enough."

"Let's not start that." Tessa waved her hand. "Do you think she'd mind if I called her Danielle? I have a real problem with nicknames. Granted, I call Zack *Zack* because if I call him Zachariah that man knows I'm upset about something. He's Zack. But he's the only person whose name I've ever shortened."

"Of course, you can call her Danielle. My god, you're the only person who calls me Louisa, for heaven's sake. My own mother rarely called me that."

"Oh, you," Tessa said. "The only reason you ever let me call you Louisa is because that's what I told you I was going to do."

We sat on the porch and began to share stories of where our lives had taken us. I watched Dani. She had glued herself to the fence. She was trading off love and attention among the horses. She was in her zone. It felt great to finally be out of that car. The trip had been difficult for her. She had always been a very active kid. To trap her inside a car for four days was more than a sacrifice for her. Being penned up gave both of us

21

too much time to fight and invade one another's space and no time to properly release our pent-up energy.

Casually, I asked, "Where's Zack? I thought he'd be here by now?" I could see the sun had already slipped over the western ridge. Sunset wouldn't be for a while, but Tessa was a creature of habit, which meant dinner was underway.

"I was wondering how long it would take before you'd ask that question." She smiled. She patted my leg and stood up from the swing. "I've got to go inside and check on dinner. Why don't you and Danielle take that Gator down to the main barn? He's down there with the farrier. I'm sure they're just about done. What's more, I can't think of anything he'll love more than to see you and your little you pulling up to the barn."

"Are you sure?" I asked. "Why don't you let me help you with dinner? I don't want to—"

"Oh, yes, you do, and yes, you will. I don't need any help with dinner. I know you're dying to see him. Go on. Get out of here. Besides, I've got stuff on the stove." She tucked her arm under mine, gave me one last squeeze at the door, and told me to get down to that barn to see the one person she knew I really couldn't wait to see.

I leaned over, brushed a kiss on her cheek, and jogged down the stairs. "Hey, Dani," I called. "C'mon, let's go down to the barn and see some more horses."

"Seriously?" Without hesitation she jumped off the fence and ran toward the Gator.

5

We rattled down the gravel road beyond the house to the main barn. As we drove away, the horses trotted along the fence line with us. Pearl, of course, had taken the lead.

Dani spun around to catch one last look before we dipped down the road. We came out of the first dip and made our gradual climb up to the top of the road. Although it had been years, I knew what was waiting for us at the top.

We took the last couple of yards in silence. At the top I cut the Gator's engine. Once it died down, we sat in silence and took it all in. Nature surrounded us as far as the eye could see. I looked behind me, and just as I remembered, I couldn't see the house anymore. I think Zack's dad must have had a clear vision long before he knew he was building a place to bestow to his only child. He had made a point of separating the house from the barns, which is why he cut the road to the barn as he had.

Shortly after making the last elbow turn before the barns, a dense grove of evergreens grew on both sides of the road. The years had added a considerable amount of growth to the trees. We took the dip in the road on the other side. Years ago when I had been at the ranch, the trees were barely taller than one of the chimneys on the house and had been the only indication that something other than land and wildlife were out here. Sitting at the top of the hill now and looking back behind us, no signs of civilization showed. No house, or gardens, or paddocks, or even the hay fields way back down at the entrance could be seen from where we were. Even the road we'd just driven was camouflaged from our vantage point.

Dani was getting restless. I didn't expect her to drink in all this with the same euphoria I was experiencing, but a pause for the grace and beauty would have been nice.

"Why are we stopping? Are we out of gas?" She gave me a worried look.

"No, we're not out of gas," I answered, laughing. "I thought it would be nice if we stopped here for a minute so you could look around and get a better idea of where we're going to spend our summer."

She looked to her left and right and back at me. "It's really pretty, Mom." And with complete disregard, she pointed to the valley below and asked, "Are those the barns? I see a couple of horses. Where are the rest of them?" A series of four buildings organized in horseshoe fashion with several fenced-off pastures lay ahead. They made a checkerboard pattern across the valley below where we had stopped. Some fenced areas were compact while others were long and wide. All lines had a common end at the hillsides in the distance. Our view didn't give the main barn the justice it deserved. A large structure from our view, yes, but I knew it housed at least twenty-five horses. I remembered the building immediately to its left. The brood mares were housed in it for birthing. I didn't recall the other two buildings to the right; new additions, I assumed. The main barn was as I remembered it, with the exception of a new coat of paint. At some point Zack must have tired of the color because he had changed it from mahogany red to hunter green. I completely ignored Dani's barrage of questions and basked in the memories until her relentless insistence interrupted my thoughts.

"Mom," she demanded.

"What?" I snapped.

"Geez. Can we go? We're just sitting up here and, like, I get it. It's pretty. I just want to go down to the barn and see the rest of the horses," she whined.

"Okay." I started the Gator and gave her a hard look. "It's very important that you hear what I have to say. You need to—"

"Here we go again," she mumbled, "more lectures." She sat back, rolled her eyes, and crossed her arms.

I slammed on the brakes and nearly dumped her from the vehicle. "Listen," I demanded. "We've been here for less than an hour, and already we're on our way to round 3. Don't start with me. I'm telling you right now, little girl, I'm not going to put up with this shit all summer long. Do you aQCURE EMAIL AND OTHER PASSWORDS me?"

She shot back one of her epic glares and acidly replied, "Sure. Whatever."

I raised my hand, hesitated, and put it back down. I bent my head down and rested it on my hands. I had a white-knuckle grip on the steering wheel. I took a deep breath and pleaded in silent prayer: "Lord, please don't make us go there right now. Please give us both the strength we need to snap out of this in the next twenty seconds so Zack doesn't witness exactly how dysfunctional we really are before we've had a couple of days to properly show him."

I lifted my head back up and kicked the Gator back into gear. I had lost my train of thought. Perhaps that was the answer to my prayer. The best thing to do right now would be to drive. At least that was one thing I had successfully proven I was capable of doing over the past few days. I pressed down too hard on the gas, and the back tires spit out some gravel. The Gator fishtailed a little before it righted and we were able to continue forward.

We continued down the hillside. When we leveled off, I cut the engine and let the Gator glide to a stop in front of the barn. The double doors of the barn stood open. Four horses were in the paddock. When they saw us, they trotted toward the gate. Dani saw them. I could see she was still upset, but knew I was the last person she wanted to talk to. We stood next to the Gator for a couple of minutes, facing off with one another, and she spoke, "Mom, I'm sorry. I know this place means a lot to you and I'm going to try. Okay?"

In spite of my anger, I put my arms around her and gave her a hug. I tucked my arm around her waist. "C'mon, I know you have no interest in meeting more people right now, especially when there are horses close by, but humor me for a few more minutes, and I promise I'll let you go see those guys over there." I nodded toward the horses gathered at the fence.

She looked at them and grinned up at me. "Okay. But you promise?"

"I promise." We walked toward the barn entrance.

Just through the doorway I could see Zack. His back was to me. The farrier who was with him straddled a hoof stand with a horse's hind right hoof in his hand. Each time he raised his hammer to strike the nail, the horse gave a slight kick and sent the nail flying. After two attempts, although I couldn't see his face, I could sense Zack's frustration.

"Oh, for Pete's sake, Buster, give me that damn hammer," Zack sputtered. He walked around the rear end of the horse and gave him a hard smack on the rump. "Jasper, if you don't knock it off, I'll drive this nail into another part of you that will make you knock it off, you

25

knothead," he said to the horse. The horse looked back at Zack and let out a loud whinny then pawed at the ground. Zack did a double take, and the horse whipped its head back around and stood at attention.

I leaned against the barn door opening and slowly started to clap my hands. "Now that's what I call authority," I said, grinning.

Zack spun around and stood up tall. The look of utter surprise on his face brought tears back. I saw a man who was years older but still in his prime of life. He had a thick head of hair. What had once been jet black was now completely gray with a few sprinkles of black. His signature handlebar mustache had also turned completely gray. His blue eyes still sparkled like a fine-cut diamond held up to the sun, and his frame remained tall and straight at over six foot three. Zack looked incredibly fit, which told me the daily demands of running his ranching operation kept him that way. A familiar, infectious smile formed at the corners of his mouth, and the look of authoritative hardness melted into kindness. He dropped the hammer and walked toward us.

He picked me up and spun me around. "Well my god! It's about damn time you got here," he said, voice booming. He spun me around again and put me down. He took a step back and surveyed the situation in front of him. "Let me take a good look at you. My god, it's good to see you. I can't—"

I stood there and collected my balance. Tears streamed down my face. I tried to choke out a "good to see you too," but the words stuck in my throat. Without hesitation, he put his arms around me. He squeezed me so hard I stumbled a little.

"Now don't you go crying like that, Lou," he said, "I haven't been waiting around here for the past few days for you to get here only for me to stand here now and watch you cry. There's plenty of time for tears when tears need to be shed," he insisted.

I let out a small chuckle and gently pushed away from him. I thought I had behaved with such bravado when we had arrived. I had been caught completely off guard when he turned around and our eyes met. Memories flooded my mind of how many times the man who stood before me had coached me through some really difficult choices.

Dani quietly stood by, leaning against a horse stall. She looked at the ground, tracing patterns in the dirt with her shoe. I looked over at her

26

and back at Zack. He followed my gaze and saw her. I saw a trace of a tear brim in his eye. He cleared his throat. "Well, who do we have here?" he demanded.

"This is Dani," I said, smiling. I reached my hand out to her. She walked over to my side and looked up at him. I stood back a little and let them size each other up.

"Go ahead. You can talk," I said to Dani. "I don't know where all this shyness is coming from, Zack, this child exceeds her minutes on her cell phone every month, and now she can't think of anything to say." I winked at her.

She walked toward Zack and held her hand out. "It's nice to meet you, sir," she said, obviously unsure about how to address him.

He threw his head back and laughed. He looked at me and back at Dani. "Well, Dani," he said. "The first thing we have to get straight is I'm not a sir. My name is Zack, and that's what everybody around here calls me if they want to get my attention. That is, of course, unless it's Tessa." He lowered his voice, looked Dani in the eye, and whispered: "Most of the time she calls me Zack. But sometimes she calls me Zachariah. I don't like it when she does that because all that can mean is I've done something to really piss her off." He chuckled. "I bet your momma calls you Danielle sometimes, huh?" He nudged her.

Dani grinned and looked back at me. "Yeah, and just like you, it's usually when I've done something really bad," she agreed, and we all burst out laughing.

"Well then, we haven't even spent ten minutes together, and we already have something in common," he said and extended his hand toward Dani.

Dani accepted his hand and shook it. She gave him one of her beautiful smiles and looked back at me. In that fleeting moment, her eyes told me she liked this guy and was maybe even a little glad to be here this summer.

"Tessa wanted us to come down to let you know dinner will be ready in about an hour. That was about fifteen minutes ago. We're going to head back up and get our things out of the car. See you up at the house?" I asked.

Dani looked at me. Disappointment was written all over her face. Zack caught it and said, "You know. The boys could really use some help finishing up these feed buckets. Dani's welcome to hang back with me if it's all right with you. She can ride back up to the house with me."

"I don't know, Zack," I said, hesitating. "We've been on the road all day and we really need to get the car—"

"Mom, please," Dani begged. "I promise I'll be careful. Please."

"Okay. I see what's going on here: two against one," I said and turned to walk away but stopped. "Forty-five minutes, or Tessa will be calling you Zachariah," I said to Zack, grinning. I blew Dani a kiss and headed back to the Gator.

Part II

6

Zack looked at Dani after Lou had gone. "Let me square a couple things away with Buster, and then you can help me with feed and water buckets. Okay?"

"Sure," she said and peeked around the corner to see if the three horses she had seen when she and her mom had first pulled up were still out there.

"What are you looking at?" Zack asked when he returned. He came up behind her and looked around the corner. "Oh, now I see what's so interesting." He smiled down at her. "Tell you what. Why don't you go out and introduce yourself. I'll finish up in here, and then we can get started on those buckets. Okay?"

"Sure!" she said much more eagerly and started to bolt toward the pasture.

"Now hold on just a minute. Not so fast," he said. "If you're going to properly introduce yourself, don't you think you should know who those guys are?"

"Oh. Yeah," she said and grinned.

"Okay. C'mere." He pointed toward the flea-bitten gray that was closest to them. "All of those guys are my newest additions. They've only been here for a few months. I've just started to blend them with the rest of the herd. They're good boys, but they've got some work ahead of them before they get their permanent jobs. Now, starting with the flea-bitten gray, his name is Cheetah. The boy standing to his right is Bull, which is short for Sitting Bull."

Bull was a gorgeous liver-and-white paint. He had one blue eye and one brown.

"And that other guy standing next to Bull, the one closest to us, that's not a guy at all. She's one of the finest ladies on the ranch, aside from Pearl." He quickly corrected himself. "Did you meet Pearl?"

"Yeah, she's really pretty."

"She sure is, honey. Anyway, that lady over there is Gandy Dancer, but we call her Dancer for short," he explained.

Dani looked over at Dancer and could see what he meant. She was big, but she did look graceful. She had a pretty, coppery coat and sweet brown eyes. Her legs were long like a thoroughbred. "Is she a thoroughbred?"

"She sure is," Zack answered, obviously impressed by Dani's knowledge. "Your momma told me you knew a little something about horses. She didn't tell me you knew how to sight breeds." He nudged her. "Now go on. Go over and say hello."

Dani ran to the fence. She was so excited to meet more of the four-legged tenants of Echo Ranch. One thing she had picked up on was the fact that every horse she had met so far was very friendly. They welcomed a stranger and didn't seem to spook when approached. She climbed up on the bottom rail of the fence and held out her hand. The three horses trotted over to her, pushing each other out of the way, certain she had treats. When they got to where Dani stood and realized she had nothing, they lost interest and did what any respectful horse would do: They each allowed her a pat or two, then one by one they turned their backs on her and wandered off toward the far end of the paddock.

"Hey, Dani," Zack called out.

She turned and hopped off the fence. She met him in the doorway with her hands stuffed in her pockets and her head bent. "I guess they weren't too thrilled to meet me after they figured out I didn't have any treats," she said and shrugged her shoulders.

"Yeah? It's not just them, honey. Horses can be a fickle bunch. As a matter of fact, they can be downright selfish and stubborn."

"C'mon, follow me through the barn and out the back. There's something I want you to see before we head up to the house."

She was confused. "Don't we have to do feed and water buckets?"

"We do, but not tonight. Honey, I've got five strong and able-bodied full-time hands down here. They earn their keep doing things just like that, among other items. I pitch in a lot of the time because the work keeps me honest, but the fact of the matter is that's why I hired them. Now come on, time's wasting, and we cannot be late for dinner." He set off at a brisk pace through the barn. Dani practically had to power walk to keep up with him.

As they passed down the center aisle, she turned from left to right to catch the names on the stalls. She saw Sitting Bull and Jasper but didn't recognize any of the other names. It made her realize that she had a

31

lot of horses yet to meet. When they got to the other end of the barn, Zack threw the double doors open and disappeared to the right. She quickly followed and saw him heading toward a large round pen. A man was inside with a long lunge line. Tethered to its other end was an incredibly beautiful horse, who, at the moment, was trying to fight whatever the man would ask him to do. The horse would take a couple of trot steps forward and pit stop. Each time he stopped, he dug his hooves deep into the footing. The horse dropped his head and pawed at the ground, then he shot off in a half canter, twisting his head side to side and up and down. He snorted and whinnied and looked like, more than anything, he wanted to stop the nonsense of being on the lunge line at once. He even kicked out when the man made him change direction.

They stopped at the far side of the round pen, and Dani climbed up onto the bottom rail. Zack leaned on the rail and called out, "Hey, Bobby, how's he doing?"

Bobby shook his head and looked irritated. He looked back at Zack. "How do you think?" he called back.

"Well, he looks like he's just not having any of it today. Go ahead and call it a day. The boys will be down soon to finish up buckets. Turn him out with Duck and Cheetah in the front paddock, and they'll get him in for feeding later."

"Okay, boss," Bobby shouted back and reeled in the lead line. The horse followed Bobby's command and stopped in front of him long enough to hear the click of the clasp being released from his halter. As soon as he took his hand away, the horse shot off in the opposite direction.

Dani was hypnotized. She watched every muscle on the horse's body ripple as he made his way around the pen. He was headed toward them. He was stunning. His coat shimmered in the afternoon light. It wasn't quite black, but very close. The only identifying marks on his body were the perfect heart-shaped star on his forehead and one white sock on his back left leg. Everything else was black, from mane to tail.

"What's his name?" Dani asked Zack.

"Poet."

"Poet," she repeated slowly. "Why Poet?"

"Well that's a long story." Zack kept his eye on the horse. "Why don't you walk with me? We need to get up to the house. I'll tell you his story on the way." Zack took his hat off, smoothed his hair, and placed it back on his head.

"Okay." She hopped down off the fence and took one last look behind her just as Poet raced past the spot where she had been standing seconds earlier. She could see his flared nostrils. His tail was straight out behind him. "Wow! He's got a lot of spirit, huh?" she said.

"Spirit." Zack laughed. "That's one way of describing him." He shook his head and placed his hand on her shoulder. "C'mon, let's head up to the house, and I'll tell you his story."

She climbed up into the truck. They backed out and headed toward the road. She turned around to watch Bobby walk Poet over to the paddock where the other horses were. As soon as Bobby took Poet's halter off, Poet took off across the field. He bucked a couple of times and galloped to the far end.

She turned back around. "So why Poet?"

"Well, his full name is Poetry in Motion," Zack began, "and aside from the spring babies, he's the youngest horse on the ranch. I picked him up at auction when he was just a baby. He's a little over three years old now. I've given him a lot of space and free time because life started for him on a real sour note."

"What do you mean?"

"He was sold at auction when he was barely seven months old. He's from Wyoming originally. He comes from good stock—really good stock—but he lost his momma when he was too young."

"What happened?"

"Like I said, he's from Wyoming originally. There's a big auction in Gunnison each summer right after the Fourth of July." He looked over at her. "Miss Tessa made me swear to her that I wouldn't bring another horse on this ranch because we already had more than enough." He shook his head. "Well, don't you know that he was at that auction? After I heard his story, I just had to buy him. My instincts told me he was meant to be here at Echo Ranch. I don't know why it is, Dani, but I get around those animals, and I lose a lot of the common-sense part of me, especially if I feel a connection." He looked over at her. "Do you know what I mean?"

"Uh, yeah," she said, smiling. "My mom thinks I'm crazy sometimes with the things I do around horses. Don't get me wrong, she likes them fine too, but I think she likes the ones that are a little older and more predictable. Like some of the horses at the barn where I train are amazing jumpers. The reason they're so amazing is they have to have a little craziness in them, but they'll do anything you want them to do as long as they think they can trust you."

"That's what I'm talking about," Zack said. "Anyway, about Poet," he continued, "like I said, he was barely seven months old and up on the auction block. That's not typically the time you want to rip a baby away from his momma. Usually you want to wait until they're closer to a year. He never had that chance. The guy that brought him to auction had four other babies around his age, different mommas, and a few older horses. There'd been a terrible fire. The barn where Poet and the other babies were typically housed burned to the ground. Most of the horses in it burned right down with it."

"Oh my gosh! How did Poet and the other babies get out?"

"Like I said, it's a little early to take a baby that age away from its momma, but the owner had started to separate them at night to get them used to being apart. On that very night of the fire, he'd moved all the babies over to another barn after feeding. The saddest part of the whole story is when word got up to the main house that one of his barns was up in flames, by the time he got down there and the fire rescue team showed up, that fire had all but consumed the barn and every living thing inside. What's even worse is the barn that the babies were in had a couple of end stalls that faced that barn. Poet was in the last stall on the end. To this day, I'm convinced that boy knew his momma was in there and he would never see her again." He shook his head and pulled his truck alongside the house.

They sat there in silence for a moment. Dani was upset by the story. She looked over at Zack and asked, "What's going to happen to him?"

"That's where you come in. See, your momma doesn't know this yet, but I'll have a long chat with her about the details later on. In a lot of ways, Poet's destiny lies in your hands this summer." He looked at her, and Dani could tell he was waiting for a reaction.

"She jerked her head around and in a panicked voice asked, "What do you mean?"

"What I mean is that Poet may be just a horse, but he's a lot like you, if I understand some of the reason you and your momma are here this summer. He's a teenager that keeps pushing the boundaries and testing waters that he's already tried. He knows they don't work, but he's a knothead, and he just keeps going back and making the same mistakes over and over again. There's one thing to keep trying something, and each time you try it, you learn a little, and you drop the stuff that doesn't work. That's called growing up. It's a completely other thing to keep going back to that same place and doing the same dumb stuff instead of moving forward. Hell, all you do then is keep slipping farther back."

Dani was indignant. "So it sounds like my mom has already talked with you about me. Looks like I don't get a say in what's going on."

"That's not what I'm saying at all. Besides, I'm talking about Poet. Who are you talking about?" he challenged her.

She thought about it a minute and asked, "So what does Poet have to do with me this summer?"

"Well, he needs a lot of love and devotion. I have nearly sixty horses on this ranch and a business to run in addition to that. The horses are a big part of that business, but they're not the only part. I like to work with the young bucks. At times I'd like to believe they're teaching me a hell of a lot more than I am them. But Poet's special. That boy has a heart that's ready to burst inside, and he wants to share it so bad. But he doesn't trust enough. He gets on fine with Bobby and me, but I can see he hasn't found his one and only yet. He's young, Dani, and so are you. Hell, you're both teenagers," he said, smiling. "I'd like to think you're a match made in heaven just waiting to happen."

She grinned up at him and asked, "So what am I supposed to do? Train him or something? I mean, I know a lot about horses, and I definitely know how to ride and groom them. I can tell when something isn't right, but I don't know how to train a horse."

"Well, I won't throw you in the round pen with him tomorrow and say, 'Go on, get to work,'" Zack said. "I was thinking that since he's primarily Bobby's job, maybe you could work together with them. Ultimately, I'd love to see Bobby take a backseat with him and you take

35

over the reins once you feel comfortable. My gut tells me you're the one who's gonna win his trust." He paused and asked, "What do you think?" He didn't wait for her to answer. "I'll tell you what. Let's get inside and have some dinner. You guys have had a long trip to get here. Why don't we eat dinner and get you and your momma settled in. You can give me your decision at breakfast tomorrow morning." He added, "Besides, I'd like to run this by your momma."

Dani thought about his proposal. She didn't want to wait for her mother's permission. "You know what? I'd like to do that."

"Okay, great. We'll talk about this again at breakfast. Now—"

"No, that's not what I meant." She grabbed his arm as he was getting out of the truck. He stopped and sat back down and looked at her.

"What I'd like to do is work with Poet this summer. His story is amazing. I just know how much love I can give him if he gives me a chance," she insisted. "There's nothing to think about. I want to do it."

"Well, all right then." Zack chuckled. "It won't be easy, you know."

"I know that. I don't even feel sorry for him. That's not what he needs. It's more like I want to give him the chance for you to see that he does have a big heart and he can share his love with you. He just never got to give his mother a proper good-bye. If that's what I get to do this summer, I can't wait to get started," she said, grinning.

"Then I suppose the only thing left to do is shake on it." He held his hand out. She met it halfway and gave him a hearty shake in return.

Dani jumped out of the truck and ran up the steps. Zack got out on his side and looked up at the stars. "Lord, tell me I haven't overstepped my boundaries." He shook his head and caught up with Dani.

He met Tessa at the door.

"Well, there you are," Tessa said, greeting them. "I thought I heard the truck pull up. C'mon, you two, you have just enough time to wash up and dinner will be ready." She stroked Dani's head as Dani slipped by Tessa into the house.

Once inside Dani stopped dead in her tracks. She wanted to go wash up but didn't know where the bathroom was. She turned back around to Tessa.

"What's the matter, dear?"

36

"Uh. Where's the bathroom?" Dani asked sheepishly.

"Oh, I suppose that would help, now wouldn't it?" Tessa said, laughing. "Zack, why don't you help Louisa set the table." She turned back to Dani, "C'mon, honey, I'll show you where you can wash up."

"Thank you, Miss Tessa."

"Tessa," she insisted. "Just Tessa, honey. You and your momma are family while you're here."

As they cut through the great room, Dani looked up overhead. The ceilings were open and beamed with knotty pine rafters. She looked toward the second level. A balcony overlooked the room. The breezeway divided one half of the upstairs from the other. On the far end, a doublewide stairway led up to the second story that looked just like something from *Gone with the Wind*. The stairs were dark. From where Dani stood, she could see the top of a wall-to-wall, floor-to-ceiling bookcase that was trimmed in that same knotty pine wood.

Dani had never seen a room so big. She looked back down the staircase and out the windows to the setting sun. The sky was awash with vibrant reds mixed with shades of orange. Wisps of violet swept across the entire western skyline. She was looking at the sunset in absolute awe through a huge bay window that was the wall of the house. An intricate, subtle etching of horses thundering across open ground with dust kicking up behind them formed a center pattern in the glass. Beneath the window, and running its entire length, was a window seat with one long overstuffed cushion. It looked like the perfect place to snuggle down with a good book on a cold, rainy day.

A couple of sofas and a large semicircle sectional with a deep burgundy plush fabric sat in the room. An end table with a cushy lounger covered in what looked like dark brown corduroy pants and a floor-to-ceiling brass lamp stood off to one side. Dani smiled to herself, thinking that was probably Zack's special seat just like her dad's back home. The most dominant fixture in the room, however, was a giant, freestanding fireplace. It divided the two rooms. Its façade was covered with beautifully polished river rock. Pictures of horses, landscapes, and mountains decorated the walls. Dani guessed that every single one of those shots had been taken on the land where she was about to spend an entire summer, and she couldn't wait to see the scenes depicted in the photos in real life. There were some photos of people too, one in particular of a man and a woman who looked like something straight out of an old Western movie. She paused on that one and turned to Tessa.

"Who's that?" she asked, pointing at the picture.

"Those are Zack's parents, Samuel and Elizabeth Calhoun," Tessa answered. "They've both passed now. They were wonderful people."

Tessa and Dani stood together in silence, and Dani tried to absorb her surroundings. It felt like she was in a dream, but everything around her was real, warm, and safe. She had an overwhelming feeling that a lot of love and happiness had happened here.

"You have a really nice home," Dani said and smiled.

"Thank you, dear." Tessa placed her hand on her shoulder. "I want you to make this your home too this summer. Now c'mon, let me show you where the bathroom is."

"Dinner's ready, you two," Lou said, interrupting the tour.

"We'll be there in a minute," Tessa answered for them. "C'mon, honey. Let's go wash up."

7

They sat down at the table, Zack at one end and Tessa at the other. Lou and Dani sat on either side across from each other. Lou's back was to the wall of windows looking out to the southwest. Dani sat across from her with the best view at the table. She looked out the windows behind her mother and could see Bobby and a couple of other ranch hands off in the distance leading a bunch of horses back in toward the main barn. She looked at Zack and asked, "How come you bring the horses in at night? Back home during summer, the barn where I ride would leave a lot of them turned out for the night. They're usually brought in during the morning for feeding and then turned back out again for the day."

"I bring my boys and girls in at night because there are some wild animals out there that come down out of the hills at night to feed, like big cats and an occasional black bear. Most of them have migrated back up into the hills, but there're some stragglers that like easy pickings and horses are just that, especially if that cat is hungry. A couple of years back, I left a few of the horses way out there," he said and pointed to the far pasture that ran below the ridgeline where the guys were leading the animals, "and the next morning when I went out to spread some fresh hay, one of them was dead."

"Was it attacked by something?" Dani asked, looking at Zack in horror.

"That's exactly what happened. We suspected there'd been a mountain lion that was prowling around the area because—Lou, did you explain to Dani the lay of this land, the preserve and all?" he asked and looked over at her.

"Uh-huh." She looked at Dani, "Remember when we driving out here and I was telling you about the BLM and homesteaders and how a lot of the land was preserved for wild animals to roam freely as well?" she reminded Dani.

"Yeah, but you didn't tell me they were killing the horses," Dani said, preoccupied with pushing some peas around on her plate.

Zack chuckled. "I'll take this one, Lou. See, Dani, even though there's a lot of land that the government owns around my place, there's an unspoken law that says I am within my absolute right to take care of a

39

situation that is bringing harm to my livestock. That wild cat that killed my horse—and it was a wild cat—had to be addressed. We tracked him up into the mountains for two days and finally found him. He was a nasty old son of a gun and a threat not only to the animals, but to my hired help and the other people that live out here. The reality of the situation is that although some tree huggers may not agree with it, people still take precedence in life as we know it. If there's a living creature out there that might ultimately threaten the life of a human being, it's got to go."

"So you killed it?" she asked indignantly.

"You bet we did," he said. "It's important to note that once we took him down, we got the wildlife and game people in here to properly dispose of his body. After that, we changed some things up. We decided not to turn the horses out down valley anymore because that ridgeline out there"—he pointed with his fork— "is known to be bear and mountain lion haven, and it was up to us to be responsible and respect their space too. So we pull the horses out of that pasture toward sundown nightly and rotate them into some of the paddocks up closer to the barn. We've got some live-in staff down in the bunkhouse not too far from the main barn. A big part of their job is to monitor the goings-on at night. We haven't had any other mishaps like that since."

Dani felt her mom watching her, waiting for some sort of reaction.

Dani thought about what Zack had told her and asked, "So did you get in trouble for doing that?"

"No way," he said. "Like I said, I did have to report it to the Colorado Department of Wildlife. They came out the day after we shot that cat and disposed of the body properly. They knew we did the right thing. They're a good bunch of people and understand that the horses are our livelihood."

"Well, I hope nothing happens to anymore horses, especially Poet," she said and gave him a worried look.

"Well, honey, let me tell you what. As long as I'm able to take a breath, I can promise you we're going to do everything we can to make sure nothing like that happens again," he said, "especially to Poet."

She smiled, scooped up a bunch of peas, and continued eating her dinner.

"You look tired, Dani," Lou said. "How about when we finish up, we go out to the car and get our things. It's been a long couple of days. I bet it feels good knowing we won't be getting up and driving again all day tomorrow. Huh?"

"Seriously!" Dani said, laughing. She looked at her mom and sheepishly asked, "Do you think it would be all right if I took a shower?"

"Of course, honey."

Lou set her fork down. "Dani, let's go out to the car and get our bags. We don't have to unpack them tonight. We can just grab our overnight bags and your backpack with your shampoo and stuff. We'll unload the rest of the stuff in the morning. Okay?"

"Okay, I can go out and get them," Dani said.

"Okay. The car isn't locked. Are you sure you don't want some help?"

"No thanks. I can get it." She pushed herself away from the table. As she got up, she looked at Tessa, "Tessa? Thank you for dinner. It was really good."

"You're very welcome, dear. Are you sure you don't need some help getting your bags?" Tessa motioned to Zack.

"You know, I'm done too. C'mon, Dani," Zack said. "Let's go get your stuff." Zack stood and winked at Tessa. "That was a real fine meal you made, Tessa. Excuse us."

Zack and Dani came back in with some of the bags and brought them upstairs. Tessa instructed them to take Lou's bag to the back guest room.

"C'mon then, woman. This little lady is about to fall asleep standing up. She wants to get a shower," Zack said.

"Okay. Okay. Hold your horses! We're coming," Tessa said, shaking her head.

They followed each other in single file up the stairs. Dani stood in the center of the railing looking down into the room. "This place is so cool!" she exclaimed. "Wait until I text Chelsea. She won't believe it." She spun around to Tessa. "Do you think it's all right if I take a picture with my phone of the room down there from here? I want to send it to my friend back home."

41

"You go ahead and take as many pictures as you like. We're going to take these bags back to your mom's room, and then we'll be back to show you where your room is. Okay?"

"Cool," Dani said, and without hesitation, she grabbed her phone out of her back pocket and began to snap away.

When they came back around the corner, Dani had plopped down on the sofa and was chattering away on her phone.

"Seriously, Chelsea," they heard her say, "This place rocks. It is sick, it's so amazing. Oh my gosh. I've already seen about ten horses, and there's a ton more. There's this one horse that's incredible. He's going to be my project this summer! His name is Poet. What?" She burst out laughing.

She held up her index finger, indicating she'd be another minute.

"Dani," Lou said. "Wrap it up. It's getting late. You still need to unpack and take your shower."

"Hold on, Chelsea." She put her hand over the phone. "Okay, Mom, one more minute, please."

"Okay, but no longer," Lou said. "Here. Give me your bag, and I'll get you unpacked."

Dani pushed her bag toward Lou with her foot and flopped back on the pillows. She was oblivious to anyone or anything as she lay there twirling her ponytail and chattering incessantly into her beloved cell phone.

"C'mon, Louisa," Tessa said, nodding towards the hall again, "I think you'll remember this room." Tessa smiled as she opened the door and stepped aside so Lou could walk in.

As soon as Lou flipped on the switch, a flood of memories came rushing back to her. While Tessa had updated the room, the furniture was still arranged as Lou remembered. She looked across the room at the queen bed that was centered on the far wall. The bed ran the length of the bank of windows that looked out across the southwestern night. A beautifully hand-stitched patchwork quilt in vibrant reds, blues, greens, and oranges covered it. The two-step foot stool still sat on the floor centered on its left side. Lou smiled at the memory of climbing up those steps only to collapse into bed each night after an exhausting day's work. At the foot of the bed there was a trunk that had a couple of throw

42

blankets arranged on its top. On the wall to the left, a door led into the full bath. Lou slowly walked into the room and thought about some of those nights when she could barely finish dinner because she had been so tired, but she would manage enough energy to get up the stairs, strip down, draw a bath, and just lay in that big soaking tub until her fingers and toes had turned into shriveled-up prunes.

"It's just as I remember it." Lou chuckled and looked at Tessa, "well maybe not exactly as I remember it. Do you remember how by the time each weekend would come around, there'd be so much of my junk thrown everywhere it's a wonder I'd find the bed each night?"

"Oh, I do," Tessa said and raised her eyebrows, "but I also knew that you were paying rent, and as much as it drove me crazy, I had to respect your space. I couldn't tell you how to keep it, especially since you were paying for it."

"Yeah, but that didn't keep you from straightening things up sometimes," Lou reminded her. "Don't think I didn't know it was you who would sneak in and clean it up when I'd leave in the morning. I'd come home at night, head up the stairs, and halfway there get a sick feeling because I was so tired but knew I needed to do at least a little pickup. I'd throw that door open, and it was like a little fairy had swooped down and folded that landfill of jeans and T-shirts and lined all my boots back up in their proper place in the closet. You'd never say a word, and neither would I, but I knew it was you!" Lou thought about that for a minute and said, "Do you know I do the same thing with Dani and her room. My god!" she whispered, "you don't suppose the messiness is genetic, do you?"

"Of course it is," Tessa said, laughing. "If that's the worst thing you experience with your child, you're a lucky mom!" Tessa laced her arm through Lou's. "Come over here. I thought for sure you would have said something about this picture." She led her over to the small section of wall between the windows to get a closer look.

Lou leaned in for a closer look. "Is that—oh my gosh! I can't believe you still have this!"

As she examined the picture, she went back to the day the picture was taken. She was standing with Eagle, Zack's horse. They were on the tabletop of the place she had named Final Fall. It was the first time Zack

43

had taken her up there, and they'd come through the last cut of the trail, which opened to a tabletop between two ridges. It was the perfect place to get a panoramic view of the surrounding mountains and valleys below. She remembered saying if a person were to take a wrong step, it would be the "final fall." From that point on, anytime Zack took a trail group up along that ridge, he would tell them the last stop was Final Fall.

Lou turned to Tessa and said, "I can't believe you still have this picture! I look so young."

Dani climbed onto the bed and flopped down. "What's that a picture of?" she asked.

Lou turned to her. "That's me and Eagle."

She pushed herself up and hopped off the other side of the bed. She examined the picture more closely.

"That's you?" Dani asked, studying it more closely. "What happened? You look so different and young."

"I beg your pardon! I'll tell you what happened. You and your sister happened!"

"What's that supposed to mean?" she asked indignantly.

"What it means is I was young once too, just like you are. It means that time and years have a way of aging people, but I can assure you that I'm not old in my mind."

She looked back at the picture. "Is that Jasper? How old is that picture?" She was confused. "How old does that make him?"

"That's not Jasper. That's Eagle, Zack's horse. He was his pride and joy," Lou said.

"Yeah."

With no further interest in the photo, Dani looked around the room. "This room is great. Is this my room?"

Tessa smiled. "It sure is, honey. This room is the room your mom used to rent from us each summer she came to work on the ranch."

"Rent? You had to pay rent?" she asked, looking at her mom in total disbelief.

"Well of course I had to pay rent! Working here was my job. I had to pay for my lodging, silly. I was one of the hired hands, but since most of the hired help were men, they lived down in the bunkhouse. Zack and Tessa didn't think it was appropriate for me to live down there with them, so they offered me this room as an alternative. They were very clear from the beginning that it wasn't a free ride. We came up with a reasonable amount that wouldn't leave me completely broke at the end of each summer."

Dani looked at her mom and then back to Tessa. "Do I have to pay rent this summer?"   They exchanged a look and began to laugh. Tessa smiled, walked over to Dani, and patted her shoulder. "No," she said and continued to the door and paused in the doorway and looked back. "There are some clean towels in your bathroom. I'll say good night and let you two get settled. Louisa, I'll see you downstairs in a while?"

"It's been a long day, long few days, actually," Lou said to Dani after Tessa left, "C'mon. Let me help you get unpacked. Why don't you go take a shower and I'll unpack your things? Dani," Lou said, looking at her daughter seriously, "you do need to understand this isn't a holiday. It's a working ranch. Everyone pulls their share. Zack and Tessa have opened up their home to us. While there are no strings attached, the proper thing for us to do is accept the gift and show our appreciation by lending a helping hand where one is needed. Clear?"

"Clear," she said, nodding. She sighed, went into the bathroom, and closed the door behind her.

Lou picked up the suitcase and started to unpack her daughter's things. She grabbed a handful of shirts. As she walked to the dresser, something fell out of them to the floor. It was a framed picture of Dani and Kylie, an image of the two of them sitting on horses. It had been taken at a weekend rally they attended a couple of years earlier. They looked so happy. They'd just finished the cross-country course, and there were still traces of sweat on both of the horses. Lou thought about Kylie and how much had changed since that picture, more so since she had gone off to college. It made Lou realize that this had been a huge adjustment for Dani too. Perhaps some of her acting out over the past year was a direct result of not having her big sister around anymore. She thought about some of the blowouts they had experienced since Kylie had left home. Before, when the pressure had gotten too unbearable, Dani always had the safe haven of her big sister's room. Somehow Kylie always managed to calm Dani down. Often when she eventually emerged

45

from Kylie's room, an apology would follow, but more often, even if an apology didn't follow, her mood improved.

Lou sighed and walked over to the nightstand. She set the photo down in front of the lamp and whispered, "Watch over her this summer, Kylie. She misses you."

She finished unpacking the remaining items from Dani's bag and paused in the doorway. She looked around the room—her room—and let out a sigh of relief. She had no idea how life would turn out tomorrow or the next day, but one thing she was certain: this was a good choice. No matter what, things would happen as they were meant to happen. Lou needed to take a step back and see what awaited her child.

Lou went down to her room and unpacked her own things. She was tired but wasn't ready to go to sleep and decided to go check on Dani. Dani had changed into a pair of sweats and a tank top. Her hair was wrapped in a towel piled high on top of her head. She had her earbuds in and was humming along to whatever song was currently blasting in her ears as she filed her nails. When she noticed Lou standing in the doorway, she took one of the buds out and said, "What?"

"I was going to go back downstairs for a while. Do you want to come?"

"Nah, I think I'm going to go to bed. I'm tired. Besides, Zack said I get to start working with Bobby and Poet tomorrow."

"Poet? Which horse is that?" Lou walked over to the bed and sat down next to Dani. She reached for the towel on Dani's head, took it off, and started to dry her hair.

"He's amazing, Mom," she said. "He's this big bay—almost completely black, but he has one white sock and a heart-shaped star on his forehead. He's huge," she added. "He hasn't been ridden yet. Bobby started round penning and lunge lining him. Zack says he's a knothead, and he needs a job," she said, grinning. "He said he's a teenager like me, and we both need a job so we stay out of trouble."

Lou thought about this for a minute as she continued to dry Dani's hair. "Well, Zack's a pretty smart guy. One thing I can say for sure is he knows his horses. If he thinks you and Poet are a good fit, then I trust him one hundred percent with his decision. Now come on, get under those covers, and I'll tuck you in."

46

8

When Lou came back downstairs, Tessa was curled up on the big sectional sofa in front of the fireplace, and Zack had kicked back in his easy chair. Tessa was crocheting. Zack had a pair of reading glasses resting on his nose, intently reading what looked like an instruction manual. Lou walked into the room and sat on the sofa next to Tessa.

"What are you making?"

"Oh, it's just a baby blanket for one of my friends. Her daughter is due to deliver the first grandchild, and what baby doesn't need a new blanket?"

"Can I see?" Lou asked.

"Of course," Tessa said as she removed the crochet hook and handed the blanket to Lou.

Lou spread the blanket out over her lap to get a better look. "Tessa," she said. "This is so beautiful! Your blankets are so special. They're a labor of love."

"That they are." Tessa picked up the blanket and gently tucked it back into her knitting bag. She took her glasses off and rubbed her eyes. "Well I think I'm going to head upstairs. I'm a little tired. I don't think I can keep my eyes open much longer. Do you mind?"

"Of course not. We'll have plenty of time to catch up."

Tessa walked over to Zack and gave him a kiss on his forehead. "Good night, honey, you and Louisa have a nice visit." She squeezed his shoulder then went upstairs.

"Good night," Zack called after her. He looked at Lou. "You must be exhausted."

"I'm tired, but I don't think I'm ready to go to sleep yet. I'm afraid if I go upstairs now, I'll just lie in bed for the next couple of hours and stare into space."

"I've got the perfect remedy," he said and smiled. He got out of his chair and walked to the bar tucked behind the fireplace. Two bar stools were tucked up under the counter. The backdrop had a big mirror with a lithograph that read Echo Ranch in a half moon across the top. On the shelf in front of the mirror were miscellaneous decanters and a few bottles of whiskey. To the right was a small cabinet stocked with wine. He settled on a bottle, closed the door, and reached overhead and grabbed a couple of glasses. He set the glasses on the table in front of the sofa and opened the bottle. He poured two glasses and said, "Let's let that sit there for a minute. We need to give it a chance to get used to its new home before we drink it up." He winked.

"Since when did you become such a wine aficionado?" Lou teased.

"Oh you know Tessa," he said. "She's made lots of trips with her girlfriends out to wine country over the years. Every time she comes back, a couple of cases from whatever wineries they visit follow on the back of a delivery truck. At first, I didn't want anything to do with that stuff, being a whiskey-and-beer man myself. A few years back, we had a big Christmas party. There was food and alcohol flowing like water. She convinced me to try some of it. So I did. As much as I didn't want to admit it, I liked the stuff—not like my beer and whiskey, but it'll do." He chuckled. "Anyway, she kept doing those trips and kept having more wine shipped here. When I realized this wasn't a passing phase, I blasted out one of the walls in the basement about a year ago and built a wine cellar. I figured I might as well build a proper place to store it so all that money wasn't just being thrown away." He shook his head. "Here." He bent over and picked up their glasses. Lou took her glass, and they clinked them together. "Welcome home," he said and smiled, tipping his glass back.

"And to you." Lou raised her glass.

They sat across from each and enjoyed the wine. Lou admired the room. As she skimmed past some of the pictures, she relaxed further into the moment.

"What do you think of the wine?"

"It's fabulous!"

He sighed. "This is a good time for me to tell you what I have planned for you this summer."

Lou looked at him in total disbelief. "What you have planned for me?"

"Yep."

"Okay. I'll bite. I didn't know I needed a plan this summer, but please tell me. I'm all ears." She sat back in the sofa and crossed her arms and legs.

He looked over at her and started to laugh. "Well, look at that, will you. Looks like Dani isn't the only one who knows how to throw a temper tantrum."

"What's that supposed to mean?"

"What it means is as soon as I told you I had a plan for you, you just sat back and bunched yourself up into a knot."

Lou wanted to be angry, but the urge to laugh was greater. "Okay," she said, grinning and uncrossing her arms and legs. She picked her wine up and sat back. "Tell me your plan."

"That's much better," he said as he reached over to a business card that was sitting on the table and offered it to her. "This is a card for one of the women that Tessa does a lot of charity work with. Her name is Carla Preston. She runs an organization in town—an outreach program."

"What kind of outreach program, smarty?"

"Well if you'd stop yappin' and let me finish, I'll tell you," he said. "It's a program for inner-city kids. It's fueled by charitable donations that come in from all over the country. There's a lot of troubled kids out there, Lou. When Carla lost her son a few years ago, it was her personal mission to do something for some of those troubled kids."

"What do you mean she lost her son? How horrible! How old was he?" Lou asked.

"He was sixteen."

"Oh my god! What happened?"

"Well I'll tell you." He got comfortable in his chair and began his story. "For the most part, this is a pretty harmless place to raise a kid, but that doesn't mean if there's trouble to be had and a kid wants to find it, it's not going happen. One night a few summers back, Justin, Carla's boy, and a couple of his buddies went out toward Estes Park to go to the movies." He shook his head over the memory. "At least that's what they told Carla they were doing. Anyway, Justin barely had his driver's license." He paused then said, "That was their first mistake because once they started driving back home, one of the things they didn't think about was the fact that Justin was pretty tanked. He had no business getting behind the wheel of that car, let alone taking those other two boys with him. One thing led to another and—do you remember that sharp S curve not too far out from Estes on the way here?"

"Are you talking about the one that drops into the ravine?"

"That's the one," he said. "Well those boys probably had the music blaring, and they had some beers in the car with them too. Lou, if I tell you the panic they must have felt in that instant when the car left the road and flew off and into that ravine." He shuddered. "I just can't imagine it myself." He sat quietly, trying to collect his thoughts. "When the rescue team, cops, and all that other business arrived at the scene, I think the thing that was most significant and surely stamped a permanent memory in each of their minds was the skid marks the tires left on the road coming out of the final turn in that curve. They went straight up to the guardrail before they plowed through on their way to the bottom of that ravine."

"Oh my god," Lou said. "That's horrible!"

"It gets worse," he continued. "I already told you Justin had to have been pretty drunk." He shook his head. "The worst part is he lived through the nightmare. The other two boys didn't make it."

"That poor child. I mean, it's terrible he was drinking and driving," Lou said, "but to have to live with the memory of being the one that was driving and his two friends didn't make it has to be a horrible reminder for him every day since."

"We'll never really know that for sure, Lou," Zack said. "See, Justin survived because his blood alcohol was so high it turned his body into rubber. Granted, there was probably a part of him that snapped into sobriety a little as they were flying through the air. It was the alcohol that saved his life—if you can really call it a life. After the accident, he was in one of those assisted-care medical places over in Grand Junction—has been ever since he was strong enough to be transported from the urgent care. He's a full paraplegic now. He's completely bedridden, and his brain—if you can call it that—is a pile of mush inside his head." He finished his story and reached for his wine.

"I can't imagine the terror of something like that happening to one of my children," she said. "How has Carla managed? Has she pulled through?"

"Well, it's been a long road back for her. I'm out of wine. I'm getting some more. Do you want some?"

"Sure." Lou held her glass toward the bottle.

Zack finished filling the glasses and sat back down in his chair. He took his time getting settled. After a long sip of wine, he set his glass back down on the table.

"What I don't understand is what this has to do with me," Lou asked.

"I'm getting to that," he said. "First, there are a couple of points I want to make. The first one is that you're here this summer because we want you to be here. I know you want to be here too. When I heard your voice on the phone a few weeks ago, I knew there wasn't time for Tessa and me to sit down and have a family meeting. There was no long-winded discussion between us or any crap like that," he said. "I took care of all that after you and I talked because I knew Tessa would absolutely be on the same page.

"Basically, Lou, we're providing a change of scenery for your kid, which will help her get some new perspective and hopefully help her pull her head out of her ass before the end of summer. There's plenty to keep her occupied. Hell, there's plenty for her to get in trouble if that's what she insists on her life's work to be," he added. "But if—"

"Zack, I didn't just finish a two-thousand-mile drive for you to tell me you're providing a haven for Dani to get into more trouble. My god! We could have—"

"Let me finish." He held up his hand. "What I meant by trouble is the kind of trouble that happens here on the ranch—crossing paths with a rattler, forgetting to close one of the gates on the paddocks and some of the horses get out—that kind of trouble." He changed the subject. "Did she mention Poet to you? I can assure you that knothead is going to keep her busier than even she can imagine. She told you about him. Didn't she?"

"All she told me is 'Zack has a project for me. Bobby and me are going to work Poet this summer because Zack said he's a knothead,' which you just said so again, 'and since he's sort of a teenager, and I am, we would be the perfect match to work together this summer.' That's what I know about Poet, Zack," Lou said. "And that he's 'amazing.'"

Zack laughed. "Well, he is a knothead, but he's a smart knothead. I'd venture to guess Dani can be quite the knothead too, and if my early observations are correct, she's a bright knothead too. Let me break it down for you. He's a three-year-old that has unbelievable promise. Bobby is beyond capable of breaking that boy and making him into one of the best horses on this ranch. Poet's different. There's something about his spirit that needs a special kind of connection because of that spirit. He needs someone that has a wild hair but understands how to read his wild hair and work with him. That someone needs to teach him how to temper it versus break it all together. In the little I know about Dani, my gut tells me she's the one for him."

"Are you telling me you're going to let my kid work with a horse that isn't even backed?" Lou asked. "Zack, she's a very accomplished rider and an even better read of the animals, but breaking a horse is a whole different—"

"Oh my god," he said. "You two really are from the same cloth. I've got your kid telling me she doesn't know how to train a horse, but she wants to do it. Now you're sitting there telling me she can ride and knows the animals, but she can't train them." He seemed truly exasperated. "I'll tell you what I told her. I'm not throwing her down in the round pen tomorrow morning and telling her to get to work. I've already had a long discussion over the plan with Bobby long before the two of you even got here. Poet demands a lot of attention and work. Bobby is going to work side by side with her until she reaches that point that she can handle him on her own. And—"

"But—"

He held his hand up. "And when she gets there—because she will," he insisted, "then she'll take him to the next step. I'm telling you right now that by the time you guys get ready to go back home, that child will be riding that boy, and the two of them will move mountains together because of it." He didn't wait for a response and launched right into his second point. "The second point is this. What Carla has to do with all this is for you. So pay attention," he said firmly. "I know you do all sorts of charity consulting. When you decided you were coming, I had Tessa give Carla a call. The week after the Fourth of July each year, we host a weeklong rally for inner-city kids from all over the country. We pitch a big-top tent in one of the lower pastures and fill it with cots and sleeping bags, tables and chairs—hell, there's even a section along the back that's set up like a kitchen with propane gas stoves and the works. The entire week we have nightly jamborees and barbecues, campfires, sing-alongs, and whatever else people think cowboys used to do. By day we have roping expeditions, play horseshoes, offer hour-long trail rides throughout the day, give riding lessons, and pretty much show off everything else a horse can do. But what's most important is we offer a place for a kid to come and leave with a memory of something he or she will have for the rest of their lives. In some cases, these kids don't have the means to get a plane ticket or a bus ticket or even a car ride. It doesn't matter. Carla gets them here one way or another."

"I'm listening."

"Carla has taken care of the heavy lifting. She starts organizing this thing each year the day after this year's event is over. Hell, the tent is still standing in the pasture, and she's on her cell phone making calls to people about what she's got planned for the next year and do they think they can donate help or money or both. She reaches out to youth homes and drug programs and churches and wherever else there's a resource that can point her in the direction of a kid that needs at least one moment of hope in his or her life. Then she sets up a lottery and blasts endless communications out to all these places all over the country, targeting the major cities and their surrounding communities. She spells out in amazing detail how the lottery will work, and in each and every one of those cities, a drawing is held on a certain day six months before the rally is going to happen. There are ten kids from each inner-city location—"

"Ten kids," Lou exclaimed. "Jesus, Zack. That's five hundred kids. Are you telling me there are going to be five hundred kids invading the ranch the week after the Fourth?"

"Hell no! Your math is correct in that it's five hundred kids, but all of them won't be here. There'll be about fifty here. Anyway, once the lottery has been held and the winning kids are contacted, she spends the next month doling the list of kids out and placing them all over the country."

"So where do all the other kids go?" she asked.

"Some of them go to beach locations; others are sent to wilderness areas, and so on. The goal is to get these kids out of their day-to-day hopelessness and into an environment where they're surrounded not only by nature, but people who care about them. This isn't to say their parents

53

don't care. Jesus, in some cases they don't even have parents. They live in orphanages or, even worse, on the streets. Don't get me wrong. It wasn't like Justin was a kid that was headed toward a life of debauchery before the accident. The fact is, he was all-American in a lot of ways. He just started taking things for granted because he could. These kids who are selected are kids that have never even had a chance to take all this for granted.

"She may not be waving a magic wand and everything is perfect once they leave, but one thing Carla is definitely doing is making a difference. This work saved her life. When I told her a little about the work you do, she couldn't wait for you to get here. She really needs some help. I thought it would be a perfect outlet for you to get a little space from Dani. At the same time, you can gain some new perspective toward the days ahead between the two of you."

"I'm not sure what you mean by that last part," Lou said.

"What I mean is you're so close to the frustrations you've shared over how she's behaving and what she's been doing that you can't see the forest through the trees, Lou. You need to take a step back and find a different path, both of you do. The best way to do that is to give you both some space."

"So you lined me up with a job for the summer, and that's supposed to make things work better for us?" Lou asked, somewhat irritated.

"No, Lou," he said. "I lined you up with a woman that's a lot like you in the sense that she hears the word *charity* and she's signing up before there's even a sign-up sheet. Get your head out of your ass and stop making this all about you. It's about both you and Dani, and, as much as she needs some direction, you need some direction too. Damn it. I know how to do that when it comes to you. Humble yourself, woman, and try it before you say no."

Lou jumped a little after his last comment. She could hear the anger in his voice. "You need to calm down. I—"

"Don't tell me to calm down. I'm sitting here trying to help, and you keep slamming the door in my face because you're stuck in a rut just spinning your wheels," he said seriously, "I love you, Lou. I can see what a terrible strain all this has been on you. I want to see that fire in your eyes again that used to light up the canyons around here. There's still a fire, but it's one that's fueled by a lot of pain and resentment. Take this opportunity with Carla and focus your energies on doing what you do beautifully—giving. Stop worrying so much about molding Dani into the person you want her to be by controlling her every step. If she turns out to be half the woman you already are, then someday you'll be able to stand back and be proud of the amazing person she's turned into. Hell, it's a given that's going to happen because your blood runs through her veins. But you need to let her figure it out, Lou, and let her make some mistakes and suffer the consequences for her mistakes."

Lou wanted to fight with him, but she knew everything he said was true and felt like she was back in a time when she had just told him about yet another screwup she had managed and didn't know how to resolve. Sometimes back then he would be furious and other times not so much, but always definitely upset. One thing he always managed to do, no matter what, had been to listen. Lou sat and thought about everything he had said and realized the majority of it was the very essence of why she had come to Echo Ranch and Zack and Tessa: she trusted them and believed in the ranch. Lou wanted to do something drastic with Dani because mollycoddling definitely wasn't working. Whisking her away from all her friends and familiar places was drastic, but the saving grace was the safety of Echo Ranch as their landing pad.

"Okay," Lou whispered.

"Okay what?" he asked.

"Okay. I'll go talk with Carla. When does she—"

He cut Lou off. "Great, because you and Tessa are going into town tomorrow to meet her for lunch." He grinned.

"Why, you old snake," Lou said, but realized that she shouldn't have been surprised. "You and Tessa had this all planned out. Didn't you? 'Oh dear. I'm tired. I think I'm going to go to bed,'" she mimicked Tessa. "Yeah right."

Lou picked up her wine glass and poured the last bit down her throat. It was nearly one o'clock, and suddenly she felt like she couldn't keep her eyes open any longer. She stood, stretched, and let out a long yawn. Zack rose and walked over to her and picked her up before she finished her stretch. He swung her around and nearly sent the wine glass he had set on the table flying across the room.

"Zack, put me down," she demanded. "For heaven's sake, I'm not nineteen anymore."

"I know, but you're still a wild filly," he said, laughing, and set her back down. "Go on. Scoot. It's late, and tomorrow's another day." He hugged her again. "I'm going up in a minute. I just want to get rid of the evidence before Tessa comes down in the morning." He motioned toward the empty bottle and glasses.

"As if she'd care," Lou said.

Lou laughed, reached up and gave him a kiss on the cheek, and headed upstairs. She thought about Carla as she brushed her teeth and got ready for bed. She was intrigued and couldn't wait to hear more about her work.

9

Daylight came spilling through Dani's room. She turned over and slit her eyes open to see where the light was coming from. She lay there for a moment then sat bolt upright in her bed. Disoriented, she looked around the room and back out the window. After a moment she remembered where she was. She grabbed her cell phone off the nightstand to see what time it was.

"Seven o'clock," she said after looking at her phone in horror. She sank back down to her pillows and yanked the covers over her head. She curled up into a ball and closed her eyes again. When that didn't work, she flipped over to her other side, straightened her legs out, and took the other pillow and placed it over her head. She closed her eyes tight and tried to go back to sleep. After another few minutes and several tosses and turns, it was clear that sleep wasn't going to return. Frustrated, she threw the covers back, sat up, and swung her legs over the bed, forgetting about the step stool. Without hesitation, she pushed herself off the bed and, when her feet didn't hit the floor, she fell. She sat on the floor, bewildered, and looked over at the step stool. "Oh yeah," she said, giggling at herself then pushed herself up from the floor.

Dani stumbled toward the bathroom. She leaned over the sink and inspected her face in the mirror. After she tapped the remaining water from her toothbrush once she had rinsed it, she stuffed the towel back into the rack. She went back into her bedroom, slid her feet into her moccasins, pulled her hoodie over her head, then walked out into the breezeway and looked down into the great room. She could hear muffled voices coming from somewhere downstairs but was hesitant to go down alone. She wondered if her mom was up yet. She looked back down the hall and decided to check.

She tapped lightly on the bedroom door and waited for her mom to answer. When no answer came, she tapped a little harder, but still no answer came. She turned the knob and pushed the door open enough to peek in. The bed was unmade but empty. She walked into the room toward the bathroom door. It was ajar, but she didn't hear any noise coming from inside. She walked up to it and, as she was about to place her hand on the knob, the door pulled away from her, and her mom appeared. Lou let out a yelp, and Dani jumped back.

"Oh my god, Dani," Lou exclaimed. "What are you doing?"

Dani laughed. "Geez, Mom, I just came to see if you were in here."

"Well you scared the crap out of me," Lou said, laughing. "Good morning, Punk, how'd you sleep last night?" Lou reached over and gave Dani a hug.

"Okay." She gave her mom a quick hug. "It was weird when I first woke up because I forgot we were here," she said, grinning sheepishly. "And that bed is so high off the floor. I forgot you have to use that stool to climb up and down on it, so I fell off."

"Are you okay?" Lou asked, looking at her with concern.

"Mom, I'm not five," Dani said, brushing Lou's comment off. "Yes, I'm okay. I just fell, and besides, the carpet is so thick in there it felt like I landed on a bunch of pillows."

"It's nice, huh?" Lou agreed. "Are you hungry? I wonder if anybody else is up yet."

"I think somebody is downstairs," Dani said. "I was going to go down before I came back here because I thought it was you." She paused and said, "But then I figured if you weren't down there, it would be awkward."

"Awkward?" Lou teased. "Dani, this is your home for the summer. Zack and Tessa are very happy to have us here. What that means is that you don't need permission to walk around the house on your own. They want us to feel comfortable. Part of being comfortable is treating this home like it's your home too," Lou said, reassuring her. "Do you get that?" She pushed a piece of hair off Dani's forehead and tucked it behind her ear.

"Mom." She pushed Lou's hand away. "Don't do that. Okay?" she looked up at Lou.

"Do what?"

"That thing you always do with my hair. It makes me feel like a baby," she insisted.

"Well you are my baby," Lou said.

"I'm not a baby, Mom."

58

Lou could see that Dani was getting irritated and wanted to diffuse the moment before they jumped into the first fight for the day. "Okay." Lou held her hands up and backed away. "Sorry. I promise not to touch your hair anymore."

"Sure. Can we just go downstairs now?"

"Yep." Lou started to put her arm around Dani's shoulder and stopped. "Is it okay if I do this?"

Dani rolled her eyes. "Yes, Mom, you can do that. I just don't want you to—"

"I know. I know. Touch your hair." Lou smiled and put her arm around Dani's shoulder.

They walked downstairs through the great room and cut through the dining room to the kitchen. Zack was sitting on one of the bar stools at the counter drinking a cup of coffee. He had his reading glasses perched on his nose and was intently reading an article in the newspaper. Tessa was on the other side of the counter at the stove making what smelled like pancakes.

"Mmm," Lou said and smiled. "What is that smell? Are those muffins?" She bent down and peeked in the oven.

"Yes, they are, dear. They are muffins, and they'll be ready in another minute or two."

Lou looked at Dani and said, "Tessa makes the best muffins on the planet. She used to make them all the time when I lived here. To this day I still don't have her secret recipe." She looked back at Tessa and winked.

"They smell really good, Tessa," Dani said.

"How did you sleep last night?" Tessa asked. "Was everything all right with your room? Were you warm enough? There's a chest at the foot of the bed that has more blankets in it if you need another one."

"I was fine. That bed is really comfy," Dani assured her.

"Well good. Like I said, though, if you get cold, help yourself to another blanket. And if you get really cold, just let one of us know, and we can fire up the stove in your room."

"Okay. Thank you, Tessa." Dani climbed up on the stool next to Zack.

59

He set the newspaper down and took his glasses off. "Good morning," he said, smiling. "Are you ready to do some work today?" Zack asked Dani.

Dani thought about this for a minute and asked, "What kind of work?"

"Oh, there are about thirty stalls that need to be mucked," he said. "Then we have some fencing that we need to repair down toward the south valley. After that, we should probably cut back some of the hay and bale it up in the east pasture. By the time we finish that, it should be close to lunchtime. We'll take a twenty-minute break and come up for some food. After that, we'll go down to the office and get organized for the trail groups coming in tomorrow." He paused and looked down at her for a reaction.

She felt sick. With everything he had just rattled off that they were supposed to do, a miserable reality set in that maybe this wasn't going to be such a great summer after all. She began twisting her fingers and, without looking up, said, "That sounds like a lot of work. I thought I was going to work with Bobby and Poet."

"Well of course you'll work with Poet," Zack said. "But that shouldn't take more than an hour or so. There's a lot more work to do besides work that knothead."

She gave him a gloomy look. "So should I wear my muck boots?"

"That's probably the best," he said and looked down at her moccasins. "You definitely can't wear them. Those slippers will get ruined before you finish the first stall, and remember, there're thirty or so to do." He nudged her.

"Yeah," she said with a sigh. "I remember." She looked back down at her hands and got real quiet.

Zack looked at Lou and back to Tessa. The silence was unbearable. They began to laugh. Dani looked up and shot a dirty look at her mother. She looked back at Tessa and Zack and couldn't figure out what was so funny.

She looked back at her mother and snapped, "What are you doing today? Shopping?"

They stopped laughing. Lou gave Dani a disapproving look. Slowly, she responded, "Actually, I'm going to go to work too. Tessa and

60

I are going into town to meet a friend of hers who has a business she needs some help with this summer."

Dani immediately looked back down at her hands, and she fell silent again.

After another moment, they began laughing again. She felt angry because somehow she understood that she was the brunt of their joke. "I don't get what's so funny," she said.

Zack reached over and grabbed one of Dani's hands. It took her by surprise, but she didn't snatch it away.

"Relax." Zack chuckled. "We're not mending fences or mucking stalls or baling hay today," he assured her. "I was thinking that maybe you and I could take a trail ride up to Bonita Ridge. It's a place—"

"Seriously!" she exclaimed. "A trail ride would be awesome."

"Yes. A trail ride," Zack finished. "In the summer, my main job is leading trail rides all over this property. That's the main part of our business in the summer months, and it's a known fact that I am the trail boss."

"Cool," she said and smiled. "So when will we go?" She hopped off her stool and turned to go back upstairs. "I should go get ready."

"Hold on there." He grabbed her arm. "Tessa here is making a nice breakfast, and the rule around here is you eat breakfast before anything else happens. There are a couple of reasons for this." He looked at her to be sure he had her attention. "The first is you need nourishment and energy to get properly fueled for the morning's work," he said, "but the most important reason is because my beautiful wife has taken the time to put it all together, and out of our deep respect for her, we'll eat and be grateful that she took her time and energy to make it." He looked down at Dani. "Understand?"

Dani felt like she'd just been subjected to yet another lecture but was too afraid to give a smart answer in return. Instead she nodded, climbed back up on her stool, and looked at Tessa. "Thank you for making breakfast for us, Tessa," she said.

"It's my pleasure, honey. Do you like pancakes?" she asked.

"I love pancakes."

"Good." Tessa reached over, set a place in front of Dani, and put a plate of steaming pancakes down next to it. They all sat there for a moment looking at the plate of food.

Zack looked to his left and took Lou's hand and then looked to his right and picked up Dani's hand. He bowed his head and said a prayer, "Oh, Heavenly Father," he started. Dani bent her head down and cocked it to the left to peek over at her mom and then across to Tessa. Everyone had their heads bowed in unison as they listened to Zack speak. "We want to take a moment to thank you for the food before us. We thank you for our health and another day of living. And we'd like to make a special thanks to you for guiding Lou and Dani to the safety of our home. Amen." Zack broke the silence. "Well, let's eat," he said. "Tessa gets real mad if you let her food get cold." He reached over for the plate of pancakes and turned to offer them to Lou first.

They sat and enjoyed breakfast. Every now and then Dani caught Lou glancing at her. Mostly, however, she was completely absorbed in enjoying her meal. Zack kept reaching over and putting another pancake on Dani's plate when he thought she wasn't looking. After the third time, Dani held her hand up. "No more. I'm stuffed," she said, giggling.

They finished breakfast, and Dani looked at her mom. "Is it okay if I go upstairs and get my riding gear on?"

"Sure. Your saddle is still in the car. My keys—"

Zack interrupted, "Well, let's hold on a second here." He looked at Dani. "Your mom told me you were one of those fancy English riders. I think that's great, but I have a situation I want to run by you and see if you can help me out with it."

Dani shot her mom a concerned look. "Okay," she said hesitantly. "What?"

"Most of those horses out there don't know much about English riding. I know there's quite a difference between that and Western, but I'm thinking I want you to try something a little different while you're here."

"But Zack," she said, giving him a worried look. "I don't know how to ride Western. Besides, that's why we brought my saddle."

"I understand," he assured her, "but can you humor me for a minute?"

She looked down at her hands. "Okay."

"See, my horses do a lot of climbing out on those trails, and some of the terrain is pretty steep. An English saddle isn't designed for a rider to take some of those steeper trails. I'm thinking about your safety today. One of the trails we're taking is pretty steep as you're climbing the last stretch up to Bonita Ridge."

"So do you think I can't handle it?" she asked with an edge to her voice.

"Honey, I believe you can handle anything that's put before you if a horse is concerned," he said and looked over at Lou and back to Dani. "Your momma has told me what an excellent rider you are. But let's try something here. Okay?" he suggested. "So here's what I'm suggesting: Tessa has a beautiful Australian saddle that's more streamlined than most of my bigger and clunkier Western saddles. See, Tessa's a lot like you because she can't stand all that bulk underneath her between her and her horse. She wants to feel the motion of the ride. So we talked about this before you guys got here and thought maybe you could give her saddle a try. If you like the ride, you can use it this summer."

She looked at Tessa. "If I'm going to use your saddle all summer, what will you use?"

Tessa leaned on the counter and smiled. "Honey, I have a couple of favorite saddles I use. I know the saddle that Zack is talking about. I'd be honored to let you use it. Honest," she said, reassuring Dani. "I want you to feel comfortable on the horses because you're going to be doing a lot of riding this summer."

"Yeah, but," Dani started whining. "Mom, if I can't use my saddle, why did we even bring it?"

"Honey, we're not telling you that you can't use your saddle. Zack is thinking of your safety," Lou said, sharing a look a look with Zack.

"That's exactly right," Zack agreed. "Besides, I have specific plans for your saddle."

"Like what?" Dani asked and looked back down at her hands.

"Like Poet," he said.

She popped her head up and gave him a big smile. "Do you mean I get to train him English?" she asked.

63

"Not exactly," Zack said then hesitated. "He does have those sleek lines, and I know what a jumper is, but he's still growing and has a lot of filling out to do. I think when you and Bobby get to the point of backing him, your saddle is going to be the perfect one to use. It's a lot lighter than a Western saddle, a nice beginner to get him used to having something on his back. I suppose it's a good thing you brought it with you so it doesn't have to just sit in the car all summer gathering dust." He ruffled Dani's hair.

She thought about this and looked at Tessa. "What's your saddle like?"

"It's got buttery-soft leather that's broken in just right, and the seat is so comfortable. It doesn't have one of those big annoying horns on it," Tessa answered, wrinkling her nose. "The best part is it has a lift in front where you can rest your hands, and the back of the seat has a lift too because it was made for a woman's butt." Tessa smiled.

Lou laughed. "What she means by that is it's comfortable around all the right curves."

"My butt isn't big," Dani insisted.

"Your butt is beautiful, Punk."

"Mom," Dani said, feeling embarrassed.

"Okay, ladies," Zack said, stopping them. "Before this conversation goes too far south, I suppose it's time we thought about heading down to the barn." He looked at Dani.

"Okay, I'll go get changed." She hopped off the stool and stopped. "Is it okay if I wear my boots? They're English tall boots. You know the kind I mean?"

"Of course you need to wear boots," he said. "I don't care if they're African bush boots. Nobody gets on one of my horses without proper foot gear."

Dani shook her head, turned, and left to get ready.

"Thank you," Dani heard Lou say to Tessa and Zack as she left the room.

She paused just outside the kitchen door to listen.

"For what?" she heard Zack ask.

"For mediating something that could have easily turned into another Cold War," Lou replied.

64

10

When Dani came back downstairs and saw that Zack was no longer there, her heart sank.

"Where's Zack? Did he already go down to the barn?" she asked. "How am I supposed to get there? Do I have to drive the Gator by myself? Aren't we going anymore?" She looked at her mother. She was sure that her regret was written all over her face. "Do I have to go into town with you guys?"

"He's down in his office," Lou said. "No, he didn't go to the barn. Yes, you're going with him. Absolutely not are you driving the Gator by yourself, and, no, you're not going into town with us." Lou paused and added, "I think that answers all your questions."

"Very funny. What's he doing downstairs? When are we going?" Dani demanded.

"Patience, my child," Lou warned her. "Remember, Zack has a business to run. He had to do a few things in his office."

"I thought his office was down at the barn."

"It is, dear," Tessa said, coming into the room. "He has a small office downstairs too. He figured since you had to get ready to ride, he'd take care of some business while he was waiting for you."

"Oh," Dani said, breathing a sigh of relief. "I mean it's not like I don't want to spend time with you guys. It's just that I'd—"

"Rather go with Zack and be with the horses?" Tessa asked, smiling.

"Yes," Dani admitted, grinning.

"Trust me, Tessa. If there's a cot and a blanket down in that barn and Dani is missing from her room this summer, we'll know where to find her," Lou said.

"Mom, you make me out to be such a freak."

"Who's a freak?" Zack asked, returning from the office.

Dani jumped when she heard his voice. She wondered how long he'd been standing behind her.

"Let me ask you something," he said, looking at Dani.

"What?"

"Do you always treat your momma like that?"

The air suddenly grew very thick, and an awkward silence spread.

65

Ignoring Dani's failure to respond, he said, "I remember one time when I was just about your age—fourteen, right?"

"Yes," she said.

"Now, I know it's hard to believe that I was fourteen once, but I was," Zack said. "Anyway, I remember my dad asked me if I'd go down to the barn and get started on mucking stalls. Hell, it was summertime. Me and a couple of my buddies already had our day planned out. We were going to grab a couple of those ponies and take off into the hills for the day. See, there's a great lake down at the end of the southern range on the property." He paused to be sure he had her attention. "It's a great place—the perfect place to spend a nice summer day, actually. It's got a rope swing and a couple of picnic tables. There are all kinds of trails to ride up into the back country if you get bored of swimming. Anyway, this day we even had a couple girls riding over to the lake to meet us. Without even thinking about the consequences, I spun around and looked at my daddy. I told him I wasn't mucking any stalls that day because I already had plans."

Zack stopped speaking, walked into the kitchen, and poured himself another cup of coffee. Lou and Tessa busied themselves clearing the breakfast dishes away and wiping nonexistent crumbs from the countertop. Zack took his time pouring his coffee as though there was no bottom to his cup. Dani stood on the other side of the counter feeling all alone and very on-the-spot. After the silence became unbearable, she asked, "What happened?"

"Well I'm getting to that," Zack said. He poured some cream in his cup and motioned for her to follow him into the dining room so he could finish his story. Dani saw Lou give Zack a look, and he waved her off.

Dani followed Zack into the dining room through the doorway.

"Have a seat," Zack said as more of a command than an offering.

Dani pulled up a chair across the table from him. She felt as though she was about to cry.

"So Samuel," he said and looked hard at Dani. "Samuel was my daddy's name. Samuel took me into this dining room right where you and I are now. He didn't want my momma to hear what he had to tell me. You see, Dani, I used to give both him and my momma a lot of lip. I could be real disrespectful. It used to make my momma cry, but it used to make him want to get his strap out so I'd have something to think about before I just went ahead and smart-mouthed him the next time."

"Your father beat you?" Dani asked, horrified.

"Hell no," he said. "He didn't beat me. It just took one or maybe two times during my entire childhood that he took that belt to me before I figured he meant business and I needed to change my way of thinking and acting. The first time he did it was the very day I'm telling you about. He was so damn angry I thought it was going to be the end of me." Zack looked out the window toward the sky, and a smile formed at the corners of his mouth to Dani's disbelief, considering he was talking about getting punished.

"Well, he gave me four good cracks on my behind. He was a big, strong man, and I was mortified. There I was, a fourteen-year-old kid and definitely thinking I was way too old to be getting a whooping from my daddy." Zack shook his head.

Barely audible, she asked, "Did he hurt you?"

"Hell yeah it hurt," he said. "What hurt more than anything, though, were his words." Zack took a deep breath. "He told me if I was so smart and had the opinion that the plans I'd made were more important than the responsibility of my chores, I could go ahead and go down to that lake. But he also said if I thought for a second I was going to take one of his horses or have a good time on his land, I had another thing coming."

"What did he do?"

"He said he wasn't kicking me out because that would be child neglect, but until I figured out how to demonstrate honest-to-goodness respect toward him and my momma and learned how to earn that respect through my actions, I wasn't a son of his. He made this rule that I was not allowed to talk to him or my momma until I figured out how to do that. What's worse, I wasn't allowed to ask them for anything. I couldn't borrow money for the movies or ride any of his horses or do any of those sorts of things a fourteen-year-old kid likes to do. No, sir," Zack said, shaking his head.

Zack took a long sip of his coffee and set the mug down on the table. He rubbed his eyes and looked out the window toward the sky.

Dani followed his gaze. The way he looked she thought maybe there was going to be an image of his father up there.

"You're wondering why I keep looking up there, don't you?" he said, interrupting her thoughts.

She looked down at her hands. She couldn't look at him. In a faint whisper, she said, "You seem like you're mad at me or something."

"I'm not mad at you," he said then got up out of his chair and came around the table and sat down next to her. "What I am is confused. See, your momma is an amazing woman. The last summer she spent working here was one of the best summers I remember." He sighed. "It was one of the saddest summers for me because I was watching someone who, when she first came to this ranch, was a lot like you. When she left, she was a lot different."

Dani wasn't buying it. "She was fourteen when she started working here?"

Zack started to laugh. "Hell no she wasn't fourteen, but she was a smart mouth and didn't really think too much about what she said until somebody put her in her place after she said it. After a couple of times Tessa—"

"Tessa yelled at her?" Dani asked, shocked.

"No. Tessa didn't yell at her, but I'll tell you something right now. Don't you ever underestimate Tessa. She's got a heart of gold, and she'll give you the shirt off her back in the freezing rain, but she will not stand for someone sassing her or taking her for granted," he warned. "C'mon, now, let me finish my story. So anyway, my daddy basically turned his back on me. He convinced my momma she had better be in alliance with him if she expected to see some changes around this place. Well, that silence from both of them lasted about a week. I couldn't ride or go anywhere with my friends or have any fun, and school had barely let out. I had a whole summer ahead of me. My greatest fear was that it would be spent with backbreaking work and total silence. It got so bad he must have clued all the hired hands in on his plan because the only time any of them would say anything to me was if they needed me to take a wheelbarrow over to the manure pile to dump it out or grab some horses out of whatever paddock they were in because the farrier was coming. They'd tell me to 'get on down to the ring, there's a group of tourists coming in. You have to help get them set up for their trail ride.'" Zack shook his head as he was remembering that time.

"At least you got to go on trail rides," she offered.

"Hell no I didn't. I had to saddle up all those horses and watch them all ride off," he said. "I had to go back to mucking stalls or haying or riding out to one of the lower pastures to mend fences all day. And," he reminded her, "I did all that in absolute silence."

"They didn't talk to you the whole summer?" Dani challenged.

"Sure they did, and I'm getting to that." He picked his coffee up, took a sip, and continued, "About a week and a half later, I'd come back up to the house after finishing my chores for the day. I was exhausted. I was so tired I practically planted my face in my dinner plate that night. I finished eating and took my dish to the kitchen. I asked permission to go upstairs to shower and go to bed. My momma looked like she was going to break down and cry for a week, but she just nodded her head. My daddy wouldn't even look at me. So I went up to my room, got my clothes off, and took a shower. I turned that water on and started to cry. The longer I stood under that shower, the harder I cried. I don't imagine I was in there much more than ten minutes, but by the time I got out and got dried off, I started in on a whole new round of tears. I climbed into my bed and was about to turn the light off and decided against it."

"What did you do?"

"I threw my covers back and went downstairs. My parents were still up. My daddy was sitting in that chair where I usually sit now in the evenings. My momma was on the couch reading a book. I had stopped crying because I didn't want any pity. I just wanted to hear them say something to me. So I stood in the doorway for a few minutes, and finally, I asked, 'Daddy, do you think it would be all right if I talked with you and Mom for a minute?' He took his reading glasses off real slow and looked over at me just standing there. He was thinking about my question and took his time answering. Finally, he told me to come in and sit down. So I walked into the room and sat on the chair across from him." Zack grinned. "It had been a while since either one of them had said anything to me. It occurred to me I didn't know what I wanted to say to them. I could feel some tears starting to come up again and wiped them away real fast. They both just sat there and didn't say a word. I stole a quick look at my momma. She always kept a tissue tucked in her sleeve. She had pulled it out making it look like she was wiping her nose, but I knew she was wiping some of her own tears away."

"What did she say?"

"She didn't say anything."

"Then what did you say?"

"Well, I said that I knew what I did was wrong—not that it was wrong to want to make plans to be with my friends, but it was wrong because I didn't care what him or Momma wanted because all I wanted was what I wanted. I said I was sorry for being so selfish, but I was even sorrier for making my momma cry." He paused to clear his throat. "It was then that I turned to him and said, 'but what I'm really sorry about, Daddy, is how you and Momma think I don't respect you and that I've disappointed you. That's when I couldn't hold it back anymore. I just opened up the floodgates and told him how much I missed talking to them. I didn't have anybody to talk, to and it was killing me a little bit more each day. The one thing that hurt the most though is that if felt like my parents didn't want me anymore."

Dani had tried holding it in, but she felt a tear trickle down her cheek.

"Sometimes I do that to my mom and dad too," she said through her tears. "It's not that I think about being mean to them—especially my mom. My dad just gets real mad and tells me I'm ungrateful and I need to pull my head out of my ass and think about what I'm doing. But with my mom it's different. I love her so much, but I get so mad at her. I don't know why. I just do." Then Dani really started sobbing.

Zack leaned over and wiped her tears away. "Dani, Dani, Dani," he whispered. "You are your mother's child through and through. I want you to understand something. I'm not your daddy, and Tessa isn't your momma. We never had kids of our own, but that woman who is your momma is the closest thing that we ever had to a child." He sighed. "She loves you so very much. What I'm asking you to do this summer is start taking some baby steps toward recognizing what an important person she is in your life. I want you to learn how to temper that wild horse inside of you when it comes to dealing with her and your daddy. Someday, they won't be around. Once they're gone, you've got to have the memories of all the joyful moments you spent with them while they were here. It won't always be easy, but you've got to start somewhere. Maybe now is a good time to think about a plan and how you can do a little each day."

Zack sat back in his chair and rested his elbow on the table. He looked out across the valley. "Now c'mon, enough of this. We've got horses to tack and ride because we've been sitting here way too long. I'm thinking today would be a good day for you to take a spin on Lucy."

"Who's Lucy? Did I meet her yesterday?" Dani asked, tears vanishing.

"Honey, if you did, you'd remember. Lucy is the prettiest redhead I know aside from the real Lucy." Zack smiled.

"Who's the real Lucy?" she asked.

He started laughing and shook his head. "Never mind. You're too young. C'mon, grab your helmet and let's head down to the barn."

11

They drove to the barn in silence. Zack pulled his truck up next to the double doors by the barn. A big hay truck was parked off to the side. A couple of men came out pushing wheelbarrows. He turned the engine off, reached over to grab a couple of folders off the seat, and looked at Dani.

"You ready to do some riding today, young lady?"

She looked at him and managed a smile. "Yes."

"Now that doesn't sound like somebody that can't wait to get on a horse," he teased.

She gave him a faint smile. "Trust me. I'm ready to do some riding."

"That's better." He popped his truck door open. "I've got to drop these files in the office."

Dani followed him into the office and sat down in one of the chairs. Zack walked over to his desk, grabbed a marker, and scratched a couple of notes on the whiteboard above his desk. She sat in the swivel chair, turning it from side to side as she checked out the photos on the walls. She stopped when she noticed one particular photo. She popped up out of her chair and walked over to get a closer look. It was an image of a younger Zack and that same horse she had seen in the photo hanging in her room. The young woman standing next to him looked like her mom. They were standing with the horse outside the barn. They looked happy. Dani looked at Zack and asked, "Is that you and my mom?"

He turned around. He set his marker down and walked over beside her to look at the photo. "That sure is. That was my horse."

"Eagle?"

"That's right. I guess you saw him in the picture in your room."

"Yeah, Mom and Tessa told me about him last night. My mom said he was a ham."

"He sure was," Zack said and smiled. "Jasper's a lot like him, but there will never be another boy quite like Eagle." He sighed. "C'mon, half the day is gone, and we haven't even gotten our horses tacked up yet."

"What time is it?"

"It's almost nine."

72

"Nine," Dani said, shocked. "If I was still back home, I wouldn't even be up yet."

"Well then, welcome to Echo Ranch. Half the day's work is done by nine o'clock," he said and patted her shoulder. "I'm going down to get Jasper and talk to the boys for a couple of minutes. There are a couple of things that need to be done around here, and I'm going to remind them of just exactly what those things are." He called over his shoulder. "Bobby is probably somewhere out there too. Find him before you just go charging into that paddock. I don't want you going around the horses by yourself for a couple of days until you get used to the lay of the land. Clear?"

"Clear," she confirmed.

When she got to the paddock, there was a gorgeous, coppery-red horse with a long sun-bleached red mane and forelock. The horse stood on one side at the fence line.

Dani held her hand out toward the horse. "You must be Lucy," she said.

Lucy leaned into Dani's hand, snorted and snuffled a couple of times, and stepped back. She nodded her head and leaned back into the fence so Dani was able to stroke her forehead. "Well aren't you sweet," she whispered. "You're pretty too."

"Hey, Miss Dani."

She spun around just in time to see Bobby tip the brim of his hat to her again. She giggled. "You don't have to tip your hat every time you see me, you know."

"Yes, ma'am, I know, but it's the right thing to do to a lady," he replied.

They stood, stroking Lucy for a couple of minutes, and Bobby said, "The boss said you're riding Lucy today." Bobby reached up and tousled Lucy's mane. "She's a fine horse. She's got one of the nicest trots on the ranch. You'll feel like you're on the softest and smoothest rocking horse you ever rode." He smiled at Dani.

"Smooth ride works," she whispered and continued gently stroking Lucy's forehead.

"C'mon through the gate here with me," Bobby said. "Grab Lucy's halter and lead line. It's hanging on the post behind you there." Bobby pointed to the fence post by the gate hitch.

Dani grabbed them and followed him into the paddock. She turned and locked the gate. When she turned back around, she could see Poet. He was running like a locomotive and coming straight toward them.

"Watch yourself there," Bobby cautioned. "Sometimes he gets a little crazy."

Poet was in a full gallop headed straight for them. It spooked Lucy, and she sidestepped around Bobby and quickly trotted off to the opposite end of the fence line. Bobby turned to Dani and motioned for her to go ahead and get out. When she turned to lift the gate latch, Poet advanced toward them again. He was in a slow trot, heading straight for Dani. Bobby looked at him and back at Dani. He reached up for his hat and took it off. He was just about to swing his arm up when Dani grabbed his forearm.

"Don't. Please," she asked him. "Let's just see what he does."

"What the?" he said, surprised.

"He's not going to hurt us," she said, trying to convince Bobby. "He's just curious. He doesn't know me. He wants to get a closer look. Please don't wave him off."

Bobby slowly placed his hat back on his head and took a stand between Poet and Dani. "Miss Dani," he cautioned, "don't do something crazy because Zack will have my head."

"I won't. I promise," she reassured him. "I just want to see what he does."

Poet stopped trotting and slowly walked toward them. Bobby was obviously of no interest to him, but Dani was. He got close enough for her to reach her hand out to his muzzle, but not close enough for her to touch him. He jerked his head back and snorted a couple of times. He stood still for a moment then extended his muzzle toward her. Dani hadn't moved her hand. She still had it extended out to him. This time she could feel his warm breath tickling her palm. She gave him a big smile and whispered, "That's right, boy. I'm not going to hurt you. I just want to get to know you. Do you smell Lucy? Is that what you smell?" she asked, coaxing him as she inched her hand out a little closer to him.

74

Poet bent his head down toward her hand. He took a half step toward her and raised his head. He let out a big whinny and pawed at the ground. He tossed his head side to side and brought it back down to her hand. He took a couple more sniffs and stepped closer. Dani inched toward him, and he jerked his head back.

She froze and began speaking softly to him, "C'mon, Poet, I know you want me to pet you. I can barely reach you, boy. Do you think it would be all right if I come a little closer?" she asked as she moved a little closer.

Poet stood as though he were posing for the cover of a magazine. His ears were pitched forward, and his head was slightly cocked. He seemed to relax a little as he listened to Dani's voice. Finally, he surrendered and bent his head down to her hand.

"That's right," she said, soothing him. "I'm just going to reach up and tickle your muzzle. She reached up to touch his nose. He jerked back slightly on first contact, but Dani didn't retreat. She waited patiently. Satisfied she wasn't a threat, he relaxed his muzzle into her hand. She tickled his muzzle and cautiously inched her hand up and around the side of his mouth to his cheek. She paused at his cheek and gently stroked it a couple of times as she guided her hand to his forelock. She brushed the hair away from his eyes. She eased her hand around his forehead and, ever so slowly, began stroking his neck. She concentrated on long, slow passes up and down his neck. After a few more strokes, he leaned into her. He let out a content sigh.

She smiled up at him. "That's right. What a good boy you are. You are the most handsome boy I've ever seen." She continued talking to him. "I'm going on a trail ride with Zack today, but I'll be back later to work with you. Would you like that?" she asked him. He looked at her and relaxed further into her strokes. "I know what you mean." She smiled at him. "I can't wait either."

He looked down at her and over at Bobby. He allowed her to give one more stroke and then lifted his head high. He bellowed a great whinny, spun around, and took off toward the back pasture.

They stood by and watched him run away. Bobby turned to Dani. "Do you know that is the first time that crazy horse has ever done something like that to anyone, let alone a perfect stranger?"

"I'm not a stranger. I'm going to be his trainer. He just wanted to get the formalities out of the way because he knows that we've got a job to do together this summer," Dani said, then asked, "Do you think it would be all right if I go get Lucy alone? I can handle her."

"Uhhh. I don't—"

"Please, Bobby?" she asked, interrupting. "She's not going to do anything bad."

"Okay," he said, "but Zack doesn't want me leaving you in any of the paddocks alone until you and the horses get to know each other." He looked back out toward the far pasture and could see Poet at the far end. "Okay, but I'm waiting right here."

"Cool," she said, "Thanks."

She grabbed the halter and lead rope and took off before Bobby had a chance to change his mind.

12

They set out toward the northwestern valley. Jasper and Lucy meandered down the gravel road and the paddock next to the main barn. Poet trotted up to the corner of the fence that intersected with the road. He whinnied a couple of times as they walked past. Lucy turned and answered him with her own whinny. Jasper couldn't be bothered and kept his eyes on the road. He was too busy maintaining his lead. They rounded the bank of pines that separated the fence from the road. They had an option to either continue straight or move out across the valley toward the ridge in the distance. Zack said that he wanted Dani to see the brood mares and their foals.

"C'mon." He gave Jasper a kick. "I want to show you something."

They trotted on, and he pointed to the large white barn. "That's where all the mommas and babies live," he told her.

"Really? How many babies are there?" she asked.

"We have three this summer—two colts and a filly. Once we get up this knoll, you'll be able to see them."

"Cool."

They continued up the road in a gradual ascent until it leveled off and was even with the barn far to their right. Dani looked over just in time to catch one of the babies running double time to keep up with its momma, trying to stay close to her side. He was a black-and-white paint, and his momma was a beautiful dark bay.

"Oh, he's so cute," she exclaimed. "Look how sweet he is, staying so close to his Mom."

As they continued down the road, Dani turned to steal one more glimpse of the baby before they rounded the next bend and began to climb again. Once they reached the top, she could see a large meadow in the distance and, beyond that, a magnificent mountain peak projected high into the sky above it.

"That's where we're taking our first trail group tomorrow. It'll be the official kickoff to Echo Ranch's summer season," Zack announced as he pointed to the mountains ahead of them.

Dani could not believe the size of the massive peaks staring back at her. She looked back at Zack. "You're taking horses up there?" she asked.

"We sure are, honey. I know from here it looks pretty scary, but once we cross this valley and get closer to the trailhead, it won't look so threatening," he said, assuring her.

"Wait a second. We're going up there?"

"Well of course we are," he said. "We always ride the trail before I take a group on it. I've been up here a few times already this summer, but since you're going to be riding with me tomorrow—"

"I am?" she interrupted.

"I figured it made sense we ride it together today before we take the group up tomorrow."

"Zack," she said. "I've been on lots of trail rides, but the ones I've been on are mostly fields and woods. I've never climbed a mountain on a horse. That looks like a really big mountain to me."

"Okay. Let's hold up here for a minute," he said, stopping Jasper. Dani pulled up on Lucy's reigns to halt her.

"I'm guessing you're not too sure about doing this trail today." He looked at her.

"Well," she said hesitantly, "it's not that I don't want to do it, it's just that it looks kind of steep." She was searching for an excuse. "Besides, what if Lucy loses her footing? It doesn't look like there's a lot of room for a mistake on that trail."

"That's what I was trying to explain. We've got at least another hour before we get to the trailhead. From here it looks like a skinny little path that's barely a foot wide." He paused then said, "But trust me. By the time we get there, that trail will look a lot wider. I promise nothing bad will happen to you. You're sitting on top of one of the finest climbers I have. She's real agile and sure-footed. She also takes real good care of her passengers."

He reached over and gave Lucy a pat. "Isn't that right, my pretty redhead?" Lucy lifted her head and whinnied.

"C'mon, we've got a valley to cross. Just wait until you see some of this place."

"Okay," Dani said, taking a deep breath and giving Lucy a kick.

They got into the open field. Zack looked at Dani. "What do you think? Are you ready to trot them out a bit? How's that saddle working for you?" he asked.

"It feels good," she said. "It's really comfortable. I thought it was going to be clunky, but it feels pretty good."

"Good." Zack rode up beside her. He reached out to her reins. "Here. Let me show you something. If you gather them up in one hand like this," he said, picking up his own reins and holding them in one hand to show her, "and every now and then when you want to adjust your direction, lay it to the right or left on either side of the neck like this." He demonstrated on Jasper. "Lucy will act on a dime for you. Another thing to keep in mind with her is she's real soft on the bit. That girl knows a good rider, and I'll tell you why I know you're a good rider."

"How?"

"Because ever since we set out, I haven't seen her bob or jerk her head once. That tells me you're listening to her as much as she's responding. I don't typically let an inexperienced rider on her because her mouth is so soft. Novice riders always cinch up the reins and pull them back real tight. What they don't realize in doing that is it's driving their horse crazy, especially her," Zack said and nodded toward Lucy. "Every now and then I read a rider wrong, and it irritates the hell out of Lucy. She turns into a right nasty bitch and scares the crap out of the person on her back. She won't toss them, but she sure will make them wonder if they're going to be tossed." He shook his head. "She gets so darn angry with their yanking and pulling on her mouth."

"So you think she likes me?" Dani asked.

"You bet," Zack said. "Let's get these two moving a little?"

He gave Jasper a kick and trotted ahead. Dani followed behind them.

"Look," she said as she pulled up on Lucy's reins and stopped.

Zack looked ahead to where she was pointing. Some of his herd was running along the ridgeline.

"That's so awesome," Dani exclaimed.

"Those are the horses we'll be using for the two different groups coming in tomorrow," he said. "See, we rotate the horses out a lot because we don't want to overwork them. That small herd up there is turned out here because we want them to get used to the ground they're going to be crossing over tomorrow. They're sewing some of those wild oats of theirs today to get them good and relaxed for tomorrow. Bobby and some of the hired hands are coming out later this afternoon to round them up. We'll stage the groups in that paddock by the barn and get everyone squared away before we head up into the back country. Remember when I was writing all that stuff on the board in the office earlier?" he asked.

"Sort of," Dani answered.

"I was making up the assignments for what horses we're going to use tomorrow. We have two groups coming in. The first one is about ten people and the second, eight." He pointed to the herd and said, "Those renegades out there kicking up their hooves will be divided up for the two groups. We'll do the actual assignments of riders to horses tomorrow once we get an assessment of who knows what about riding."

"That sounds like a lot of work, and confusing too," she said. "I mean, what if you put somebody on the wrong horse—like Lucy?"

"Sometimes that happens. All we can do is fix it and hope nothing bad happens." He gave her a serious look. "Before we take anybody up into these hills, we do assessments. We take them down to the south pasture."

"Which pasture is that?"

"The one I was telling you about at dinner last night."

"You mean the one you said you don't let horses in because there are wild animals that could hurt them?"

He chuckled. "Well it's not like we're going to be doing assessments beside mountain lions and bears. They don't just come out in broad daylight because they want some fresh horse meat to nibble on. This isn't some darn zoo, you know. We use that area because it's wide open and there's lots of space for the horses," Zack explained. "There'll be about eight of us doing the assessments. We'll divide into groups with a couple of riders each. Once we put them through some courses and make sure they're comfortable with the mount we've chosen for them, we'll be ready to ride. It's a safety thing, Dani." He looked at her in complete seriousness and said, "If we make a bad judgment call of their abilities, and we figure it out when we're halfway up that trail, things could get ugly. Bottom line, I take my business and the safety of the visitors real serious."

80

"I'll take it serious too," she promised. "Just tell me what I'm supposed to do."

He smiled at her and looked back to the herd just as it dropped down over the other side of the ridge into the ravine. "I'm sure you will. Let's go. We've got a lot of ground to cover. Besides, we need to get back in time for you to work Poet later on."

He gave Jasper another kick, and they headed off toward the mountains.

13

Zack and Dani had made it to the first plateau on the mountain. Zack guided Jasper around a grove of aspens and waited for Dani and Lucy. When they came to the opening on the other side, Zack halted Jasper and turned to Dani.

"This is as far as we'll go today. This is the ride we're going to do tomorrow," he said. "Let's head down there. We'll give these two a rest and have some lunch."

Dani looked down to where he had pointed at a beautiful meadow surrounded by pines. Dead center, a stream ran through the meadow with wild flowers on both of its banks.

"That's really pretty," she said.

"It sure is, honey. This is God's country." He smiled. "Long before we showed up, all this belonged to Indians. I've tried with all my might, just like my daddy did, to respect this land as much as I'm sure they did. It's a sad story what was done to those nations."

She felt a little awkward because Zack looked upset. They sat on top of their horses watching the stream trickle through the valley below. She was a little hungry but didn't care. It occurred to her that just five short days ago she was thousands of miles away from here and incredibly angry over the fact that she wasn't going to see one of her friends all summer long. She thought about the battles she had waged with both of her parents and the horrible thoughts of just how much she hated them leading up to leaving for Colorado. She remembered the mood she had been in when she and her mom first started the drive. She had made a silent promise with herself to make sure her mom knew how, no matter what, she wasn't going to have any fun. Now, she wasn't so sure about that. She was on a horse on top of a mountain, and all she could see for miles in every direction were more mountains and incredibly blue skies, and she could feel the warm sun on her back. As much as she wanted to hate her situation, a tiny voice inside her head told her she was crazy if she hated any of this.

"Are you hungry?" Zack asked.

"Hmmm?" she said, snapping back to reality.

"Food? Do you want to have some lunch?"

"Sure."

82

"Let's set up in that meadow. We'll take the gear off the horses and let them graze. Tessa packed a nice lunch." Seemingly as an afterthought, he said, "If you want, I've got a couple of fishing poles in my saddle roll. You want to try and catch something?"

Dani smiled. "I used to fish with my dad."

"Yeah? When was that?" he asked.

"Honestly, I can't remember. I just know I did because he has this picture of me when I was real little holding a fishing pole." She grinned. "There's a ridiculously small fish dangling on the end of it."

"Was it a minnow?"

"No," Dani said. "It was bigger than a minnow. I don't know what kind of fish it was. I just remember the picture."

"Well it was probably a minnow," Zack insisted.

"Whatever," she said, giggling.

"What is it with you kids and that word?" he asked.

"What word?"

"*Whatever.*" He put his hand on his hip and cocked his head to the side. "I mean, like, whatever." He rolled his eyes, mimicking her.

Dani laughed. "Seriously? You did not just do that!"

"Oh yes, I did. Duh!" He rolled his eyes again.

"Oh my god, you totally can't mean it."

Zack started laughing with her. "C'mon, I'm starving. Besides, I can't wait to see you with a fishing pole in your hand."

"Bring it on," she said. "I bet I catch more fish than you do."

"You're on." He gathered up Jasper's reins and gave him a kick.

Dani and Lucy fell into step behind them as they began their descent down into the valley.

Once they dismounted and untacked their horses, Zack gave Jasper a gentle slap on his rump. Jasper trotted off toward a particularly lush patch of wild grass, and Lucy followed close behind him. Zack took the saddle blankets and rolled them out, arranging them side by side on the grass. He grabbed his saddlebags and took out a thermos and a couple of paper cups. Plastic containers with baked chicken and a crisp green salad and a paper bag with homemade bread and cheese appeared as well. He arranged everything on the blanket. "That Tessa sure knows how to make a meal, doesn't she?" He offered Dani a chicken leg.

"Thanks." She took a bite. "This is so good. It's totally better than the chicken my mom makes!"

Zack nearly choked on the bite he had taken. "Why? Is she a bad cook?" he asked, laughing.

"She's not a bad cook. It's just that I don't think she's ever made chicken like this. Besides, my dad cooks way more than she does."

She took another bite.

"Zack?" Dani said.

He was looking out across the stream. "Yeah?"

"It's pretty here. That was a nice trail we rode to get here. Am I going to go with you guys tomorrow?" she asked.

"Of course you are," he said. "That's part of your job this summer. You didn't think Poet was going to be the only job, did you?"

"I don't know." She looked down at her hands.

"Well that would be like working at a country club," he said. "I was serious when I said there's a lot of work to be done. I fully plan on having you help out with mending fences, baling hay, and whatever else needs doing around here," he assured her. "You're as much a hired hand as your momma was years ago."

Dani thought about this. "So you're saying my mom used to do all that kind of stuff?"

"She absolutely did and was darn good at it—one of my best workers. Your momma is a pretty amazing woman. I can't tell you how much it means to me that she's come back to see Tessa and me. I'm so proud of what she's done in her life. Getting to know you confirms what I believed the day she left years ago."

"What's that?"

"That she would be a fine mother too. You're a good kid—like your momma was. You need to figure out that no matter what she and your daddy do, it's all because of the love they have for you and your sister. Do you get that?" he asked.

"I guess."

"You guess?" he said, raising his eyebrows. "Well how about this? Your momma and Tessa are in town today meeting with another friend of ours. Her name is Carla, and she's a pretty spectacular person too. As a matter of fact, she's one of Tessa's best friends." He paused.

"Anyway, a couple of weeks from now there will be one hell of a party on this ranch. Tons of kids will be here—some your age, others a little younger, but none of them older than sixteen. They'll come from all over the country and spend the week here. For some of them, it will be the first time in their lives they saw something more than a grimy city street or dinner from a dumpster. The reason—"

Dani cut him off. "Dinner from a dumpster? What's that about?"

"It's about survival, Dani. It's about the only life some of these kids know. It's about hopelessness in a hopeless place. For one week in some of these kids' entire lives, the whole lot of us try to give them some hope with no strings attached."

"What does this have to do with my mom?" she asked.

"It has a lot to do with her," he insisted. "Like I said, they're in town with Carla right now. Your momma is gonna be her right-hand man for the event this year. Now I know you know that's what your mom does for work. Maybe she gets paid to pull a lot of those charity events together back home, but I'd venture to guess if she didn't get one copper penny for this one—which she won't by the way—she'd still put all of herself into the work." He plucked a piece of sweet grass out of the ground. He stuck it in his mouth and concentrated chewing on it.

"What does that have to do with loving me and Kylie?" she asked.

"Well, honey, it doesn't directly, but it does have its place," he said. "You see, your mom has so much love to give—always has. Sometimes her giving is to a fault, but don't you ever confuse that with she does it because she has to. She and your daddy would do anything out of love for you and your sister, even when you think they're doing it to punish you. God blessed the two of you when he chose your momma and daddy for you. All I'm saying is try a different pair of glasses on the next time you want to scream your head off at her. That's all." He smiled. "Now c'mon, finish up that salad so we can go catch some fish. I just know I'm gonna whup you in that department."

He gathered up the trash and stuffed it back into his saddlebag. He stood up and stretched. He reached down, grabbed the fishing poles and a plastic container with some fresh bait, and walked over toward the edge of the stream.

85

Dani sat there and watched him walk away and thought about what he had said. Some of it sort of made sense, but what was still perplexing was that she couldn't figure out why every time he talked with her she didn't feel lectured when he was done. She decided that she would have to think about that one for a while. She shook it off, popped up off the blanket, and followed him down to the stream.

14

"There you are," Tessa said, smiling. "Are you ready to go?"

"Absolutely. I can't wait to see the town again," Lou said. "It feels like I've come home again. Don't get me wrong. We love our life back East."

They were approaching the final curve before they dropped down into town. Lou asked Tessa, "Is this the curve?

"Yes, it is," Tessa answered. "This is the place where those two boys and Carla's boy lost their lives—well the two of them, literally, and Justin, well"—she shrugged her shoulders and sighed—"life as he once knew it." They drove through the curve in silence.

As they approached the exit, Lou asked, "How is Carla doing now? After Zack told me what happened, all I could think about is how I couldn't imagine anything like that happening to one of my children."

"Well she has good days and sometimes bad days," Tessa said. "She still goes over to Grand Junction three or four times a week to sit with Justin. He's been in that center now for nearly three years. She and Frank can't seem to get to the next phase, whatever that might be. The doctors have long since confirmed that Justin will never wake up and live a normal life ever again. It's still too painful for them to consider alternative measures. The fact of the matter is that Justin is their child, and no parent ever wants to bury their child." Tessa shook her head. "What makes me so proud of them both is how they've managed to rise up again and embrace their lives. In a warped sense, the tragedy that struck is the very one that brought them back to life again. When Carla started her charity, it was pretty rough going at first." Tessa smiled at the memory. "She was clear from the beginning that it had to involve kids, but she didn't have a lot of insight as to how she was going to do it. By the grace of God, what she did have was a community of friends that were right here for her. All she had to do was ask. When she figured that out and started asking, they came in droves to help. She does an amazing thing for a lot of kids, Louisa," Tessa said, beaming with pride for her friend. "She's giving kids a chance—a ray of hope, actually. Many of them never had— or may never have—such a thing again in their lives. I'm convinced—as she is—that she's getting a gift far greater in return than the one she's giving." Tessa pulled into the parking space and turned off the ignition.

They walked down Main Street until they got to the coffee shop. Carla was already inside, sitting in a corner booth. She saw them come in and waved. Tessa waved back, and they made their way to the booth. Carla climbed out of the booth to greet them. She was tall and lean. Her hair was dark brown and cut in a stylish bob. As they approached the booth, the corners of her mouth turned up into a welcoming smile, exposing perfect white teeth. She had a beauty mark above the corner of her mouth on the left side. Her eyes were a magnificent dark blue. She was fit and casually dressed. Even though she wore a white T-shirt and jeans, it looked as though she'd spent hours meticulously grooming herself. Tessa made the introductions. They placed their lunch order and, once the waitress walked away, slipped into the comfort of getting to know each other before talking business.

After their lunch dishes were cleared away, Carla reached down on the seat next to her and pulled a few files out of her briefcase. She handed one across the table to Lou and the other to Tessa.

"Tessa," she began, "I've put an outline together for you similar to what we did last year. I've done a slight modification on the menu, though. I think there was a lot of pork left over, so I'm thinking of cutting that portion considerably. I've already coordinated the quantities with Smitty's." She paused and looked over at Lou. "They're a local butcher in town that donates all the beef and pork"—she looked back to Tessa—"and he's in agreement. I think we're still going to need the amount of beef we had last year and maybe some more. Bottom line, that part is squared away."

Tessa read the outline and took her glasses off.

"Carla, this looks great," Tessa said. "I like the idea of doing finger-size desserts versus the larger sizes we've done in the past. I think it's going to be a lot easier if everything is set up with more of a grab-and-go style."

"Exactly." She looked at Lou. "We have some church groups bake unbelievable amounts of cakes, cookies, and brownies. What seems to keep happening each year is we have a ton of half-eaten cakes left over. Ultimately, we end up throwing a lot of them away come the end of the week. We're able to salvage some and make donations to a few shelters here in town, as well as down in Grand Junction, but a lot of it just goes to waste. It's a shame because it contradicts the whole concept of what we're doing."

"I think that's a great fix," Lou agreed.

"Tessa, why don't you take that file with you and give it a good scrub," Carla said. "We can talk at some point over the weekend and fine-tune whatever areas you think need attention."

"That works for me," Tessa said and looked over at Lou. "I'm usually the one in charge of anything and everything to do with the kitchen we set up in the tent. I don't do any of the food preparation or anything like that. We have a few catering companies who not only donate their time and labor, but also provide a handful of chefs that make outstanding barbeque, chili, and everything else that a real cowboy cookout is supposed to have. It's an amazing time, Louisa. I'm so happy you and Danielle will be here to experience it this year."

"I can't wait," Lou said. "Carla, I am in awe of what you've done for so many needy kids. Zack was telling me about the first year and how much this event has grown since then. What was your inspiration?" As soon as Lou asked the question, she had immediate regret. She wished she could take her words back. "Oh my god! I'm such an idiot. I'm so sorry, Carla. I didn't mean—"

"It's all right. I'm sure Zack and Tessa have told you about Justin." She looked away for a moment, composed herself, and continued. "You're a mother, so I'm sure you can imagine the pain and sorrow both Frank and I have endured since that horrible night a few years ago." She waved her hand. "I don't want you to walk on eggshells around me. What's more, I certainly don't want you to feel awkward. It's a time in both of our lives when, if we had the power to do so, we would race to whatever clock we needed to and stop those hands and turn them back by the seconds it took for things to go as terribly wrong as they did that Friday night." She paused and reached into her purse. She was digging around in search of something. She smiled and pulled out a travel pack of Kleenex. She held them up. "I never leave home without these." She cleared her voice, "As I was saying, I don't know that Frank and I will ever be the same again. We also don't know what the future holds where

Justin is concerned. What I do know is that this woman sitting next to you saved my life. In turn, her efforts enabled me to save Frank's and my life as we know it together. What none of us will ever be able to achieve, however, is to save Justin's life."

Tears streamed down her face. She stopped trying to dry them.

"When I started this charity, I didn't know where it was going to go," Carla said. "The one thing I was very clear and certain about from the beginning, however, was that no matter what I did, it would be for the love of my son. He was such a giving and warm soul. After the first year of doing this event and experiencing such exuberance and love from so many complete strangers, I knew this was my calling. It was something that, if Justin was able to be a part of it, he would have been so proud of his mom and dad." She wiped her tears.

Tessa reached across the table and took Carla's hand. The three of them sat quietly. No words were necessary. After another moment, Carla gently pulled her hand away. She dabbed at her eyes again and tucked her packet of Kleenex back in her purse. She sat up a little taller and brushed back a few stray hairs that had fallen across her forehead. "As I was saying," she said and smiled at the two women, "who wants a margarita?"

They all laughed. Tessa reached back across the table and patted Carla's hand. They talked a while longer, covering the highlights of what needed to be done in preparation for the event. They had coffee and shared stories about their lives and talked about nonsense, the economy, and just how all of their lives really were. It was close to three o'clock by the time they wrapped things up.

Carla pointed out that only one other table was still seated. "My gosh," she said. "It's a good thing we're not paying for this table by the hour. Look at this place. We've been hogging this booth for hours. I've got to get going here shortly. Frank and I are going to meet some friends for dinner in Grand Junction tonight. I want to stop by the home and see Justin too. I better get going." She scooted her way out of the booth and stood.

Carla hugged Lou. "When Tessa told me an old friend of the family was coming with her daughter to spend the summer, I had no idea just how much of a friend you were. I've heard so many stories about you over the years, especially from Zack. He talks about you like you're his daughter, you know." She smiled. "I cannot wait to meet Danielle. She sounds like an absolute doll. I always wanted a daughter. You don't mind if I borrow her once or twice this summer to take her shopping and shower her with clothes and makeup, do you?"

"You just said the two most magical things in Dani's world," Lou said, "makeup and clothes. The child can want for nothing more than those two very important commodities. There are times when I truly think she was born into the wrong family because she clearly has that gotta-have-gimme-I-want gene, and she doesn't get that from me."

"I don't know about that one, Louisa," Tessa challenged her.

Lou spun around. "What? When did you ever see me lavish over makeup and clothes?" she asked, laughing.

"Well let's see, I seem to remember a girl that couldn't wait to get paid so she could go racing off to town to buy yet another pair of boots and jeans and whatnot."

"Well that was different," Lou said and waved off the notion. "Okay. I confess." She held up her hands. "Carla, it was an absolute pleasure. You can have Dani for a day of shopping and lavishing. I can assure you she won't refuse."

"Great," Carla said. "I look forward to that. Now I really have to go." She gave Tessa a quick peck on the cheek and headed for the door.

They left shortly after and walked back to the car.

They drove in silence most of the way home. When they came upon the curve, Lou looked over at Tessa and asked, "Do you suppose Carla thinks about that awful night for Justin every time she drives this part of the road?"

"I'm sure she does, dear," Tessa said and sighed. "I know Zack and I do. For nearly a year after the accident, you could drive this section every day and the entire roadside would be littered with mementos that covered every inch of the guardrail and shoulder. There were flowers and pictures and teddy bears and crosses and just about everything you could imagine. There was even a letter jacket with Justin's name stitched across the back of it." She shook her head. "He was loved by many. What was beautiful about this community was how everyone joined together to assure both Frank and Carla that their little boy may be gone in many respects, but he will never be forgotten."

They came along the final stretch of highway by the Echo Ranch entrance, and Tessa slowed to make the turn under the archway. Lou looked to either side as they drove up the drive to the house. She sighed.

"What's wrong, dear?" Tessa asked her.

"Nothing," Lou said, "absolutely nothing. Today has been a perfect gift. I cannot think of anything that I'd rather be doing than what I'm doing right now." She smiled and rested her head back on the seat.

"Well that's what we want for you and Danielle as long as the two of you are here," Tessa said and finished the drive up to the house.

15

Zack and Dani chose a spot on the stream where a small waterfall was trickling down over a pool of rocks. "See that there?" he asked, pointing to the swirling pool.

Dani followed the direction of his finger. She wasn't sure what she was looking at but nodded.

"When you're fishing," he explained, "especially in streams and rivers, you want to find a spot like that."

"Why?" she asked.

She put her hand above her eyes to shade them from the sun.

"Because of the rocks down underneath the water," Zack answered. "Fish like to congregate in little pools and around rocks like that. There are all kinds of food sources for them in places like that."

"If I throw my line down there, I'll catch a fish?"

"It's not quite that easy," he said. "Fishing takes a lot of patience. You have to play with your line in a certain way so it entices the fish to want to come a little closer and ultimately grab on to the bait so you can hook him."

"I think it's disgusting that anything would think a worm is appetizing." She scrunched her nose.

"Do you like spaghetti?" he asked.

"Huh?"

"Spaghetti. Do you like it?"

"Duh. What kid doesn't?" she said.

"Well, what if a fish saw you eating spaghetti?" Zack asked. "He'd probably think you were eating worms too. Do you think he'd think that was disgusting?"

"Seriously?" she said, laughing. "First of all, a fish isn't going to see me eating anything. Even if he did, do you honestly think he's gonna wonder if I like it?" She rolled her eyes. "Whatever."

She shook her head and looked back at her line that was just sitting down near the center part of the stream in one of the pools Zack had pointed out.

"I'm just messing with you," he said.

He jiggled his line a couple of times and let it settle down again. After a few moments, he reeled it in and checked the bait. Satisfied, he pulled the reel back in slow motion and brought it forward. He gave it a quick snap at the same time he released the bale, letting the line and bait skyrocket across the stream. It landed twenty feet beyond Dani's.

"I was thinking," Zack said.

"About what?"

"Well just about how nice it is to have you and your momma here. It's been a long time since I've just taken a day and headed up here to do some fishing." He smiled at her. "I should do this more often."

He glanced down the stream and could see Jasper and Lucy standing side by side, tails swishing and heads down in the grass, grazing away.

"Look at those two over there." He nodded toward the horses.

Dani followed Zack's nod.

"I think it must be great to be a horse," Dani said. "I mean, if I was a horse, I wouldn't have to clean my room or go to school. All I'd have to do all day is stand in a field full of grass or roam around a place like this. I wouldn't have to worry about makeup or what I was going to wear, and when my hair needed brushing, somebody else would do it for me."

"What about work?"

"Geez, Zack. I don't even work now. I'm not old enough." She shook her head and pulled on her fishing line because she thought maybe it was the right time to do so.

"These guys work."

"Yeah, but if you're describing work as having to walk up and down these hills and run along the ridge like the ones we saw on the way up here, then I would definitely want to be a horse."

He smiled and jiggled his line again, but there was still no action. He pulled back and reeled it in. When he popped the lure out of the water, the bait was gone. "Son of a gun," he muttered.

"What's wrong?"

"What's wrong is there's a thief in that water. Look at my lure," he said and pointed. "The bait was stripped!"

He took his hat off and smoothed his hair back. He placed it back on his head and reached for the bait container.

"How come there's no fish?" Dani asked.

94

"Okay, smarty, I was gonna ask you the same thing," he said, pointing to her line. "I was wondering if you were going to leave your line in the water all afternoon or you were thinking about maybe checking your own bait."

"You're the one who told me I had to have patience," she said. "I'm just waiting for a fish to bite so I can pull him in."

"Well you're not supposed to just let your line sit out there without working it every now and then."

"Sorry," she said sarcastically and jiggled her pole a couple of times, then began to reel the line back in. "How's this?"

All of a sudden her line stopped. She tried to pull her pole and couldn't understand why the line wouldn't reel as fast as it had a moment ago. "Zack?"

"Yeah?"

"It's stuck."

"What's stuck?" He looked over at her pole.

The tip was slightly bent toward the water. He dropped his pole and stepped over to her.

"It's not stuck. I think you just may have hooked something," he exclaimed. "Reel some of that slack in real slow. That's right. Just keep turning that little lever so you get all that loose line in so it's kinda tight."

"Like this?" She looked at him.

"Exactly like that. Now give your pole a couple of yanks straight up."

Dani snapped the pole straight up a couple of times and looked back to him for further instruction. "I can't move it. I told you. I think it's stuck on something."

"That's good. Hold on. Now reel some more and hold off for a minute."

She followed his instructions and yanked up a couple more times. Her line was nearly to her side of the stream. As she was pulling up, a fish jumped out of the water.

"Oh my god!" she screamed and dropped her pole.

"Don't drop the pole!" he said, laughing, and quickly ran to it.

He grabbed it up and finished reeling it in the rest of the way then pulled the rest of the line out of the water. The fish on its end was flipping its tail back and forth as it dangled helplessly.

Dani stood in amazement and started squealing. "I caught one! I caught a fish! What do we do? What do we do now?" She hit his arm and laughed.

He reached out to calm the brown trout. He wasn't much more than a baby. When he managed to wrap his hand around the fish, it instantly froze.

"Well, darlin', we can't keep him anyway. First of all, he's way too small, and second of all, it's catch-and-release only around here."

"What does that mean?"

"It means if you catch something, you have to release it."

"That's a stupid rule. What's the point of fishing if you have to throw it back?" she asked.

"It's for the sport."

"That's dumb."

"You're a girl. Girls just don't get it." He shook his head and slipped the hook out of the fish's mouth. He turned and held the fish out to her. "Here. Throw this baby back to the water. His momma is probably going crazy right about now because she can't find him."

"Ew! I'm not touching that." She backed away.

"Dani," Zack said. "That's part of fishing. The person who catches the fish is also the person who throws him back. Now c'mon, take him," he insisted.

The fish was getting agitated and started to flap its tail from side to side. She cautiously reached out to take him. When Zack placed him in her hand, she turned with lightning speed and torpedoed him into the water. Zack reached over and gave her a pat on her shoulder. "Good lord, the way you chucked that fish back into the water, I wouldn't be at all surprised if he has a headache for the next three days," he said, laughing. "It's official. Now you can tell your friends you caught a fish when you were in Colorado this summer."

He took his hat off and wiped his forehead again. He placed it back on his head and looked around.

"I suppose we should think about heading back. I told Bobby we'd be back around four so you can work Poet. Are you ready to go?"

"Sure." She bent down and picked up her pole. As she stood back up, she looked at Zack and proudly announced, "Wait until my mom hears I caught a fish."

They wound their way back down the trail to the lower valley and stopped.

"Why are we stopping?" She asked.

"Well I've been thinking. I've been watching you ride today. I just wanted to tell you that I think you're a natural. You just took to that saddle like nobody's business. I'm real proud of you for doing that."

"Really?" she asked, smiling ear to ear. "I mean, it's definitely different from my saddle, but I kinda like it. I think you were right about using this one instead."

They trotted on and Zack let her head out in front, holding back on Jasper.

16

They headed up the last stretch of road to the main barn. Dani looked over toward the round pen and could see Bobby was already working with Poet.

"Oh no," she said, her heart sinking.

"What's wrong?" Zack asked.

"Look," she said and pointed to the round pen. "We must be late. Bobby's already working Poet."

"Hell, we're not late," Zack said, reassuring her. "He's just trying to get that knothead calmed down for your first lesson with him. Trust me, that boy can be worked for two solid hours straight, and he still would need another three before you turn him out."

"Are you sure?"

"Positive. Bobby just took him out a little early to get a pulse on his temperament today. The last thing I want to happen to anyone, especially to you, is serious injury. I told you: Poet is a teenager. He has some wild hairs that need to be tamed."

"Zack?"

"Yeah?"

"Don't you like Poet?"

"Well of course I do," he said. "Why would you ask something like that?"

"I don't know. It just seems like every time you talk about him you call him a knothead."

Zack responded with obvious care and tact, "Well let me tell you how I really feel about that boy. I already told you his back story. What I didn't tell you is the absolute, without a doubt in my mind, reason I bought that horse is because he chose me as much as I chose him. Hell, some people may look at the reasoning like I was purchasing a rescue or something." He shook his head and halted Jasper, which made Dani follow his lead.

"Did you?" she asked.

"Hell no," he shot back. "He sure as hell is not a victim. That horse has more pride than Mount Rushmore. I don't have one single solitary victim of an animal anywhere on this ranch. Granted, Poet is a handful, but when I call him a knothead, well that's just my way of saying he's stubborn. He's got a will of his own, mainly because he's still fairly young, but mostly because he doesn't have a defined job to do yet." He turned to Dani. "That's what you're gonna teach him—a job."

Dani sat on Lucy quietly, thinking about what Zack had said.

She asked, "So is it like he's my horse this summer?"

"That's exactly what that means. Now remember," he reminded her, "at first I want you to work with Bobby so you can get some solid and basic training knowledge under your belt. Bobby's a fantastic reader of horses. He's an even better teacher. You follow his lead and pay real close attention to everything he has to tell you and show you. Before long, he's gonna look at you one day and say 'Dani, go ahead and take care of Poet on your own today. Zack has other things he wants me to do.'"

"Seriously?"

"Honest to God."

"Cool," she whispered.

He reached over and took Lucy's reins from her.

"Here, give me those reins. Why don't you hop off and head over to them now. I'll take Lucy with Jasper and me the rest of the way up to the barn. Okay?"

"Huh? I thought you said it was the person—"

"I know what I said." He held his hand up. "And don't think this is going to happen every time you ride. Everybody is responsible for the horse they ride. That's part of the job. However, Bobby already has Poet ready to go. As a matter of fact, the work he's doing right now would be a good thing for you to watch. I think it's important you get over there and get started."

She stood on the ground next to Lucy and looked up at him as though she were waiting for further instruction.

"Well, why are you just standing here? Get going," he commanded.

She smiled, spun around, and took off in a run toward the ring. She stopped short and turned back around.

"Thanks, Zack," she yelled over to him. "I had a great trail ride today, and I caught a fish!" She didn't wait for his response.

When Dani reached the round pen, she climbed up on the bottom rail. She was concentrating on what Bobby was doing in hopes of being able to do something other than watch at some point.

"Hey there, Miss Dani," Bobby called to her.

"Hi, Bobby, how's he doing?"

"So far so good, he seems a little quieter today. I've been lunge lining him for about fifteen minutes." Bobby gathered up the excess line, adjusted the tension on the lead, and dropped the excess line back on the ground.

"I'm about finished with his left lead, and then I thought it would be a good time to have you join us. I think the sooner you two get acquainted, the sooner Poet will realize you're here for the long haul." He looked over at her and asked, "What d'ya think?"

"Sure," she exclaimed. "Just tell me what I have to do."

She climbed up on the second rail and swung her leg over the top, balanced, then swung her other leg over to sit on the top rail. She relaxed and studied Bobby's technique. Poet was doing great. He lost focus for a moment when Dani was situating herself on the fence but got right back to it after she had settled down.

"Did you see that?" Bobby called out.

"What?" Dani wasn't sure what she was supposed to have seen.

"When you were climbing up there, he started to lose focus. That's good. It means he's comfortable having you around. He's not much for strangers. There seems to be a connection already established between you two. Let's try something."

"Okay."

"I want you to get down off the fence slowly," Bobby instructed. "And stand in place for a minute or two. Don't jump, just climb down."

With her back to them, Dani turned around and climbed down the fence. She glanced over her shoulder once to see what they were doing. Poet slowed his canter. Bobby cracked the whip, which spooked Poet a little. Poet pit stopped and turned his head toward Dani. Bobby whispered something, which made Poet's ears flicker forward. He cocked his head and turned around until he had her in his sights.

"Easy, boy," Bobby said, reassuring him.

100

Dani intently watched from the sideline. She was listening to Bobby but couldn't take her eyes off Poet. She was afraid to say anything for fear it would spook him.

"Okay, Dani, I'm going to start to bring his lunge line in toward me. When I have about four feet of slack between him and me. I want you to take a few steps toward me here in center ring. Don't look at him; look at me. After you take a few steps, stop."

"Okay. Just tell me when you want me to move," Dani answered.

"Go ahead and take those steps now," Bobby instructed.

She started walking slowly toward Bobby and made a point to not look at Poet. She could feel him staring her down and desperately wanted to look at him, but knew she couldn't.

"That's good. Hold up there for a minute," Bobby directed. He turned back to Poet and gave a quick snap of his whip.

"C'mon, boy, get up."

Poet lifted his head and spun in the direction of the tug Bobby gave the lunge line. Initially he tried to turn his head back toward Dani, but with lightning reflex, Bobby snapped the whip again, and Poet immediately obeyed the command. He kicked out a little before easing into a trot. His circles were smaller than they had been when Dani first got to the ring.

"I'm gonna halt him in a minute and pull him in," Bobby said. "I'll make him stand next to me. Once he's by me and stops fidgeting, I want you to walk out to us the rest of the way and stand on this side." Bobby pointed to the ground to his right. "I'm gonna have Poet over here." He tapped on his left thigh. "When you get out here, we're just gonna stand for a bit real still and quiet."

"Got it," Dani said.

"Good. I'm gonna pull him in now. Make sure you pay close attention to what's going on. If he spooks, he could rear, buck, or both. Be prepared. Okay?"

"I will. I am," she answered nervously.

"Take a couple of deep breaths and calm yourself. You know enough to know a horse can sense fear a mile away. If you've got the jitters, this ain't gonna work."

Dani took a deep breath and wiggled her arms by her sides. She cracked her neck, straightened up, and took another deep breath then blew it out slowly. "I'm ready when you are, Bobby."

He looked back to Poet. Hand-over-hand, he slowly pulled the horse to him. When they were barely a foot apart, he dipped under Poet's chin between the lunge clip and his neck. As he came up on his other side, he pushed Poet's head away and ran his hand down the length of Poet's body. Dani intently watched as Poet's skin flickered against Bobby's touch. Poet kept trying to turn his head to see what Bobby was doing. Each time he tried, Bobby applied more tension to the line.

Dani walked toward them. She fought the urge to whisper words of encouragement to Poet because that was not what Bobby had told her to do. Instead, she kept repeating over and over in her head, *It's okay, boy. It's okay. I'm not going to hurt you. That's right. It's okay.* When she got to Bobby and Poet, the three of them stood together in silence for what felt like an eternity. She looked far ahead of her to the distant mountains and focused on a couple of circling hawks. She felt an intermittent breeze. An annoying wisp of hair had slipped down from underneath the brim of her helmet, barely touching the tip of her eyelash and forced her to blink.

"That was really good," Bobby whispered. "Now take a couple of steps away from me. Slowly turn once you're in front of me so you're facing me. Make your movements smooth, not jerky."

Poet's ears began to twitch, and he tried to turn his head toward Dani as she stepped out. Bobby was prepared and pulled the tension on his line a little tighter, forcing him to look forward.

"Perfect," Bobby whispered. "Now walk toward me until you can take his line out of my hand."

She walked toward him and slowly extended her hand. Once she had the line and Poet felt the tension relax, he immediately turned his head toward her. He let out a soft snuffle. In the next breath, he jerked his head back.

Worried, she looked at Bobby. She didn't know what to do next. Bobby had made a point to stay between Dani and Poet through the whole process. She looked over Bobby's shoulder and saw Zack leaning on the fence, studying the entire scene. Bobby said, "I'm going to step out from between you two. As I'm stepping out, I want you to hold onto Poet—not too tight, but not a lot of slack either. Tell me when you're ready."

"Ready."

"When I start to move forward, follow around behind me. What we're trying to do here is trade places, but you never want to stand dead square in front of a horse, especially a young horse. If he rears up, it'll happen faster than you can blink your eyes. Then, what's gonna happen when he comes down?" Bobby looked at her, expecting an answer.

"He's gonna trample me," she answered.

"That's exactly right."

Dani felt as if they were getting ready to do a square dance. Bobby came shoulder to shoulder with her as she passed him, going toward Poet. When she was at Poet's left side with her back almost completely to Bobby's, she did a half turn. She readjusted the tension on the line and let Bobby turn and come back up next to her on her left side. They had successfully traded places.

Poet stood at attention the entire time. Once situated, Dani let out a deep sigh of relief. She smiled and looked up at Poet. He turned his head slightly and let out another snuffle.

"I want you to walk him to the outside of the ring. Take him around once and make sure you let him know you're the boss. Do not give him even half an inch on that line. Understand?" Bobby asked. "He knows what 'walk on' means, but he definitely knows the person leading him is the person who sets the pace. Do not let him bully you. Got it?"

"Yep," she said bravely. "Should I go now?"

Bobby nodded and stepped away from Dani.

She took another deep breath and softly said, "Okay, Poet, walk on." She took the first step and gave the line a slight tug. Poet bowed his head until it was even with her shoulder and began walking alongside her to the opposite fence line. Each step was tenuous at first. After two or three more steps, she relaxed into her own stride and let a little slack out of the line. They got to the outside ring and turned. She saw Zack was still leaning on the fence, watching her every move. She was nervous. She didn't want to make a mistake with him watching her. It felt like she was being evaluated. If she didn't do everything exactly right, she wasn't going to get pinned for this round. Right around the halfway mark, Poet

103

stopped. He jerked his head up. Dani's heart leapt into her throat, but she knew she needed to remain calm. She tightened the tension and firmly said "walk on." Once they'd completed their first revolution, Bobby told her to bring Poet across the diagonal and change direction.

"That was great," Bobby said, praising her. "We're gonna wrap things up in here, but I want you to walk him into the barn. Put him on the cross ties and groom him down. Bring him back to the center here and set him up like we did before. Do you remember the drill?"

"Yep," she said.

Dani finished her circle and proceeded back to the center. When she got to Bobby, he reached out and took the lead from her.

"It's not that I don't think you can do it, but I'm gonna get him in the barn," Bobby said. "You can get him on the cross ties. We're gonna do what we did today for a few more days. Little by little, we'll introduce a few new things. I have to tell you, though, you're a natural. He's real comfortable with you. You seem to be pretty calm around him too."

"Seriously?" she asked, all smiles. She reached up and tickled Poet's muzzle. Poet leaned into her touch for more.

"Okay, let's go. I want to show you a couple of techniques I've been teaching him on some ground manners. Believe it or not, he's pretty good on the cross ties. I think it's because I've been doing that with him for over a month now. He still has a tendency every now and then to get a little separation anxiety if you leave him alone. That's unacceptable." Bobby shook his head. "He needs to know that sometimes you have to walk away, and he just has to have faith that you'll be right back."

Just before they passed through the double doors, Dani looked back toward the round pen. Zack was still leaning on the fence watching them go.

"Hey, Zack, you coming?"

"Be right there."

"How'd I do?" she asked Zack.

"You did good—strike that," he yelled over. "You did fantastic." He smiled, took his hat off and waved it as further assurance.

104

17

Lou and Tessa were sitting on the porch when Zack and Dani returned to the house. Zack barely had time to put the truck into park before Dani threw the door open and went running up the steps.

"Hey, Mom. Hey, Tessa," she said once she got up to their chairs. She turned to her mother and asked, "Can I get my cell phone? I want to call Chelsea."

"Hi, Dani," Lou said, smiling. "What's that? Oh, I had a great day. That's so sweet of you to ask. How about you?"

"Mom," Dani said anxiously, putting her hands on her hips. "It's just that I had an amazing day. I miss Chelsea, and want to tell her about Poet."

"Did the saddle work okay for you, Danielle?" Tessa asked.

"Huh? Yes! Thank you so much. Zack said I can use it all summer if it's all right with you. It's really comfortable."

"Of course you can, dear. That's why I offered it in the first place." She reached down and tucked her knitting back into its bag. "Dinner should be ready in about thirty minutes. You two have time to take your showers if you'd like." She stood up on tiptoe and gave Zack a peck on the cheek once he got up to the porch.

"I think I might just have to do that," he said, smiled, and returned the kiss.

"How was the trail?" Lou asked.

"Great. We went up Bonita Ridge to Crooked Creek and had lunch. I brought a couple of fishing—"

"Oh yeah!" Dani said, cutting Zack off, "Guess who didn't catch a fish today?" She stood behind him, pointing.

"Thanks a lot," he said to Dani. "You know, don't think you're so high and mighty because if you call what you caught a fish, I'm gonna have to take you out again and show you the difference between a fish and the minnow you caught today."

"That is so not true," she said, giggling, "Mom, I caught a fish, and I swear it was bigger than a minnow." Dani looked at Zack and rolled her eyes.

Dani went back to her original agenda: "Mom, can I please have my cell phone?" she begged. "I want to call Chelsea and tell her about Poet!"

"Yes, it's in my bag on the chair right inside the door. But—"

"Thanks," she said as she shot through the door.

"Wait," Lou said.

Dani stopped, but didn't look up. She was too busy dialing Chelsea's phone number.

"Yeah?"

"Not too long. Dinner is almost ready, and you definitely need a shower before dinner."

"Okay. Okay."

"And," Lou stopped her again.

"What?" Dani demanded.

"Watch your tone," Lou warned. "Take those boots off out here on the porch. They're filthy, and I don't want you tracking that mess all over the floors inside."

She sat down on the top step and pulled her boots off as she waited for Chelsea to answer. Seconds later a smile popped up on her face. "Chels! It's me! Hi!"

She tossed her boots next to the railing and looked back over at her mom. She pointed up in a gesture of asking permission to go to her room. Before she disappeared, Lou said, "Five minutes, then get in the shower."

Dani gave Lou a thumbs-up and disappeared.

Zack sat down in the chaise across from her. "That's some kid you've got there, Lou." He smiled and shook his head.

"That's one way of putting it."

"Well, if you two will excuse me, I'm going to put some water on for the spaghetti," Tessa interrupted.

"Did you say spaghetti?" Zack asked.

"Yes. Why?"

"Oh, nothing. I can't wait until Dani hears we're having spaghetti." He chuckled to himself.

"Tessa, do you need some help?" Lou asked, starting to get up.

106

"Sit, dear. For heaven's sake, it doesn't take two people to put a pot of water on to boil. Everything else is ready. Sit and relax with Zack. I'll be back in a few minutes." Tessa turned to Zack. "Watch your time because you still have time for a shower before dinner."

"You bet. I'm just gonna sit for a minute."

"So you guys had a good time today? What's with the spaghetti reference?" Lou asked.

"We sure did," Zack said, smiling. "Ah, it's nothing. You had to be there." He changed the subject. "I think she was a little apprehensive when we first started out and she realized I was gonna take her up Bonita Ridge. Do you remember how steep the first part of that climb is?"

"I sure do." She grinned and said, "What I remember more is how scared shitless I was the first time I had to come back down that hill." She laughed at the memory. "What'd she do?"

"She was a real trooper. When we were trotting across that valley and I told her where we were headed, the look on that child's face was priceless. She got real serious and quiet like she was getting ready to put her final affairs in order." He laughed. "She tried to pass it off like she wasn't scared, but her expression was a dead giveaway. She was asking all sorts of questions like how wide the trail was and was it as steep as it looked from here and stuff like that. It was pretty funny." He shook his head.

"Well good for you." Lou reached over and gave him a slap on his shoulder. "I need all the help I can get when it comes to scaring some sense into my kid. If a terror ride on a trail is going to assist with some attitude adjustment, I say you take her on every steep trail there is on this ranch. The steeper, the better."

"You should have seen her working with Poet and Bobby this afternoon," Zack said.

"Yeah?"

"She's a natural. I don't know what it is about her and that horse. I'm telling you there is some definite chemistry between them. She got a little upset with me because I kept referring to him as a knothead. She told me it made her think I didn't like him. I set her straight. I told her the only reason I call him a knothead is because he's stubborn. I even added her momma probably thinks she's a knothead sometimes too."

"I'm gonna go take a shower. Why don't you go in and grab a bottle of red to have with dinner? Check with Tessa and see what she recommends. That woman has been all over wine country and definitely knows what's what."

"I believe I will," Lou said. She watched Zack walk to the door and asked, "Do me a favor?"

"What's that?"

"Check to see if Dani is still on the phone when you get upstairs. If she is, give her a reminder knock on the door to wrap it up and get in the shower. If you don't tell her I asked you to do that, she'll hang up immediately." Lou sat back in her chair, picked up her file, and went back to reading.

18

The days began to stack one on top of the next. As she sat on the porch drinking her coffee one morning, Lou realized nearly three weeks had passed since they had arrived. Dani had made some minor improvements, particularly where her attitude was concerned. Lou wasn't so delusional to believe in such a short period of time the abominable teen with whom she'd driven out West was suddenly and completely gone. What she did notice, however, was a calmness beginning to surface more often. Dani still had an innate ability to rise to the occasion of potential battle whenever her mother delivered an answer she didn't want to hear, but instead of immediately spiraling into an obscenity-spewing adolescent, she was learning how to process the *why* that belonged to the *no*. She would still walk off in a huff, but it was a quiet departure in comparison to a few months earlier.

Fourth of July was around the corner. The following week, Echo Ranch would transform into a hub of activity around Carla's charitable event. Teens from disadvantaged backgrounds would converge upon the property. They would arrive with little more than the clothes on their backs and a lot of wonder about what was in store for them. For one glorious week, they could check their troubles at the door. They would have food, shelter, new clothing and toiletries, and a place to take a shower. They could ride horses or swim in the lake. Games and activities during the day and bonfires where they could roast marshmallows and sing songs under the star-filled Colorado nights were all planned. The goal was to occupy the campers' attentions every waking moment to distract them from their sorrows and worries. Carla's mission was clear. For one week, these kids got to be kids. In some cases, it was the first time they would have ever had such an opportunity.

Lou too charge of the event tent, which meant she was responsible for its setup and contents. When the week was over, she'd take care of the break down too. Everywhere she went, her cell phone was attached to her ear. She was in her element, which made her feel more at ease. She had a purpose greater than policing her daughter every second of the day, which felt good. Everything felt right. She was looking forward to seeing Carla again and meeting Carla's husband, Frank. Tessa had invited them for dinner, and they were bringing along Amy, a girl close to Kylie's age who would be one of the counselors at the event. Lou finished helping Tessa with the dinner preparation as Dani and Zack returned from the barn. She heard the front door open, and, as she made her way to the great room, she could hear them talking.

Tessa smiled and brushed Dani's hair off her forehead. "Now why don't you go upstairs with your mom and take your shower. I've got a couple more things to do before everyone gets here. I can't wait for you to meet Amy.

"Who's Amy?" Dani asked.

"Oh, you're going to like her. I think she might be the same age as your sister. She's home from college for the summer. She worked here last summer, and she's going to be one of the counselors at the event. Maybe the two of you can pair up and work together." Tessa looked at Lou. "Louisa, isn't Kylie going to be a sophomore next year?"

"She sure is."

"Well there you go. She is the same age as your sister."

"Cool." Dani hopped off the stool. She walked over to Zack, gave him a hug, and looked up at him. "Zack, we're cool."

Zack watched her leave, turned back to Lou and Tessa, and said, "Did you hear that? We're cool." Relief had spread across his face.

19

Lou walked into the great room smiling. "Hello, everyone."

Zack stood up. "It's about time, you two. I was beginning to think you went to bed."

Dani was standing behind her mother at the foot of the stairs.

"C'mere," Zack said, motioning them over to him. He turned to Frank and said, "This is Lou Croft and her daughter, Dani. Ladies, this is Frank," he said. "Lou, you already know Carla, and this is Amy. This is Dani and Lou." He turned back to Dani and held out his hand. "Get on in here and have a seat. Lou, you want a glass of wine?"

"I'd love one," she said and sat down on the sofa next to Carla. "Hi there. Listen, I promised Dani we wouldn't talk shop tonight." She looked back toward Dani just in time to see her face flush. "Honey, c'mon in and have a seat. Amy, this is Dani. I heard you just finished your first year of college?"

"Yes, ma'am," she said, smiled, and reached out to shake Lou's hand. "It's nice to meet you." She looked at Dani and gave her a little wave.

Dani smiled back and sat on the arm of the sofa next to Lou.

"My other daughter, Dani's sister Kylie, just finished her first year of college too. She's actually doing a summer internship at a horse center in Upstate New York."

"Wow. That's awesome," Amy said. "I don't have an internship this summer, but I'm working part-time for Zack." She looked over at him. "I used to work here during the summer when I was still in high school. I'd like to do something with horses some day when I get out of college. It's been great to have the opportunity to work here."

"This is great," Lou said. "I wish Kylie were here to meet you. I think you two would have a lot in common."

"So, Dani," Amy said, looking over at her, "Do you ride?"

"Yeah, I've been riding since I was six—mostly English."

"Me too," Amy exclaimed.

"You women and your fancy English riding." Zack shook his head. "Hell, English, schminglish." He chuckled. "I say throw a saddle on a horse and ride for pity's sake."

"Now, Zack, don't be so judgmental," Tessa cautioned. "I think English riding is beautiful and graceful. I've often thought about trying it." She smiled at the girls.

Frank piped in, "Personally, I'm with Zack. I just don't think those English saddles were meant for a man's seat. I mean, they're so darn tiny."

"That's what I'm talking about," Zack agreed.

"Whatever," the girls said simultaneously.

"Okay, everyone, dinner is just about ready," Tessa announced. "Do you ladies want to give me a hand in the kitchen?"

They settled into their seats around the table. The procession of passing dishes and silverware against china, along with the buzz of conversation, was heaven on earth for Lou. She glanced around the table. It warmed her heart to see Dani and Amy engaged in constant chatter with each other by the time dessert was served. She looked out the window and could see the sun had dipped down over the ridge, and stars were already beginning to twinkle in the sky.

Dani turned to Zack and asked, "Do you think it would be okay if Amy and I took one of the Gators? We wanna go down to the barn."

"I don't mind, but it's up to your momma," he said.

"Mom, is it okay?"

"I suppose," Lou said, "but not too late."

Dani popped up out of her seat and turned to Amy. "C'mon. Wait until you see Poet. He's amazing," Dani exclaimed. "He's my project this summer. Bobby is teaching me how to train him," she explained as she pushed her chair back under the table.

"Are you kidding? You must be a pretty awesome rider if you're working him," Amy said. "He's not exactly the most cooperative horse."

"It's okay. You can say it," Dani said and looked at Zack. "He's a knothead."

Amy laughed and said to Zack. "I can't believe you're still calling him that."

"We just started working him with the bit. It's in for about an hour each morning before we turn him out, then we put it back in after he feeds for another hour," Dani explained. "He was pretty mad the first couple of days. He seems to know what's coming now, and he's doing pretty good." She turned to Lou and said, "See you later, Mom."

"Hold on a minute," Lou looked at Amy. "I don't have a problem with you two going down to the barn." She gave Dani a stern look, trying to impress upon her the importance of what she was saying. "Under no circumstances are you allowed to drive the Gator. It's dark out there, and I don't what any accidents. Understood?"

Dani looked down at her feet and mumbled, "Understood."

"Okay. Go ahead, and have fun, you two."

"Oh, wait," Carla called after them.

They stopped in the doorway. "Yeah?"

She looked back at Lou. "Amy and I were going to go to Grand Junction tomorrow. She wanted to see Justin, and then we were going to do some shopping afterward. We were wondering if it would be all right to bring Dani with us. I heard we may get some rain." She looked at Zack. "I thought you could do without her for a day."

"I'm fine with that," Lou said. "Do you want to go?"

"Ah, yeah. I mean, hello? Shopping?" Dani grinned.

"I told you. Makeup and clothes." Lou shook her head.

"Perfect," Carla said. "We'll pick you up about ten."

"Sure," Dani smiled. "See ya."

"Thanks, Lou, I think those two will have fun with each other. I cannot wait to buy her something girly," Carla said and smiled.

"Oh, trust me. You will regret those words."

"How about we all go back into the great room?" Zack suggested.

20

They came up over the crest of the hill and cruised down around the stand of pines. The moon was high above them, looking like a giant yellow pie balancing on top of the ridge in the distance and casting its golden light on the road ahead of them. The barn doors stood open. As they approached, Amy took her foot off the gas and glided to a stop. She put the Gator in gear and cut the engine. They could see light coming from the office. As they walked into the barn, they saw Bobby sitting at the desk. He looked up from his paperwork and took off his glasses.

"Hey, Miss Dani. I was—"

He stopped midsentence when he saw Amy standing behind her. "Well I'll be darned." He smiled and stood up. "Miss Amy. Zack told me you were back. I hear you're gonna help out this summer." He walked over to her and gave her a big hug.

"That's great," he said, then looked at Dani. "What's going on? What're you two doing down here?"

"Mom and everybody are back up at the house. We didn't want to sit around and listen to adult stuff." She looked around the barn. "Is Poet in his stall?"

"He sure is. As a matter of fact, you can probably go down and take his bit out," Bobby told Dani. "He's had it in since you put it in earlier. I think he's had enough for one day. Besides, I bet he'll be happy to see you."

"It is so great to be back here. I love all these horses. You're lucky," Amy sighed and stopped in front of Lucy's stall to give her a scratch.

They got to the end of the aisle and turned to the right. The second stall was Poet's. His back was to the stall door. When he heard them coming, he jerked his head up away from his hay and toward the stall door. He saw Dani and poked his head out of the stall.

"Hello, boy," Dani said and reached her hand up to let him sniff her.

He bobbed his head up and down. She reached up, tickled his muzzle, and stroked his cheek. "What do you think? Should we take that bit out for a while?" she asked him.

114

"He's gorgeous," Amy said with a sigh. "He was a big boy last year, but he looks like he's grown even more!"

"Isn't he awesome?" Dani reached up to the buckle on his bridle, released it, and slipped it over his head. He blew out a soft breath and nickered. "Yeah, that's right," she said, continuing to talk to him. "You know what's coming next, don't you?" She reached up and slid the bridle over his ears. He pawed the ground. "That feels good, doesn't it?" she agreed. "Now put your head down," she instructed and gently pushed down on his nose band so she could slip the last part of the bridle over his ear. As soon as she got it over his ear, the bit slid out into her hand. She gathered up the tack and hung it on his stall door. "Let's give him a good groom down. Grab that box on the floor over there," she said to Amy, pointing to the box sitting between his stall and the next.

Dani released the latch on his door and reached up to his chest. She applied some pressure so she could get him to back up. Amy followed her into the stall and secured the latch behind them. Poet looked back and forth at the two of them. He bent down to Dani's shoulder and tried to nibble a piece of her hoodie. She pulled back and giggled. "Stop that. You can't eat my shirt." She turned to Amy and asked, "Can you hand me that curry comb? I'll start over here, and you take his right side. There's a couple of curry combs in the box."

They stood on both sides of Poet. Dani smiled and looked over his back to Amy. "I love this horse."

"He's pretty amazing," Amy agreed.

"I wish he was mine."

"It seems like he wishes he was yours too," Amy said. "He's so calm. I swear he wasn't like this last summer. The only people who had anything to do with him were Bobby and Zack, especially Zack. It wasn't like he was a crazy horse, but Zack was real specific. He didn't want anyone messing with him. I just can't believe this is the same horse."

"I wish I could have known him last summer because even the first time I saw him, he just seemed like a big baby to me. He definitely tries to challenge me, but it's like we understand each other," Dani explained. "Bobby and Zack even tell me that they've never seen him respond to somebody like he does for me."

"That's because he trusts you," Amy said.

"Yeah, maybe," Dani said, shrugging, then bent down to grab a comb to do his forelock and mane. She reached up and grabbed the clump of hair between his eyes and started gently combing through it. Poet bent his head down to her. "Thanks, boy," she said, smiling at him and giving him a kiss on his cheek.

He nickered.

"You're such a ham," she said.

"So how do you know Zack and Tessa?" Amy asked.

"I didn't. My mom has known them for years. She used to work here when she was younger—a lot younger."

"Yeah?" Amy asked. "Cool. So why did you guys come here now?" Amy asked.

"I don't know," Dani answered quickly. "Hand me one of those hoof picks."

Amy reached into the box. An awkward silence grew between them. Dani had lifted Poet's rear leg and was concentrating on picking his hoof. After a moment, she gently put his leg.

"Most of the reason is because of me," Dani admitted.

"What do you mean?"

"Like my mom and dad think I'm a mess, and they don't like my friends," she mumbled.

"Why not?" Amy asked.

"Because we always get into trouble."

After the girls finished grooming Poet, they walked down to the barn office. Amy sat in Zack's chair, and Dani settled into the chair opposite her on the other side of the desk. They grabbed a couple of bottles of water out of the refrigerator. Dani took a long sip from her bottle and set it down on the desk.

"About a week before school got out my mom finally gave me permission to go to the mall with Chelsea without her." Dani rolled her eyes.

"Your mom used to go to the mall with you and your friends?" Amy asked.

"Yes," Dani said. "We went to the Jewelry Pavilion to look at some earrings and junk. Next thing I know, Chelsea snatched a pair and stuffed them in her pocket. I couldn't believe she was going to steal

116

something because I never did anything like that before," Dani assured Amy. "When we got back out in the mall and started to go to another one of our other favorite stores, I hear this person behind me say, 'Excuse me, miss, did you pay for those earrings in your bag?' Chelsea heard it too. She tried to pull me into running with her. The lady called out a little louder, 'I wouldn't do that if I were you, miss.' That's all I needed to hear. My legs felt like jelly, and I just froze in my steps. Chelsea kept trying to pull me away. When she realized I wasn't going to go with her, she dropped my arm." Dani looked at Amy, "I honestly think for a second there she was going to bolt without me."

"Some friend," Amy exclaimed.

"She is my friend—my best friend, actually."

"I'm sorry. It's just that friends don't do stuff like that to friends. I don't even know this Chelsea, but based on what you just told me, it sounds like she's a little more concerned about herself than what any friend may need," Amy said, justifying her original remark.

"So what did your mom do when she found out?" Amy asked.

"Oh, she made me go back to that store," Dani explained. "I had to explain what happened, and the manager agreed my mom could pay for them then we could leave. As we walked back to the car she kept asking me if I knew how lucky I was and that sort of stuff. When we got to the car, she reached into her purse and pulled out the bag with the earrings. She turned to me and told me to put them in right there."

"Really?" Amy said. "Why?"

Dani looked at Amy. "I mean really? I was already wearing some earrings. When I pointed that fact out to her, she just gave me a creepy smile and told me she was well aware of that, but obviously, the earrings I stole were far more important and that's why I stole them. She told me she was going to take all my earrings, including the pair in my ears, and donate them to some thrift store. Then she told me that the ones I stole would be the only earrings I could own and wear for the rest of the time I lived under her roof. I had to wear them every day from that point on."

Amy glanced at her ears." Are those—"

"Yep. I've had these stupid earrings in every single day since I stole them," Dani said. "Just like she said she was going to, she took all my other earrings away. You know what?"

117

"What?"

"I don't even like these earrings—mostly because they remind me of that time every time I wear them. If I'd have known I was going to have to wear them every day, I don't know that these are the ones I would have stolen."

They looked at each other and began to laugh.

"Oh my gosh," Amy said and bolted out of her chair.

"What?"

"It's 10:30," Amy said. "We've been down here for nearly three hours. C'mon, we should get back."

"It didn't seem like we were down here so long," Dani commented as she secured the barn doors and dropped the latch back into its cradle.

They climbed into the Gator, and Amy swung it around. She pointed it toward the hilltop and gave it some gas. As they rolled forward, she said to Dani, "You know. I'm real glad you're here this summer. I'm looking forward to hanging out with you, and I definitely can't wait to see you work Poet."

"I'm glad you're here too. I really miss Kylie. You're a lot like her. We're still going shopping with Carla tomorrow, right?" she asked.

"Definitely."

When they reached the hilltop, the moon cast its light along the path in front of them. They could see the house's outline against the night sky from the light of the moon. They pulled up next to the porch, and Amy killed the engine. Zack and Frank were sitting on the porch smoking cigars and talking. The girls climbed the steps and sat in the chairs opposite the two men.

"It's about time you two showed up," Zack said, turning to Dani. "Your momma was just about ready to get in my truck and go down looking for you." He winked at her. I ran some interference. I sent her down to the cellar for a couple more bottles of wine.

"Thanks, Zack," Dani said. "I owe you one." She turned to Amy and said, "I'm going to head inside. I'm getting tired."

Frank rose and told Amy they were going to head out soon too.

They helped gather up glasses and went back inside. Fifteen minutes later, they were all back on the porch saying thank you and good-bye and finalizing shopping details for the next day. Dani stood on the porch and watched Carla, Frank, and Amy drive away. She gave one last wave to Amy and turned back to her mom.

"Mom?"

"Punk?"

"Amy's really cool. I'm glad she came tonight." She smiled at Lou, gave her a peck on the cheek, and went back inside.

21

Lou stayed on the porch for a few minutes longer. She leaned on the rail and looked out across the valley toward the mountains. She looked up at the moon in search of its man, took a deep breath, and let it out slowly. Just as she was about to turn, a shooting star swept across the sky. She smiled and whispered, "Yeah. I know what you mean." Not waiting for a reply, she turned and went back inside.

Lou walked toward the kitchen and could hear Zack and Tessa's muffled voices. She stood in the doorway and watched them at work side by side at the sink. Tessa was rinsing dishes and handing them to Zack. There was a tenderness to their teamwork that reminded her of how she and Jake were sometimes.

"Hey, you two," she said. Thanks for a lovely dinner. It was so nice to meet Frank. Amy seems like a lovely girl. Dani was really taken with her." Lou smiled. "Okay, you guys. Good night."

"Good night, dear,"

She got to her room and changed into some lounging pants and a tank top. She went into the bathroom, washed her face, and brushed her teeth. She climbed into bed and sank down deep into the fluffy pillows then reached over and turned off the light. After a few moments of tossing and turning, she realized she couldn't fall asleep. She reached back over and turned the light on, then picked up her phone and dialed home. She absently counted one, then two, and when she got to the fourth ring, she was about to hang up when a groggy "hello" came through from the other end.

"Jake?" she said, smiling into the phone.

"Mhmm. What time is it?" he asked.

"It's late," Lou said. "Jake? Do you want me to call you back tomorrow?"

There was no answer.

"Jake?"

"Yeah?"

"I was thinking."

"Uh-oh," he said, apparently wide awake. "That makes me nervous when you start your sentence with that."

"It's not a bad thing," Lou said. "I was just wondering when Kylie gets home from her internship."

"I think she said a couple of weeks before she goes back to school. Actually, she'll be home before you guys. Didn't you say you were going to head back the second week of August?"

"Yeah."

"So what'd you have in mind?"

"Well, I don't want Dani to know anything about this, but I was thinking maybe we could fly Kylie out here a week before we're leaving to come back. It'd be a great surprise for Dani. It would be great to give them some time together out here. I think it would be a blast for both of them. Besides, I'd love to drive back across country with the two of them. I haven't spent any time with Kylie, and I don't know if I can stand seeing her for only a week or so before she has to go back to school once we do get back."

"That sounds like a great idea," Jake said. "How about I give her a call tomorrow and find out when she's getting home, and I'll set things up after that? Lou?"

"Yeah?"

"How are you doing?"

She choked back her tears. "Oh, you know, I'm good."

"Lou?"

"Hmmm?"

"How are you really doing?"

"I'm so scared to say I'm doing okay because I really am okay. It's been such a long time since I've felt this good that I'm afraid to say it out loud for fear that it will vanish once I do," she said, her voice shaking.

"Ah, honey, it's okay," Jake said, comforting her. "Grab onto that feeling and run with it. You deserve it, and there's nothing wrong with being scared. My god, the hell we've been through the past couple of years. I know what you mean about being afraid when something good happens. It's like waiting for someone to come up from behind and pull the rug out from underneath you the moment your guard is down and you say things are great."

"Thank you for understanding," Lou said. "I love you."

"Love you too. Good night, Lou."

121

"Good night, Jake."

She hung up the phone and set it back on the nightstand. She lay there for a few minutes, staring at the ceiling and thinking about their conversation. She smiled and told herself again that things were good. She decided to leave it at that and reached over and turned out the light, pulled the blankets up over her shoulders, and sunk lower into her pillows. The last thing she thought about before drifting off was how very happy she was to be back at Echo Ranch.

22

Carla and Amy came around the next morning to pick up Dani. A light rain was falling across the valley. Summer was in its groove. The fields and aspen were lush green, and the wildflowers were in full bloom. The creek that ran through the property had settled down to a calmer flow once the spring runoff had come and gone. Lou stood at the windows in the great room with her cup of coffee, daydreaming over the beauty of the vast landscape before her.

"What's your plan for today?" Zack asked, interrupting her thoughts. "I wanted to do a run up to Final Fall. I thought it would be a good day to do that. One of the groups coming in tomorrow has some pretty experienced riders. I figured I'd take them up there but should check the trails one more time."

Lou remembered the first time she had ridden that trail. The last stretch of trail was a challenging climb and definitely not for the novice rider.

"I don't know about Final Fall, Zack," she said, wavering. "It's been quite a few years since I've ridden a trail like that. I'm pretty rusty."

"My god, woman," he said. "I'm almost seventy years old. If anyone should be a scaredy-cat over climbing some of those trails, it should be me."

"I'm not scared. I'm just a lot more conservative than I used to be," she said, defending herself.

"Then it's set." He grinned. "It shouldn't take us more than a couple of hours to make the climb. We can head out about noon and definitely be back by four or four thirty at the latest. Besides, Tessa has been dying to take a ride with you. No time like the present, right?"

He gave her a gentle slap on the back and turned away before she could come up with more excuses. She went back to the kitchen and sat on one of the stools. Tessa was finishing up the breakfast dishes.

Lou felt a tug on her heart. For the first time since she had returned, the reality struck her that Tessa wasn't a young woman anymore. She was still stunning and had aged more gently than most women Lou knew. She was fit, the epitome of grace and poise, and an accomplished rider too. Lou remembered watching Tessa in awe many times as she glided across valleys and stepped trails with such ease. Lou

123

knew that Tessa was very particular about her mounts. She expected command performance, and her horses willingly gave it to her. She had a natural confidence about her every time she gathered up her reins and gave a command. Lou could see how much a ride today would mean to Tessa.

"I can't think of anything I'd like more than to ride with you and Zack today," Lou said. "Did he tell you where we're going?"

"He sure did," Tessa said, turning around to glance at Lou. "He loves that place, and so do I."

Lou noticed how Tessa's eyes twinkled when she mentioned Final Fall.

"Do you know, of all the places on this ranch a person can ride, that is the one place that Zack truly holds closest to his heart," Tessa told Lou. "He said it reminds him of you. Through the years, every time he'd come back from a ride up there, he'd always tell me he 'had a visit with Lou today.'" She sighed. "We've missed you many times from then to now, Louisa. It's nice to come full circle with you. I know Zack is enjoying every moment since you've been back. I cannot even begin to express how happy I am, and that Danielle—well Louisa, it's like turning the hands of time back and watching you grow up all over again. She's magical."

"Thank you, Tessa," Lou said. "She is something else. That's for sure."

Lou thought about the drive to Colorado and the miles of anger she and Dani had shared in that car. She remembered the day they had pulled in under the main entrance to Echo Ranch and the flood of yesteryear that had washed over her. This place was not only Lou's hope, but her daughter's hope too. In the weeks since they had arrived, she could not only feel the changes, but see them. Calmness had enveloped her child, and although Lou tempered her hope, she gained comfort from the knowledge there had been many waking hours since they arrived that her head hadn't been filled with doubt and apprehension. She found herself looking forward to her days. A wet towel on the floor didn't matter anymore. She was learning how to step back and let her daughter figure things out.

"Well all right then," Tessa said, reaching across the counter and patting Lou's hand. "I'm going to go up and get ready. Zack said he'd meet us down at the barn."

Tessa glanced out the window toward the sky. Lou realized that it was nearly eleven. Most of the storm clouds had disappeared. The signature Colorado bluebird sky was rolling its blanket out in the aftermath of the storm, as though it was preparing for their ride.

"Look at that," Tessa said and pointed down valley.

Lou looked to where Tessa pointed and saw a beautiful double rainbow stretching over the remaining gray and fading into the blue on both ends until it eventually disappeared.

"Now there's a sign," she said, smiling as she walked away.

They got to the barn just as Zack finished tacking Jasper up. Bobby had set Black up on the cross ties for Tessa and Duck for Lou.

"It's about time you two showed up," Zack said, shaking his head. "Time's wasting." He pointed toward a saddle on the rack outside Duck's stall. "Lou, don't hesitate to ask for help if you don't remember how to saddle up a horse," he teased.

"Very funny. I think I can manage things just fine, smarty."

"Honey," he turned to Tessa, "let me give you a hand with that."

"Thank you, dear," Tessa said and stood back to let Zack swing her saddle up on top of the blanket on Black's back.

"It's a fine day for a ride," Zack said, smiling. He stood in the barn doorway admiring the sky.

He gathered Jasper's reins and led him out then busied himself with minor tweaks and adjustments while he waited for the ladies to join him. When they led their horses out a few moments later, they lined them up side by side. Bobby came out behind them with a mounting block and set it on the ground next to Tessa.

"Here you go, Miss Tessa, let me give you a hand."

"Thanks, Bobby," Tessa said and stepped up onto the mounting block and swung her leg over Black. She adjusted her seat, gathered up her reins, fixed her hat, and smiled back down at him. "All set."

"Okay, Miss Louisa." Bobby carried the block over to her and set it down. "You're next."

"Thanks, Bobby," she said as she climbed into the saddle.

125

After Lou finished mounting, Bobby picked up the block and backed away from between the horses, and they headed out across the eastern meadow.

"I figure we'll take our time crossing over here," Zack said. "That'll give the city girl a chance to get her riding legs back."

Lou shook her head. "It may have been a while, but I can assure you I still remember how to ride a horse, Mr. Calhoun."

"You just let me know when you're finished with this wimpy walking stuff, and we'll move on to something a little more exciting," Zack said, then without waiting for a response, he gave Jasper a kick and cantered off. Tessa followed his lead, and before long, she was cantering alongside.

Lou halted Duck, gathered up her reins, and adjusted the chin strap on her hat.

"Well, boy. I suppose it's time," she said, taking a deep breath and giving him a kick. He immediately set off at a fast trot. She gave him another kick, and after a few choppy strides, they relaxed into a comfortable canter. At first Lou was reluctant to go too fast or hold the canter too long. She pulled back on the reins a little to get the feel for Duck's mouth. Each time she applied the slightest pressure, his reaction was instant. He'd slow at once and break back into a trot. After doing this with him a couple of times, she realized he knew exactly what he was doing and that he would follow her lead. She eased the reins and gave him another kick. He transitioned back into a canter and was able to catch up with Zack and Tessa.

They covered the ground without much conversation. She couldn't believe she was here and felt a moment of sadness when she thought about the years that had passed. Why hadn't she ever brought her family out here? Why had the years passed so quickly? Why had it taken chaos in her family to finally push her into coming back? The trailhead appeared ahead of her. The sky was completely blue, and the sun was warm against her back. She was on a beautiful horse and with people she loved dearly. Today was a time to wash everything away and just enjoy. She settled a little deeper into her seat and gave Duck another little kick. He accelerated slightly and pulled ahead of Tessa and Zack.

She turned as she passed them and said, "I'll see you guys at the trail."

When Zack and Tessa met Lou at the trailhead, she could see that Tessa had either been crying or gotten something in her eye, but Lou chose not to mention it. Zack pulled Jasper alongside Duck and Lou, reached over, and gave Lou's knee a pat. His smile told her that they were as happy to be with her as she was to be with them; it said he regretted the many years that had passed as well, but that he was grateful to have this day and her be part of it. Lou returned his smile and fell in behind Tessa as she passed.

The three riders took the winding trail up the switchbacks until it began to level off toward the top. Lou could feel her heart pounding in her chest because she knew they were coming up on the final climb to their destination. She wasn't sure if it was out of fear or the anticipation of seeing Final Fall again. They stopped for a minute to collect and adjust. On one side of the trail, a sheer wall of rock rose, and the other was a long fall down the ravine to the valley. She subconsciously hugged the wall with Duck. He was amazingly agile, and she had faith in his sure-footedness. She followed closely behind Tessa and Zack as they led. She watched Jasper's tail swish back and forth and then disappear around the bend. Following close behind, Tessa maneuvered the turn while Lou brought up the rear.

When she came into the clearing, she halted Duck and looked up to the sky. A lone hawk dove and floated in circles around one of the mountain peaks in the distance. Periodically, he let out a shrill call before diving again toward the peak. Just before it looked as though he would plunge to his death, he would level off and swoop upward again, gracefully flapping his powerful wings. A soft breeze mixed with sunshine brushed her face. She hopped down off of Duck and walked around to his front. She led him across the tabletop to the small grove of trees where Zack and Tessa had tethered their horses.

"Go ahead and take his saddle off. Take his bridle off too, but make sure you put his halter on and tether his lead to that tree on the other side of Jasper," Zack instructed.

Once Duck was squared away, Lou walked over to Tessa and helped her with the saddlebags. Zack walked ahead of them and spread a couple of blankets over a small patch of grass.

"This is wonderful," Lou exclaimed.

She sat down on the blankets and helped Tessa lay out lunch. Tessa had packed chicken salad, homemade bread, fruit and cheese, and a couple of bottles of wine from their private stock.

"Tessa, you've outdone yourself," Lou said, smiling.

She pulled some cups out of the bag and handed them to Tessa.

"Thank you, dear."

Tessa poured each of them a glass of wine. They raised their glasses and lightly tapped them together.

"Salud!" Zack said, smiling then taking a sip. "So, Lou, is it still like you remembered it?"

"It's spectacular. I can't tell you how many times I've dreamed of this place over the years. Sitting here with the two of you right now is truly a dream come true for me," she said and took another sip of wine.

"It's our gift too, dear. What a wonderful day," Tessa said.

"I don't know what I would be doing right now had I not gotten in touch with you when I did, Zack."

Zack smiled and raised his glass to her.

Lou laughed. "I'd like another glass of wine, and let's just sit here for a while and watch time go by." She smiled and reached her glass out to Tessa for a refill.

They enjoyed their lunch and reminisced about growing older. Lou shared some of her experiences of the years after leaving the ranch. She told them that she felt like she had arrived at that place in life where she was on the threshold of completing one of her more difficult circles in life. She was grateful to Zack and Tessa for assisting in her passage.

After a time, they gathered up the remnants of lunch and packed the saddlebags. They went back to their horses and tacked them up. The afternoon had been spectacular. The breeze that swept across the tabletop was perfect: not too strong, yet strong enough to offset the heat from the afternoon sun.

They took their time winding down the mountainside. Lou could hear the chitter-chatter of conversation among the chipmunks as well as the river sounds coming up from the gorge at the basin of Final Fall. She tried to commit every image around her to memory because she knew there would be times long after she left that she would need to draw from this experience. She was happy, which was what she wanted to remember most.

23

"It's been a long time since I remembered feeling this good," she told Tessa as she led Duck into the paddock.

Tessa took Black's halter off and gave the horse a pat on the rump. The horse trotted off after Duck. Tessa followed Lou out of the paddock and turned back to secure the latch.

"Me too, Louisa," Tessa said, smiling and slipping her arm around Lou's waist as she came up next to her. "Where did Zack go?"

"He said he needed to finish up a few things before the groups come in tomorrow morning. I was thinking maybe you and I could go sneak a peek at what Dani's been up to with Poet before we head back up to the house."

"That's a great idea. You go ahead. I'll be there in a minute. I just want to check with Zack about dinner, and I'll meet you over by the round pen."

"Sure."

Lou walked back around the outside of the barn. When she came around the corner, she saw Dani and Bobby in the ring with Poet. She stopped for a moment to watch from a distance. She saw that they had managed to put a saddle on him, and, from her vantage point, he looked like he was handling it just fine. She continued to walk to the pen then climbed up on the bottom rail and rested her arms over the top. She pushed the brim of her hat a little further back on her head and watched her daughter and Bobby. Dani's back was to her, which was good because Lou didn't want to be the reason for Dani to lose her focus. Tessa climbed up on the fence next to her.

Poet did tight figure eights to Dani's commands. Dani looked like a natural. Each time he got to the point of transition, Dani would maneuver the line and give it a little tug then tell him to walk on, encouraging him the entire time.

"That's it, boy. Good boy," Dani said.

As she was making her turn with him, she saw Lou and Tessa standing on the fence. She gave them a quick smile and went right back to her job. Bobby was on the opposite side of the ring on the inside, leaning against the rails. Every now and then he would tell Dani to try this or do that, and just like Poet did for her commands, she would follow Bobby's command.

"That's good," he encouraged her. "Let out a little on the line, and give him some room to do some cantering and change directions. I want him to feel those stirrups slapping his sides so he gets used to different touches. You're doing great with him. He actually looks like he's enjoying himself."

"I think you're right," Dani said. "He seems like he's getting a little bored with the figure eights, though. I can feel him slowing down and not paying as close attention as he was when we first started. Tell me how much line I should let out."

"Give it about a foot, foot and a half. Before you do that, halt him, and bring him into you," Bobby said. "Make him halt completely where he is and collect himself first. Once he's standing still, start pulling him into you."

"Halt him now?" she asked.

"Yep."

"All right, boy, slow it down," she told Poet.

She gathered up a little of the line and gave it some tension. At first Poet wasn't sure what she wanted him to do, so he pulled his head back.

"No, boy. Easy," she said, coaxing him and gathering a little more line up in her hand. She used the technique Bobby had shown her the first day they worked together. Each time she got a couple of wraps in her hand, she dropped the excess by her side and gathered a little more up. "That's it, boy." She continued her process.

"Okay, Dani, that's real good, but he still isn't standing still," Bobby reminded her. "Give the line a couple of quick tugs and tap the side of your leg at the same time. He knows that means stop because that's what I've been telling him since the beginning. Go ahead and try it now."

She followed Bobby's instructions and gave the line two even tugs then immediately tapped her leg. Poet's ears did a pitch forward, and he stopped. He stood completely still and turned his head slightly toward her. He snuffled and let out a deep sigh. Dani smiled.

131

"Good boy," she exclaimed. "Okay, boy, I'll bring you to me now, so let's walk on real slow," she whispered.

Poet stood in place then bobbed his head up and down. He pawed at the ground and began casually walking toward her. His head bent downward, which was a good sign because it meant he was relaxed. When he got about a foot away from her, he let out another sigh of contentment. She dropped the lunge line, walked up to him, and slid her hand up under his chin. She stroked him a couple of times and continued to slide her hand down the length of his neck. He reached over her shoulder and tried to nibble on her shirt. She started to giggle and pushed him back.

"Hey. That's my shirt, silly," she said and giggled. She reached up and gave him a kiss on his muzzle and said, "I told you that you're not supposed to eat my clothes." She gently pushed his head away again.

Bobby walked out to the center. When he finished his instruction, and started to walk away, Dani reached up and unclipped the lunge line then gathered up the reins to his bridle. She walked him over toward Lou and Tessa. She was wearing a smile that Lou hadn't seen in what felt like years.

"What do you think?" she asked, beaming.

"I think the two of you are absolutely amazing," Lou said and reached over the rail to stroke Poet's face. "You are quite the man, Poet." She turned back to Dani. "And you," she started to say and could feel tears stinging her eyes, "you are just amazing."

"Oh my god," Dani said, starting to laugh. "Are you crying?" She looked over at Tessa and asked, "Why is she crying?"

"Because that's what mothers do when they're proud of their children, dear," Tessa explained.

"Yes, I'm crying." Lou wiped at one of the tears.

"Why?"

"Because I've never seen such magic up close like this, and the fact that it's you makes me so proud."

"Yeah?" Dani wrinkled her brow. "You've seen me ride lots of times, Mom."

"I've never seen you work with a horse the way you are working with Poet. Watching the two of you truly is like poetry in motion. It was a beautiful moment to behold, Dani."

Dani started to laugh. "Seriously? That's his name, Mom. Of course, it was like that."

"I know that's his name," Lou said, smiling, "but I think he's living up to it with you at the reins."

"Louisa is right, dear," Tessa agreed. "Zack knew what he was doing when he named this horse. I think since you've gotten here, you've brought the definition of his name to life."

"Punk, I think you're doing an amazing thing with him. I was watching how he responds to your commands, your touch, and you. That tells me he thinks you're pretty fantastic too." She reached back up and stroked his forehead. "Don't you, boy?"

Poet bobbed his head up and down, which made them all laugh.

"See? I told you." Lou smiled. "Hey! How was shopping today?"

"It was awesome."

"Yeah? Did you buy anything?"

"Oh yeah. I'll show you when I get back up to the house. I have to go back and finish up."

"Okay, Punk. We're heading up to the house. See you up there in a while."

"Yep."

She started to walk away and stopped. "Where's Zack?"

"He's in the office in the barn. Why?"

"Just wondering. Tell him to come out and see Poet with his saddle on if he wants."

"Sure," Lou said.

They climbed down off the fence and headed back toward the barn.

24

Later that evening, as Lou helped Tessa finish cleaning up from dinner, Dani poked her head into the kitchen.

"Why don't you go in and sit with Zack? I can get the rest of this," Tessa suggested.

"I think he went up to take a shower, which is exactly what I'm going to do. I smell like a horse from our ride today." She waved her hand past her nose.

Upstairs, Lou stopped outside Dani's door. She could hear the shower still running and shook her head. She wondered if either of her children would ever realize ten-minute showers existed.

Once she was in her own room, Lou turned the shower on and waited until the steam began to rise. She slipped out of her clothes, stepped into the shower, and stood in front of all the jets. The warm beads of water wrapping their heat around her felt good. When she finished her shower and walked down to Dani's room, she could see the light coming out from underneath the door. She lightly tapped.

"Dani, can I come in?"

"Yeah."

Dani was sitting on her bed, pulling stuff out of the shopping bags spread out on the bed.

"Wow! Looks like you bought out the stores today."

She grinned. "Carla said we weren't leaving until we hit every store because she always wanted to have girls to shop for."

"It looks like she accomplished her mission. Let's see what you got."

Lou climbed up onto the bed next to her.

"Check this out."

Dani picked up a denim skirt and grabbed a cropped T-shirt with a silk-screened image of horses thundering across a prairie.

"I like that," Lou said, taking the shirt from her. "I didn't know you would still wear something like this."

"I know. But it looks cool with that skirt, doesn't it?"

"Absolutely."

"And look at these." Dani held up a pair of earrings that were long silver feathers. "Do you think it would be all right if I changed these earrings?"

Lou thought about the mall incident as she inspected the new earrings in her hand. It was interesting to her that Dani was asking permission before she just went ahead and did the act.

"These are pretty." She gave her daughter a serious look. "I guess it'll be all right, but do you know why I did what I did with the earrings you're wearing?"

Dani was obviously apprehensive to answer at first because, Lou imagined, she really wasn't ready for one of her mom's lectures.

"I mean, I know you were really mad, and I know what I did was wrong. It's just that I don't even like these that much. The worst thing is that every time I wear them, I hate them even more."

Lou set the earrings down on the bed next to the skirt.

"I suppose it would be all right if you changed them."

"Thanks, Mom. I saved the best for last." Dani grabbed the large box and flipped the lid off. Inside was a pair of cowboy boots. They were chocolate brown with scrolled leather up each side. "Aren't these awesome?" she asked. "Carla took us into this huge store that had tons of boots everywhere. Amy and I were going crazy trying a bunch on. I ended up picking these out because I can wear them with all kinds of stuff."

She jumped off the bed and slipped them on to model them for her mother.

"What do you think?" She looked at Lou for approval.

"I love them. They're perfect."

Dani kicked them off and climbed back on the bed. "We had a blast today."

"I'm glad."

She got quiet and looked down at her things. "You know, we stopped at that hospital where Carla's son is."

"Yeah?"

"It was sad. I mean, he looked so small in that bed."

Lou hesitated because she didn't know how much Carla had told Dani about her son. "Do you know what happened to him?"

"Amy told me. It's awful."

"Yes it is. It's a tragedy—maybe one that could have been avoided if those boys had taken the time to think about their actions before just doing what they did."

"I know."

They sat quietly for a moment.

"Mom?"

Lou looked at her. "Yeah?"

"I tried drinking once."

Lou stiffened but didn't say anything because she wanted Dani to keep talking. Learning something about her child, especially something she didn't want to know, was hard.

"Yeah? When was that?" she asked cautiously.

"I don't know. It was before school got out. It was at a sleepover."

"So what happened?"

"I don't know. I mean, we were all up really late, and Kendra's mom and dad were sleeping. We were all in the basement, and Kendra said she had some beer if we wanted to have some. We got a couple of cans and passed them around."

"Yeah?"

"It tasted gross, but I did it because I wanted to see what it was like."

"How much did you guys drink?"

"I don't know, maybe a few cans. I mean it wasn't like we got drunk or anything."

"Did you think that was a smart thing to do?"

"I don't know," Dani answered, and Lou could tell her questions were beginning to irritate Dani. "I mean it wasn't like we were out driving a car or anything. Besides, I didn't drink much because it tasted disgusting."

"But, Dani, do you understand that it was wrong for a couple of reasons?" Lou said. "One, you were doing something you knew you shouldn't have been doing, and two, you are all underage. What do you think would have happened if Kendra's parents found out or, worse, all the other girls' parents?"

"They would have been mad." She glared at her mom.

136

"Do you think her parents found out?"

"I don't think so. I mean, if they did, Kendra never said anything, and neither did her parents. Mom, I don't drink all the time. I mean, I haven't done that again since then."

"Do any of your other friends drink?"

Dani hesitated. "I don't know."

"Dani, I'm not going to sit here and lecture you." Lou reached out and took Dani's hand. "Look at me, please."

Dani looked up at Lou.

"Can you do something for me?"

"What?"

"Can you work with me and help me work with you?"

"I don't know what that means."

"What it means is there are a lot of times when I want to help you, but I can't because you won't talk to me. Right now, what you've just told me is great," Lou said, reassuring her. "I know you're not a perfect little angel, and I know your friends aren't either. But what you all did could have gone very wrong. I don't condone children drinking or lying, and basically, that's what happened that night. Not only was it wrong, but you put Kendra's parents in a very dangerous position. That's not fair to them. Your dad and I can't guard you all day every day, but it's our commitment to keep you out of harm's way whenever we can. For us to do that, you have to start talking with us when you are faced with a situation you know is wrong but don't know how to get out of it. That's why we are here for you, and that is why we are parents. Do you understand?" She watched Dani think about this for a moment. "I suppose this feels like a lecture, but I really want this talk to be different."

Dani looked back up at Lou. "Okay," she said hesitantly. "You're not going to call Kendra's mom. Are you?"

"No. I'm not going to call her mom. I do want you to know, though, that you've put me in an awkward place because if it was me, I'd want to know. You also need to know that if that sleepover was at our house and I found out all the kids were drinking, I would call all the parents. That's what responsible parents do—not to get the kids in trouble, but to inform the parents—because we care. That's all any of us want for our children. We want them to know we care."

"Yeah, I guess," Dani said.

Dani began picking up her things and placing them back into the bags. She tucked the last item away and set all the bags on the floor by the closet. She climbed back up into bed and crawled under the covers. She looked up at her mom.

"I'm going to sleep. I'm tired."

"Okay, Punk, I'm a little tired myself," Lou said and tucked the covers up under Dani's chin, then leaned over and kissed her forehead. "Sweet dreams, Punk."

"You too, Mom. Good night," she said and turned over, tucking her hands up under her pillow.

Lou paused at the door and watched Dani for a moment. It had been a good day. She flipped off the light switch and went downstairs.

"Hey, you two, I think I'm going to call it a day," Lou told Zack and Tessa once she got downstairs. "It's been quite some time since I've been on a horse that long."

"Well we're glad you had a good time, dear," Tessa said, smiling.

"Don't think that's the only time you're riding this summer," Zack warned.

"I know. I wouldn't think of it."

25

They spent a quiet Fourth of July on the ranch. The following week was a scurry of activity. Volunteers helped with cleanup and preparations being made in the south valley where the bulk of summer camp activities would be held. The tent company came a few days prior and raised the tent, which would be home for the next week to fifty kids from all over the country. An all-hands meeting was called the day before their arrival, and all the volunteers were given assignments.

Shortly before noon the next day a large tour bus pulled under Echo Ranch's entrance archway. Inside were kids ranging in ages from twelve to fifteen years old who were about to embark on the experience of a lifetime. The bus made its gradual climb up past the main house and dipped down around the bend toward the south valley, where it pulled up alongside the tent. When the driver cut the engine and the sound of the air brakes being let out made a final *shoosh*, the doors opened, and droves of children poured out. The volunteer counselors stood with their clipboards in hand, ready to welcome each child as he or she stepped off the last step. They busied themselves gathering their groups.

Dani was with Amy and her group and felt a little overwhelmed.

"You'll tell me what I need to do, right?" she asked.

"Of course, silly," Amy assured her. "Just stick with me. I've got your back."

Dani watched Amy look back to her clipboard and recheck the names.

"Nine. There's only nine," she said, looking at Dani. "We're missing someone." She looked at Dani and back to the bus. Toward the very back, seated by the window, was a boy.

She handed her clipboard to Dani. "Here. Hold this. I'll be right back."

Amy climbed up into the bus and made her way back toward the last seat, and Dani watched Amy as she sat in the bench across from the boy, who looked like he was about the same age as Dani.

Dani walked along the bus to where Amy was talking to the boy to see what was going on. Through the open bus window, she heard Amy say, "Hey there. It's time to get off this rig and get ready for some fun. Why are you still sitting here?"

The boy didn't look up at her; rather, he pulled his hoodie around him a little tighter, crossed his arms, and made a point of looking out the window, intent on assessing the goings-on outside.

"Hello?" Amy said. She stood and leaned on the seat. "My name is Amy. I'm going to be your counselor this week. We should get going. The rest of the group is waiting on us."

He turned his attention back to her and stared at her with a blank look.

"What's your name?" she asked.

"Charlie." Dani could hear them talking through the bus window.

"Hi, Charlie," she said. "I'm Amy." She extended her hand to him. "How old are you?"

He looked down at her hand and back into her eyes. He shook his head and stood. "Fifteen."

When he didn't shake Amy's hand, Amy stuck it in her pocket.

"Well, Charlie, it's nice to meet you. You are going to have an amazing time. But in order to do that, the first thing we need to do is get off this bus."

Dani began to worry about Amy and went around to the steps of the bus. She climbed up to the center aisle and began to go back to where Amy and the boy were talking. She watched as the boy gave Amy a dirty look and popped up out of his seat. He reached down on the floor in front of him and grabbed a dirty canvas bag. He tucked it under his arm, inched his way out of the seat, and stepped into the aisle, making a point of nudging her as he squeezed by her and walked toward the door. As they stepped off the bus almost together, Dani smiled up at Charlie. Just like Amy had done, she held her hand out to him.

"Hi," she said. "Welcome to Echo Ranch." She smiled with her outstretched hand and looked at the bag he was clutching in his arms.

He ignored her gesture and smirked. He shook his head as he walked away to join the group standing behind her.

Dani dropped her hand and looked at Amy. "What's up with him?"

"Don't make a big deal out of it. Dani," Amy said, brushing Charlie's behavior off. "Let's take our group over to the registration center and get them signed in. We can talk about this later."

"Did you see what he did?" Dani asked again, refusing to let it go. "He acted like I wasn't even here. I mean, I thought we were supposed to make these guys feel like they were a part of something great, and he's acting like he's going to prison."

"Chill," Amy said firmly. "You don't know his story. Sometimes that has a lot to do with how a person acts here. Just let him be. It'll be fine. Trust me," Amy assured her. "C'mon. We're the last group to sign in, and lunch service has already started."

Amy didn't wait for a response and went back to the group.

Dani was incredulous. She couldn't believe Amy was taking Charlie's side. Dani decided that Charlie had to be the rudest kid she had ever met. Who did he think he was, anyway, Dani wondered, and why didn't Amy care about his behavior?

"Whatever," Dani mumbled and went to join the group.

Dani knew that Lou was inside the tent with Tessa, assisting with the final kitchen prep. As she walked into the tent, she could hear the laughter and commotion of the kids arriving. A welcome lunch kicked off the event. Dani knew that her mom was really looking forward to the endless activities and excitement that would consume the air and grounds of the ranch. Trail rides, swimming, games, campfires, sing-alongs, hiking, and whatever else they could come up with to wear these kids out each day had been arranged.

"I think we're ready," Dani heard Tessa say while smiling. "It's going to be wonderful."

Dani was still angry as the group made its way into the lunch tent, so she didn't pause to talk to her mom. Amy and Dani had taken the kids to the sleeping quarters after sign-in before going to lunch. Dani had shown the six girls their side, and Amy showed the four boys theirs. Dani was secretly glad that she hadn't had to deal with the guys, especially after what had happened on the bus with Charlie. As far as she was concerned, she didn't care if she had anything to do with him the entire week.

By the time they got to lunch, the dining area was filled with children of all ages. The counselors were easy to identify in their neon T-shirts and busied themselves organizing the groups and escorting them to their respective tables. Dani saw Amy and her group at a table in the middle of the tent. She joined the group at the table then followed them over to go through the lunch line. After they made it through the lunch line and got settled back at the table, they joined hands as Amy led grace. Dani was horrified to discover that she had sat next to Charlie. She gave him a sullen look and held her hand out to him again.

"Do you want to take it this time, or are you going to be a loser the whole week?" she whispered.

He gave her the same smirk from earlier, grabbed her hand, and squeezed it hard.

"Ouch!" she hissed. "What's your problem?"

"Trust me. I'm not the one with the problem," he said then bowed his head for grace.

Dani squeezed Charlie's hand back as hard as she could then bent her head as well. She didn't hear much of the prayer because she was furious she had to sit next to him. She made a mental note that she was going to let Amy know in no uncertain terms that this would be the *only* time this week she was going to do this, and if Amy didn't like it, that was just too bad. Dani felt like she had made enough sacrifices in her life for the sake of this summer; she refused to have this kid wreck the rest of her time at Echo Ranch.

As they ate their lunches, Amy encouraged the members of her group to share a little about their lives. Dani made a point of turning her back to Charlie and went out of her way to listen intently to the rest of the group.

When Amy looked to Charlie and asked him to share, Dani stiffened and turned around a little so her back wasn't as obviously pointed in his face, but she still refused to look at him.

"Charlie, right?" Amy asked, smiling. "Why don't you tell us a little about yourself?"

Charlie reached down on the bench next to him and pulled that dirty bag he had been clutching ever since he arrived a little closer. He scooped another hearty portion of macaroni and cheese into his mouth and made a point of chewing on it for what seemed like forever.

Dani could see out of the corner of her eye that he was angry that Amy called on him. She decided to mess with him. "C'mon, Charlie," she said. "It was only a bite of mac and cheese. Really? Swallow already." She sneered and rolled her eyes.

He glared back at her and threw his fork down. He started to push himself away from the table and Amy held her hand up.

"Dani," Amy said sternly. "That was totally out of line. Apologize."

Dani whipped her head around, and her jaw dropped. "What? I'm not apologizing to him. He's the one that should be saying he's sorry."

"Do it now," Amy demanded.

Dani glared at her and shot a look back at Charlie. "Sorry," she mumbled and crossed her arms.

"Okay. That's better," Amy said. "Now, Charlie, tell us a little about you."

He looked down at his plate and back at Amy. He seemed determined to get this out of the way quickly so he could get out of the tent. Despite her anger, Dani noticed that he wasn't a bad-looking kid. He had unruly, curly brown hair with bangs that came down low over his eyebrows. Every few minutes, he jerked his head to flip his hair away from his eyes. His eyes were dark brown. Dani had noticed when he took that big bite of macaroni and cheese his teeth were perfectly white and straight. He had a lanky build, was tall, and could definitely stand to put on a few pounds, in Dani's opinion.

"There's not much to tell," he said, looking at Dani with what she was beginning to believe was his signature smirk. "My parents are dead. I'm from Kentucky. I live with my aunt in a trailer and have two brothers. I don't know where they are now because they were farmed off shortly after my parents died. I haven't seen or heard from them in a couple of years. I'm here now because my aunt told me I had to come. What else do you want to know?" He stared straight into Amy's eyes.

Dani could actually feel anger resonating from his body. She was struggling with her feelings because, on one hand, she felt sorry for him. On the other, she couldn't figure out why anyone wouldn't be thrilled to be at a place like Echo Ranch. When she looked up at him, pity must have been written on her face.

"What're you looking at?" he snapped.

She flinched. She wanted to punch him but opted for a kinder approach. "I'm sorry your parents died. If I lost my parents, I'd be totally sad."

"Yeah, well, don't be sorry. They did it to themselves," he said and pushed himself away from the table. He grabbed his bag and stomped off toward the exit.

Dani watched him go and looked back toward Amy. "So what now? Do you think maybe now he owes me an apology?"

Amy shook her head and sighed.

"Okay, everybody, grab your plates and toss them in that can at the end of the lunch line over there. We'll meet you outside the tent back by the registration tables in a minute."

Dani got up to follow the group and Amy told her to wait.

"Dani, I need to talk with you for a minute."

Dani stopped and sat back down. She immediately folded her arms tightly across her chest and shook her head. "What?" she asked, rolling her eyes. "Let me guess. I suppose I owe Charlie yet another apology?"

"No. You didn't do anything wrong," Amy said. "But honestly, neither did he."

"Are you kidding me?" Dani shot back. "Did you not see how totally rude he was to me just now? I tell him I'm sorry his parents died and he acted like I told him to drop dead too."

"Sometimes it's too painful for someone to show people how they really feel when they've lost somebody they love," Amy said.

Dani listened to Amy but refused to say anything.

"First of all," Amy said, continuing despite Dani's silence, "none of these kids are losers, and I don't want to hear you say that again." she said and slapped her hand on the table. "These kids have had incredibly difficult lives, and if any of them ever heard one of us refer to them as a loser, it would wreck them. The point I was trying to get across to you is that it's pretty clear that Charlie hasn't come to terms with losing his parents. He's angry because he can't understand why they're gone. We don't know how it happened, and we may never," she said sternly, looking at Dani, "but it's up to him to tell us if he feels like telling us. In the meanwhile, our job this week is to make sure all of these kids have a

144

great time. We need to make their experience one that is going to give them some new perspective on the fact that life can be good. If there are some of them that aren't ready to get there yet, that's fine too, but at least we tried. You had better understand right now, though, that it's not up to us to judge. Clear?"

Dani looked down at her hands. She couldn't understand why Amy was getting mad at her. She hadn't felt like this since she'd left Virginia. She remembered the drive out here and how pissed she was at her mother most of the way. Most of the drive out to Echo Ranch, she couldn't wait for the day when she would be able to get out of that stupid car and away from her mom and have her own space. Once she got to Echo Ranch, each day was better than the one before it, and she had even started to see her mom as a person. Amy's lecture made her feel like she was back in the car with her mom again. She was angry.

"Fine," Dani said. "I won't call him or anyone else a loser, but I'm not sitting back and letting somebody treat me like I'm a loser either."

Amy smiled at her and rested her hand on Dani's shoulder. "Deal. Now, can we please go and find our group? We're supposed to take them on a trail down to the lake this afternoon."

When they came out of the tent, Lou and Tessa were walking toward them.

"I'm going to go catch up with my group," Amy said to Dani. "I'll see you in a minute. Okay?"

"Sure."

Lou and Tessa looked at each other and back at Dani. "Is there something you want to talk about?" Lou asked Dani.

Dani looked at her mother and Tessa.

"I don't know," she said.

"I think that's my queue to go check in with Carla," Tessa said. "I'll see you over at the barns in a while." She turned to Dani and said, "Have fun on your trail ride this afternoon."

"Thanks, Tessa."

Lou was all too familiar Dani's stance: arms tightly folded, and a dark expression   "C'mon, Punk, let's go have a seat and you can tell me what's going on," she said, coaxing Dani to sit down with her.

145

Dani dropped her arms to her sides, rolled her eyes, and followed her mother back into the tent. When they got to one of the tables, she plopped down at the end of the bench across from her mother. Dani braced herself; fully expecting her mom to ~~immediately~~ jump in with questions. Instead her mom busied herself sweeping some remnants of crumbs from the table to the ground. After another moment, Dani broke the silence.

"I don't know why you thought it was going to be such a great idea to help Amy this week. These kids are creeps," she grumbled.

"Dani," Lou said. "Why would you even say something like that?"

Dani said, "Because it's true. I mean, they're not all creeps. Just one of them who's in our group is. His name is Charlie, and he's really mean."

"Why don't you tell me what happened?" Lou said.

"It's not one thing, Mom. He's been a real jerk since he got here. I mean, he got off the bus, I told him welcome and held my hand out to shake his, and he practically knocked it out of the way."

"Did he hit you?" Lou asked seriously.

Dani looked at her mother and rolled her eyes. "No, he didn't hit me," she said. "He just ignored me." Lou didn't respond, so Dani continued, "Then he got in the tent, and Amy stuck me at the end of the table right next to him for lunch. She thought it would be brilliant for each of us to tell a little something about ourselves, and when we got to him, he told us how he lives with his aunt because his parents are dead and his brothers are—"

"That's terrible. What happened?"

"I'm getting to that," Dani insisted. "That's what I said too."

"What?"

"After he said that, I told him that I was sad for him that he lost his parents and his brothers were gone, but that's not my fault." She crossed her arms again and let out a long sigh. "Anyway, he got mad and told me he didn't care and left. So I told Amy he was a loser, and then she got mad at me."

Dani felt like she was going to cry, but refused to let the tears fall. Lou sat silently for a moment then said, "Dani, I think I understand what happened, but it looks like it hurt your feelings. I'm sure Amy wasn't trying to punish you. She's worked this event for a couple of years and, because of that, knows more than you do about these children. I'm sure she was trying to help you understand Charlie's feelings. These kids don't have a life anywhere near the lives you and Kylie have. It sounds like Charlie needs a little more time to fit in. What do you think?" she asked and smiled.

Dani concentrated on kicking at the ground with the toe of her boot. She wouldn't look at Lou, but Dani had heard what she said. Dani was not ready to let Charlie off the hook. She also knew that Amy was counting on her just as much as the rest of her group.

Dani decided she'd spent enough time talking about this and needed to catch up with the group so she could prepare for the trail ride. "Okay, Mom," she said. "I get what you're saying. I promise I'm not going to do something stupid. But I'm staying away from Charlie for now too. Maybe I wasn't the nicest, but he wasn't either. I'm going to help Amy."

She stood to walk away and Lou called out to her.

"Hey, Punk?"

"Yeah?"

"I'm proud of you," Lou said and smiled.

Dani gave her a faint smile, turned, and walked away.

26

A few days later Amy and Dani led their group down to the main barn where some of the ranch hands had already tacked the horses for them to use for the ride. Each group would take at least one trail ride as a group. For some of the children who demonstrated greater comfort around the animals, they would have an opportunity to join in on some of the daily one-on-one clinics.

Dani saw Bobby standing off to the side by the barn entrance and walked over to him.

"Hey, Bobby," she said. "Who am I riding today?"

"You're on Miss Lucy. You'll do sweep, and Amy will lead. Lucy loves sweep."

"Okay, awesome. I'll go check her gear, and see you later tonight. Will you be at dinner?"

"Yes, ma'am," he said.

As Dani made her way toward Lucy, she stopped to pet Bull. "Hello, Mr. Handsome. Are you ready to ri—"

She stopped short when she saw the person standing on the other side of Bull.

"You're riding Bull?" she asked incredulously.

"You got a problem with that?" Charlie snapped.

"The only problem I have is he doesn't take very well to inexperienced riders."

"Who said I didn't have any experience?"

Dani raised her eyebrow suspiciously. "You know how to ride?"

"Duh," Charlie said. "I only lived on a thoroughbred farm in Kentucky and probably worked more horses than you've ever seen in your entire life."

"Whatever," Dani shook her head and walked away.

Dani could feel Charlie watch her go. She heard him say, "C'mon, boy. Let's head out." She turned around and watched him as he gathered up his reins and led his horse to the courtyard in front of the barn. Most of the group was assembled. Dani led Lucy over to the mounting block and adjusted her stirrup, checked the girth, and with confidence, mounted Lucy. She gathered the reins, gave Lucy a gentle kick, and maneuvered around the group until she came up alongside Amy. Once she stopped, she turned toward Charlie, gave him a smug grin, and turned back around.

Amy circled Dancer up around to the front of the group. "Listen up, everyone, there are a couple of rules we need to go over before we get underway." Satisfied she had the group's attention, Amy cited the dos and don'ts for the trail ride.

"Nobody—and I mean nobody—steps out of line from the trail," Amy instructed. "Echo Ranch has some of the finest and smartest horses you'll ever ride, and they know their job like champs. Their job is to get you to the lake safely, and they'll do just that. Don't try to tell them what to do because they already know what to do. If you start messing with them, you'll just make them mad. If anybody has a problem, you call out to either me, Dani, or Tom, and we'll be there in a flash to help you out. You already know Dani and me. That guy over there"—she pointed to the man at the back of the line sitting on Beau— "is Tom. He's taking up the rear, and Dani is going to do sweep, which means she'll be walking up and down alongside the group for the entire ride. I'll be lead. The lake is beyond the south pasture, which is beyond the tents. It'll take about forty-five minutes to an hour to get to the lake. We have all kinds of fun planned for everyone once we get there. Any questions?" She scanned the group, and they silently stared back at her. "All right then, let's head out." She gave Tom a nod and looked to Dani and gave her a nod. She turned Dancer around and called over her shoulder, instructing the riders to fall in behind her, single file.

They made their way back down toward the tents, and once they were on the other side, they eased onto the trail. Amy purposely set a leisurely pace to accommodate the novice riders. True to form, Colorado painted up one of her prettier blue skies to welcome her visitors. The temperature was resting comfortably in the 80s, and the warm summer breeze surrounded the riders like a comforting blanket.

Dani relaxed into Lucy's motion and was enjoying her job. This was the first trail she had been on without Zack at the lead and enjoyed the role of sweep. She felt important and took her job seriously. She continuously looked up and down the line to be sure everyone was safe and paying attention. Occasionally she saw a saddle slip or a rider who wasn't reining properly, and she rode up beside him or her, made a few suggestions, gave a big smile, and then dropped back to continue her sweep. She made a point of holding back from Charlie enough so she could watch him without his knowing. She noticed Bull was fidgeting a lot and finally gave in to her urge to say something to him about his technique.

She rode up alongside Charlie. "If you ease up on his reins a little, he'll stop that annoying bob with his head," she suggested.

Charlie looked over at her and begrudgingly let out on his reins a bit. Like magic, Bull relaxed his head and pressed on.

"Thanks," Charlie mumbled. "He's got a really soft mouth, huh?"

Dani felt pretty victorious, but decided against showing it. "Yeah, he has a great story, that horse. His full name is Sitting Bull. Do you know who that was?" she asked.

Charlie looked at her, made his signature smirk, then said, "Uh. Yeah. I'm not stupid."

She let out an exasperated sigh. "How come you're so mean? I'm just trying to talk to you, and every time I try to be nice, you turn into a creep."

Charlie continued to look straight ahead.

"See? You can't even answer me." Dani gathered up her reins and was about to give Lucy a kick, and Charlie reached his hand out.

"Wait."

Dani was confused. "For what?"

"What's his story?" Charlie asked.

She looked up toward the front of the group and glanced behind her. Satisfied everyone was okay, she eased up on Lucy's reins a bit and walked alongside Charlie and Bull.

"Sitting Bull was one of the greatest Indian warriors who ever lived. Zack, the guy that owns all this," she said and waved her arm, "told me when he bought Bull, he reminded him of Sitting Bull. He said Sitting Bull had a lot of pride and was very calm and wise, and that's how he"— she nodded to the horse—"acted the first time Zack saw him. Paints are a traditional Indian horse, so it seemed to be a perfect fit; he thought it was the natural choice to name him that."

Charlie looked down at Bull, and gave his neck a scratch. "You are quiet and wise, huh, boy?" he whispered barely breaking a smile.

150

"Wow," Dani said, grinning.

"What?" Charlie scowled.

"You actually do know how to smile," she said, teasing, but kindly.

"Very funny," Charlie mumbled.

"Yeah, well, it's a lot better than what you were giving us when you first showed up," she teased further, emboldened by Charlie's more stable reaction to her first attempt to draw him out.

She checked the line again and looked back at him. "I'm going to do a pass. Be right back, okay?"

"So who said I was keeping you here?"

"Whatever," she said and trotted off to the front of the line.

27

They made it to the lake in the midafternoon. After the horses were squared away, their group mixed with the other two groups, who had already arrived by way of a hayride. Squeals of laughter from campers' nonstop plunges into the cool, clear lake from the rope swing and the intermittent clang of a horseshoe landing a dead ringer filled the air, and footballs, Frisbees, and a wiffle ball game induced plenty of smiles. Amy pulled up a spot against a tree near the horses and began reading her book.

Dani canvassed the crowd, trying to figure out what she wanted to do. She was about to take a walk to the other side of the lake and join the people fishing when she saw Charlie sitting by himself at the opposite end of the lake. She took a deep breath and opted to make one more attempt to break the ice. She stopped to tell Amy where she was going.

Amy looked up from her book and shaded her eyes from the sun. "What's up?" she asked.

"Nothing."

"Don't even tell me you're bored," Amy said, laughing. "Look around. You have your pick of things to do!"

"Yeah, I know." She looked down toward Charlie.

Amy looked over her shoulder toward him and back at Dani. "Oh, I get it," she said and grinned.

"What?" Dani asked indignantly. "You get what?"

"You want to break the ice with angry boy," Amy said, giggling.

"Now who's judging?" Dani snapped.

"Chill, Dani," Amy said. "I think you should go talk to him. Seems to me you two have a lot in common." She reached her foot out and nudged Dani's leg.

"Stop it," Dani said. "We don't have anything in common."

"Yeah, you do. You both have an angry streak, which is why you know how to push each other's buttons so well."

"That's not funny."

"C'mon, Dani, go on. Go talk to him. He looks lonely. Besides, if anyone can pull him out of himself, it'll be you," Amy said, trying to encourage Dani.

"Whatever," Dani said. "I'm gonna go fishing."

152

"Suit yourself." Amy didn't wait for a response. She returned to reading.

"So that's it?" Dani asked.

"Hmmm?" Amy looked up at her and grinned.

"Forget it," Dani said and turned to leave.

"Geez, Dani, grow up," Amy said.

Dani spun around. "What's that supposed to mean?" she demanded.

Amy shut her book and set it down on the ground next to her. "What it means is you know as much as I do that you want to go down and talk to Charlie. He's interesting, and clearly he needs a friend. I think the best thing you can do for that kid is let him know that maybe he found the first friend he's had in a long time even if he doesn't know how to approach the situation. You do. You're funny, nice, and friendly—most of the time—and he looks like he could use a friend right about now. Besides, that raggedy bag he's been clutching ever since he got here looks like it could use a friend too."

Dani giggled. "I know, right? What's up with that bag, anyway?"

"I don't know," Amy said, "but it's definitely something that's pretty important to him. Go on. Go talk to him and leave me alone. This book is really good, and I want to get back to it." Amy went back to reading and didn't look up again.

As Dani approached Charlie, she could see him take something out of his bag, but she couldn't tell what it was; it looked like some sort of picture. As she got closer, he looked up and quickly stuffed the item back into his bag.

"What?" he asked, looking up at her, obviously agitated.

"Geez. Nice to see you too," she said sarcastically.

"Yeah, well don't you know when somebody chooses to be by themselves, it means they don't want anybody else around?"

Dani crossed her arms and glared at him. She let out a deep sigh, shook her head, and turned to walk away.

"Wait," Charlie said.

She stopped and turned back around. "What? Did you have some other snotty thing to say to me before I left?"

Charlie grinned and looked down at his bag.

"What's so funny anyway?" she snapped.

He looked back up at her. "I wasn't going to say something snotty. It's just that—"

"You need a little more time to think of something?"

"No, I just don't do very good with crowds." He looked back down at his lap.

Dani shifted her weight and uncrossed her arms. "So do you think it would be okay if I sit down, or are you going to throw a rock at me?"

He looked up at her and she smiled.

He smiled back, which eased the tension. "Nah," he said. "Besides, I don't see any rocks close by."

"Very funny."

"You can sit down."

She sat down across from him in the grass. Neither spoke for a few minutes.

"So how come you're not swimming or fishing or something?" she asked.

"I don't know. I guess I don't feel like it."

"Me neither," Dani confessed. She reached down, plucked a long piece of sweet grass, and stuck it in her mouth.

Charlie watched her and grinned. "You're a regular cowgirl, huh?"

"Huh? Oh! She grabbed the grass out of her mouth and tossed it. "No," she said, "but don't knock it until you try it."

"Whatever."

"So why are you so mad all the time anyway?"

"I'm not mad. I just don't like people," he said.

"Oh. I guess I should go then," Dani started to get up.

"You can stay if you want. It doesn't matter to me," he said and shrugged.

She sat back down and crossed her legs. She picked another piece of grass and went to put it in her mouth, but saw that he was watching her. She tossed it aside, which made him laugh.

"What?"

"You're addicted to that stuff, huh?" he said, teasing.

"No," she said, "it's just something to do." She looked at him, then immediately looked back down at the ground. She smoothed her hand over the grass and didn't know what it was about him that made her feel so anxious. She thought about that bag and decided to ask even if it made him mad.

"So what's with that bag?" she asked and nodded to the canvas bag by his side.

"It's personal."

"Are you sick or something?"

"Huh?" he said, glaring. "I'm not sick."

"Well you're holding on to it like it's your life, so I thought maybe you had some kind of magic medicine in there or something," she teased.

He grinned and looked at her. "Like I said, it's personal."

Dani sighed and began to stand up again. "Whatever." She stretched and looked over at the kids who were fishing. "Well, this is boring. I'm going to do something. Want to go fishing?"

"Nah."

"Okay, see you later," she said, turning to leave.

"Wait."

Dani turned around and looked at him.

"You can stay if you want."

"What for? You don't want to talk or anything. This is boring."

"So maybe if you sit back down we can talk for a while. I don't know," he said, sounding as if he might be offering friendship.

Dani thought about this and opted to sit back down. She stared at him until he looked back up.

"What?"

"So talk," she said, grinning.

"About what?"

"Anything."

Tentatively, Charlie began to open up about his life in Kentucky. At first his words were forced, and his thoughts seemed scattered. He wasn't making much sense. He would start talking about his parents, then skip to life with his aunt, and circle back to his brothers. Dani had a million questions, but for some reason, she was more interested in just

155

hearing him talk. She guessed that it had been a long time since anyone just let him talk, and she was glad she could be the person to let him do just that.

After some time, he eased into making some sense of his complicated life for her. He told her how he had lost his parents. When he and his brothers were much younger, his family had lived on his maternal grandfather's ranch. They had owned a beautiful spread of land, and his grandfather had run a thoroughbred breeding program. Although many of the horses were of fine stock, none of them had ever made it to the Derby, but they had paid the bills. His parents worked on one of the local tracks and spent most of their days assisting trainers, maintaining barns, and hob-knobbing with wealthy people. As Charlie became old enough to process what was going on behind the scenes, he began to realize that both his parents were hopelessly hooked on all kinds of drugs.

The problem got worse. Sometimes several days passed when they wouldn't come home. Some of his fondest memories before that were the times his parents had taken him and his brothers to the track with them. They had spent entire days in the barns with some of the most amazing Derby contenders. But as things got worse with his parents' drug use, so did the quality of their home life. When his parents had bothered to come home, Charlie and his brothers would lay awake at night and listen to nonstop shouting and fighting between his parents and his grandfather.

Then one day, his parents didn't come home. The days turned into weeks, and late one night after about a month, a pair of policemen showed up at the house. They told his grandfather that his parents had been found with a few other people in a dope house just outside of Shepherdsville. Charlie wasn't sure of the details but over time learned enough to know that they had found his mother first and his father soon after, both of them dead with needles stuck in their arms.

His grandfather had been crushed by the news, and, after that, he seemed to age overnight. He spent most of his days sitting in his rocker on the front porch. Toward the end, Charlie had to carry him out of that chair to bed most nights. His aunt Julie, his mother's sister, had made it a habit of checking in on them. Eventually, she had taken Charlie and his brothers away to live with her. She was a family outcast and lived in a dumpy little trailer on the outskirts of town. After a while, caring for three boys got to be too much for her. Social services must have heard about the boys when they all quit going to school because that was when they came looking for the boys. His aunt Julie promised to turn things around, but what Charlie didn't know was that she had agreed to give up his younger brothers and had promised to send him back to school on a regular basis.

She had convinced Charlie that going back to school was in his best interest. He came home one afternoon from school, and when he walked into the trailer, he knew something bad had happened. His aunt Julie had been sitting on the couch crying. When she calmed down enough to tell him that his brothers were gone, something had just switched off inside of him. He had decided then that he was going to keep going to school and make something of himself because some day he was going to find his brothers and get a place of their own.

When school let out for the summer this year, he had already gotten a full-time job at the local grocery store. When he had come home from work one night, Aunt Julie was dancing around the living room singing "You're going to Colorado. You're going to Colorado." He thought she had finally cracked, until she explained what she meant. Then he remembered that midway through the previous school year, he had brought home a flyer to his aunt Julie about this event. She must have filled it out.

"So that's how I ended up here," he said and sighed.

Dani thought about the story and realized that the only time she had ever been exposed to anything like that was when she saw it in a movie or on television. She couldn't believe that real people had real stories like the one Charlie had just relayed.

"That's some story," she said quietly. "I'm so sorry."

"Don't," he said and held up his hand. "Don't say you're sorry. I am so sick of people saying they're sorry." He punched his fist into his thigh.

"I don't feel sorry for you. All I was trying to say is that it makes me sad to hear your story," she said, trying to make him understand the difference.

"Yeah, well. That's life. Besides, I decided a long time ago that that's what they wanted to do with their lives. Not me. I'm going to do great things so I can help my brothers out."

"Do you know where they are?"

"Nah," he said. "My aunt Julie knows where they are, but she says I need to concentrate on making a better way for me right now. She promised they're in a better place and that they're safe. It pisses me off, but there's a part of me that knows she's right."

He looked back down at his bag.

"So," Dani paused, "What's in the bag?"

"It's a picture."

"Of what?"

"Me and my brothers."

"Can I see it?"

Charlie looked at her and back at the bag. She could tell that he wanted to show her but understood that he also didn't want any pity. "I'll show it to you, but you have to promise not to do some stupid girly thing like cry."

"Whatever," she said and held her hand out.

He pulled the flap open and reached into the bag. When he had the picture in his hands, he scooted up next to her to show it to her. "This is Johnny. He's seven, and that's Frankie. He's ten." He smiled at her, "That's me. I was twelve."

Dani did the math and realized he hadn't seen his brothers in three years. She couldn't imagine what she would do if three years passed without seeing Kylie.

"Wow. They're really cute," she said, smiled, and handed it back to him.

"If you say so," he said and chuckled.

"What? Is that too girly?" she asked and nudged his shoulder.

He smiled. "Nah. I guess it's all right." He took the picture back and tucked it back into the bag.

They sat quietly, watching water ripples sweep the lake each time the breeze touched its surface. The afternoon sun was warm on their backs. They'd been out there for nearly two hours. When Dani turned to check on the group back up at the lake, she could see most of the kids had gone. Their group was the only one left.

"We should head back," Dani said. "Looks like Amy is starting to round everybody up."

She stood up, brushed her hands off on her pants, and started to walk away. Charlie popped up from the ground and fell into step next to her. On the walk back Dani shared a little information as to how she ended up at Echo Ranch. By the time they rejoined the group, she had decided maybe Charlie wasn't such a creep after all.

"Hey, guys. We're just about ready to go," Amy said when she saw them. "Dani, make sure you check your gear, and help Charlie with his. Tom is just about done with the rest of the crew. Give me a heads up when you're ready, and we'll hit the trail." Amy winked at Dani then walked away.

Dani rolled her eyes and walked off toward Lucy, who was tethered to the tree next to Bull. As she led her into the open and mounted, Charlie mounted Bull. He led him around to Dani's outside and paused next to them.

"I'm falling in with the group. I'll see you on sweep on the way back." He grinned and didn't wait for a reply.

Dani blushed and turned Lucy in the opposite direction and headed toward the back of the line. Amy did one final head count. Satisfied everyone was ready, she raised her arm and gave the motion to walk on.

Later that evening after taking her shower and crawling into bed—even though she was exhausted—as soon as Dani's head hit the pillow, her mind began to race. She wanted to dislike Charlie, but she had a stronger urge to want to get to know him better. She wondered if she made the effort to get to know him, would he turn out to be a total jerk anyway and make her feel even worse by the time he left?

She rolled across the bed toward her nightstand and reached up to turn on the light. She sat up in bed, pulled her knees up to her chest, and wrapped her arms around her legs. She let out a deep sigh and smiled when she thought about the time she spent with Charlie at the lake earlier that day. She wasn't quite sure why she was smiling because he definitely wasn't the friendliest guy she had ever met. Yet there was something about the way he trusted her, when he showed her the picture of his brothers. She knew exactly where he was coming from when it came to distrusting people. She felt that way often toward her parents—particularly her mother—especially over the previous year.

She thought about some of the other kids in her group and mentally tried to match them up with some of her friends back home. Even though her friends managed to get into trouble, it was nothing compared to some of the kids at the camp. She thought about Chelsea and wondered what she was doing. Dani hadn't heard from her much since the Fourth of July. They used to call or text each other constantly if they weren't together. She felt a pang of anger when she thought about that and wanted to blame her mother for bringing her to Echo Ranch for the summer. Granted, Dani had to admit, even to herself, that she loved being around the horses, but she did miss her friends. They were probably having the best summer ever, and she was missing out on every moment.

Dani reached up, gathered her hair into a ponytail, and pulled it over her shoulder. She absentmindedly stroked it, feeling angrier the more she thought about her mother's decision to bring her to Colorado. When she reached for her cell phone on the nightstand, she remembered she didn't have it—another one of her mother's ideas. Lou had established the rule the day they got to the ranch: Dani wasn't allowed to take her phone to bed with her the entire time they were at Echo Ranch. She was permitted to use it when she came back up from the barns each night, but had to give it back to Lou before she went to bed.

She kicked her covers off and jumped out of bed. She stood by the window and looked out across the dark night then at the picture of her mom, Zack, and Eagle. She focused on her mom's image, gave her a dirty look, and shook her head.

"Why did you do this to me, Mom?" Dani asked. She wanted to grab the picture off the wall and throw it across the room. She shook her head and looked up at the night sky. Millions of stars winked at her. She looked toward the eastern range and could see the faint silhouette of the peaks against the night. She glanced back over her shoulder at the alarm clock on the nightstand. It was nearly midnight. In less than eight hours she had to be back at Amy's side with their group to begin another day.

160

She climbed back up into bed and reached over to turn out the light. She pulled the covers up over her shoulders, turned over onto her stomach, snuggled down deeper into her pillows, and let out another sigh. The last thing she remembered before drifting off was to consider the possibility of letting go of some of her anger. She hated the way it made her feel. The fact of the matter was that she and her mom would be at Echo Ranch for another month, and nothing Dani could do could change that. Maybe she would try to focus on some of the good things, like Poet, and not worry so much about other stuff.

28

Dani slowly opened her eyes the next morning to the sound of a distant buzzing. She lay there for a moment trying to figure out where the sound was coming from and sat bolt upright in her bed when she realized the sound was her alarm clock. She looked out the window and could see dawn breaking over the south pasture and the outline of the event tent taking shape against the light of dawn and wondered what camp had in store for her. Everything looked beautifully still and quiet at the moment.

She threw the covers back and hopped off her bed. She flipped the light on as she went into the bathroom and leaned into the mirror for a quick inspection. She ran her fingers under her eyes to wipe away the smudges of yesterday's eyeliner and reached behind her to turn the shower on. When the steam began to fill the bathroom, she stepped into the shower and stood motionless under the stream of water, luxuriating in the heat cascading over her body. She quickly lathered up, washed her hair, rinsed, and decided she was done. As she brushed her teeth, she thought about the prior day—Charlie, in particular. She tapped her toothbrush on the side of the sink, spit and rinsed, and placed it back in the holder next to the sink. She took one final look in the mirror after she got dressed and headed downstairs in search of Amy.

As she passed through the dining room, the little green light on the coffeemaker was the only light coming from the kitchen. She remembered trying coffee once and thought it had tasted like dirt, no matter how much sugar and cream she put in it. She put a couple of slices of bread into the toaster. As she waited for them to cook, she went over to the window and looked down valley. The sky had amassed an explosion of pinks and violets to replace the gray she had seen earlier from her bedroom window. She watched the sun as it steadily climbed over the eastern range and snuffed out the light of one lonely star. Her toast popped up, and she smeared some butter on the slices. She wrapped them in a paper towel and headed through the kitchen to the front door.

As she stepped out onto the porch, she saw Amy sitting on the far end in the swing. She walked over and sat down next to her.

"Good morning," Amy said.

"Hey," Dani grunted and took a bite of her toast.

They sat quietly, watching Pearl on the far end of the paddock. Pearl's head was bent down to the grass as she grazed peacefully in her little corner of paradise, not a care in the world, her tail swishing slowly back and forth.

"So what's the plan today?" Dani asked.

"We're taking our group over to the barns for a tour. Zack will be there. He needs to brand a few of the horses he added to the herd this year. He thought it would be a great experience for the kids to watch," Amy said.

"Cool. I've never seen a horse getting branded," Dani said.

"Seriously?"

"Yeah. I mean, I've seen stuff like that in movies, but not in real life." She looked at Amy. "Does it hurt them?"

"I don't know. It probably stings some, but Zack knows what he's doing, and he definitely doesn't do it to hurt them," Amy assured her.

Dani thought about this for a moment. "I guess." She watched Amy take a sip of her coffee. "How do you drink that stuff?" She scrunched her nose. "Doesn't it taste like dirt?"

"Not really. I load it up with sugar and cream, and it tastes pretty good. I started drinking it when I went away to college. It helped a lot when I was cramming for exams. After that, I got used to it," Amy said.

"Well I still think it's awful." Dani finished the last bite of her toast, brushed her hands on her pants, and asked, "Is Zack letting some of the kids help him brand the horses?"

"I don't think he'll let them do it alone," Amy said, "but knowing him, he'll probably let them assist if they want. Since we've been doing this event, Zack has always tried to mix the program up each year—you know, give the kids new experiences and let them figure out what they like and don't like. It's all about them the entire week. Our job is to make sure they leave with a good feeling come week's end."

"Well I bet some of them will leave the same way they came," Dani grumbled.

"Anyone in particular?" Amy asked, nudging Dani's shoulder.

Dani looked at Amy and could feel her face flush. "What do you mean?"

"Like maybe angry boy?" Amy asked, grinning.

"Stop calling him that!" Dani insisted. "His name is Charlie. Besides, who said I was talking about Charlie?"

"C'mon, Dani, I saw you guys down at the lake yesterday— looked like you two were getting along just fine."

"Whatever." Dani jumped up off the swing and spun around. "Anyway, he's part of our group. What are we supposed to do, leave him alone in the tent all day?"

"Somebody has a cru-ush," Amy teased.

"I do not!" Dani turned on her heels and walked away. She stopped at the stairs and looked back at Amy. "Are you coming or, are you going to make me walk down to the tent?"

"I'm coming," Amy said, shaking her head and getting up off of the swing. She came up alongside Dani and ruffled her hair.

Dani reached up to swat at Amy's hand. Before she could connect, Amy scooted past her down the steps, climbed into the Gator, and backed it around to the steps.

"You coming? Breakfast starts in ten minutes," Amy said.

Dani stood on the stairs looking down at her, stewing for a moment, but she decided to shake it off. She skipped down the steps and plopped into the seat next to Amy. As they pulled away, Dani asked, "Do me a favor?"

"What's that?"

"Please don't tease me about Charlie. I hardly know him, and it's embarrassing."

"I'm sorry, Dani, I didn't mean to embarrass you," Amy said.

"Well you did," Dani mumbled.

"Okay. No more teasing about angry boy," Amy said and grinned.

Dani tried not to break a smile but couldn't help herself. "Whatever," she said and crossed her arms.

By the time they got to the tent, breakfast was in full swing. They could hear laughter and commotion as they approached the entrance. As they walked inside, Dani headed toward the buffet line while Amy checked their assigned table to see if any of their group was there yet. Some of the group were already seated and gobbling up their breakfast.

Once situated back at the table, Dani bent her head and closed her eyes. Before Amy began the prayer, Dani whispered, "Morning." Charlie didn't respond. As they dropped their hands and began to eat, Dani wanted to say something but didn't know what to say. She played with her eggs and pushed the potatoes around on her plate. She had been starving when they got to breakfast but lost her appetite somewhere between the walk to the table and grace. She stole a sideways glance at Charlie. When she noticed he didn't seem to have any problem with his appetite, she felt irritated. He seemed oblivious to her as he attacked the mound of eggs on his plate and came up for air long enough to take a gulp of milk before plowing back into his food.

Dani set her fork down and looked at Charlie. "What's your problem?" she asked.

Charlie was about to take a bite and set his fork down on his plate. He looked at her and smirked. "No problem here."

Dani furrowed her brow. "Sure doesn't look like that to me," she snapped.

"Sounds like you're the one who has a problem," he said.

"Yeah, well, I don't," she said. Dani stood up and grabbed her plate. She expected him to say something. Instead, Charlie picked his fork back up and continued eating. When Dani wouldn't leave, he seemed to become annoyed.

"What?" he asked and looked at her.

"Nothing. I just thought that—"

"You thought what?" he asked.

"I thought that maybe we could talk about what we're doing today," Dani cautiously answered.

Charlie dropped his fork and shook his head. "Okay, Dani, I'm all ears. Why don't you tell me all the fun things we're doing today. Goody! I can't wait."

"Oh my god. You're such a jerk," she said as she shook her head then walked away in a huff.

Amy said, "Hey, guys, if you are finished, go ahead and drop your plates in the trash. We'll meet out by the registration tables. The hay wagon should be there or will be soon."

When she tossed her plate in the can, Dani didn't realize Charlie had followed her. When she turned around, she nearly fell over him. She quickly regained her composure and, thinking she was giving him a taste

165

of his own medicine, intentionally knocked his shoulder as she walked past him out of the tent. Once outside, Dani stood back and watched the group gather as the hay wagon pulled up alongside the tent. She could see already that signs of new friendships forming were everywhere among their group. As the last few stragglers made their way up into the wagon, she took one final look over her shoulder. Satisfied nobody was left behind, she looked back to Amy and gave her the nod to head out.

On their way to the barns, Dani made a point of not looking at Charlie even though he was seated directly across from her. He sat against the backboard with his arms folded, staring down at the floorboards. He seemed to be refusing to look at her too. He wasn't even looking up at any of the incredible scenery around them. The silence began to grate on Dani's nerves. She made a point of raising her voice and saying, "You know Echo Ranch is huge. All these mountains and valleys are part of a big conservation project here on the Western Slope. That's what we call this part of Colorado," she matter-of-factly added. Confident she had everyone's attention, she continued sharing her knowledge. "When I first got here, Zack, the owner, took me on a trail ride up those mountains over there." She pointed to the winding trail in the distance that was carved into the mountains beyond the barns. She heard a few of the younger kids utter oohs and aahs. "Anyway, from here it looks like it's a pretty dangerous climb, but it isn't. Things look smaller than they really are once you get to them."

"Duh," Charlie mumbled.

Dani heard him but refused to acknowledge him. "Over there," she said, pointing, "beyond the main barn on the hill is the brood mare barn. That's where all the mares and their foals live. Three new babies were born this year." She looked toward Amy and asked, "Are we going to be able to go see them today?"

"Absolutely," Amy answered. "We're going to watch a branding demonstration first and tour the main barn. Lunch will be set up by the brood mare pastures and barns, so we'll see all that later today." She gave a nod at Dani for her to continue.

"Anyway, that's one of my favorite parts of the ranch. Wait until you see how cute the babies are," Dani said.

They pulled up to the main doors of the barns, where Zack and Bobby stood in the doorway waiting to greet everyone. Charlie waited until everyone was off the wagon then slowly stood and hopped over the side rail down to the ground. Dani walked up alongside him. They looked at each other for a moment before Charlie shook his head, turned, and walked away to join the rest of the group. Dani was hurt and angry. She wanted to punch him but was conflicted. She wanted to get back to that place they had shared yesterday when they had been down at the lake. She thought they were becoming friends. Now, based on Charlie's signals, she didn't know what to think.

29

The second wagon pulled up to the barn, and another group of children poured off. Once everyone was situated around the entrance, Amy, Dani, and the other counselors stood alongside Zack and Bobby.

"Okay, everyone, listen up," Amy said and placed her hand on Zack's shoulder. "This is Zack Calhoun, the owner of Echo Ranch." She turned to Bobby and smiled. "And this is Bobby Compton; Zack's number 1 ranch hand and foreman." Bobby took a slight step forward and tipped his cowboy hat to the group. "These guys are going to give us a branding demonstration this morning. Before we start, I want to go over a couple of rules. Please make sure you pay attention to what's going on around you. As I'm sure you figured out yesterday, Zack has a fine herd of horses that are gentle and kind, but they're still horses. That means they're unpredictable. Sometimes, what you and I think are the simple things are situations that can frighten them. If they get spooked and you're not paying attention, you run the risk of getting hurt. I'm not saying this will happen today. I just want you all to respect the fact that these animals are a lot bigger and stronger than any of you, and it's important to pay attention." Amy scanned the group and turned back to Zack. "Okay, Zack," she said, "Looks like we're ready to get started." Amy took a step back and let Zack take over.

"Thanks, Amy," Zack said and paused for a moment to look over the group in front of him. "First off, I want to welcome everyone to Echo Ranch. We're glad you're here, and I hope everyone is having a great time so far. Like Amy said, before we go on the tour, we're going to show you guys how we brand a horse. We brand our horses because we want to make sure they have some sort of identifying mark on them. It lets strangers know they belong to somebody. There are a couple of different types of branding a rancher does with his animals. Here at Echo Ranch, we freeze brand our boys and girls. We know it's not the most pleasant experience for the animal but believe it's not as painful as using a burn brand. We—"

"How come you don't tattoo them?" Charlie called out.

Zack looked at Charlie. "What's your name, son?" He asked.

When Charlie looked around and saw all eyes on him, he regretted opening his mouth. "Charlie," he answered.

"Well, Charlie, that's a good question. Some of the horses we've picked up at auction over the years do have tattoos. The problem with tattoos, though, is over time they fade out or get so distorted you can't read them anymore. That becomes a problem in identifying your animal if the situation presents itself to have to do that. Sure, tattoos are a permanent mark, but so are burn and freeze brands." Zack paused then asked, "Charlie, how do you know about tattoo branding?"

"I've spent a lot of time around race tracks, and all those horses are tattooed," Charlie muttered and looked down at the ground.

"Well that's interesting," Zack said, "Why don't you tell us a little more about your race track experience?"

Charlie snapped his head up and looked at Zack. "It's not like I know that much," he answered, his tone defensive.

A few of the kids giggled at his response, which obviously angered Charlie. He turned to leave and nearly knocked a boy standing behind him over.

"Hold on there, son. I wasn't trying to make you feel silly. I really am impressed," Zack insisted. "I'm a horseman, and when I meet another horseman, I know there's something he'll tell me that I didn't know the first thing about. You said you've been on race tracks. I can assure you I don't know much about that. I think we'd all be interested in learning what you already know."

Dani sensed Charlie had never seen so many people in one place showing an interest in hearing what he had to say and could feel the awkward silence. Charlie let out a sigh and began to talk. Dani could tell he was choosing his words carefully and wondered if Charlie drew from his memories of the track and happier times when he was younger or thought about his grandfather and the early days when his parents were with him and his brothers. She was sure that he remembered countless hours both of his parents spent educating the boys about the way a race track operated. He described the layout of the barns and tracks and explained the importance of hooking the horses up to the cool-down walkers after an intense breezing. On race days the air was electrified in the barns as everyone prepared for the excitement of the first race. The thing he said that he remembered most about a horse being tattooed was the trust that animal had with its handler.

Charlie explained how the handler would take hold of the animal's upper lip and curl it back so all you could see was the soft, wet skin on the inside of his lip. The horse would stand perfectly still while the handler prepped its lip because it trusted him. Charlie said that a person could tell the horse was spooked because its eyes would bug out and its whole body would tense up, but it still stood perfectly still for its handler. Dani wondered if Charlie used to trust his parents like that and figured that after they died and his grandfather was gone, the last straw for him had been when his brothers were taken away. When that happened, she figured he made a promise with himself that he was never going to trust anyone ever again. She could see his sadness. He finished his tattoo explanation and looked around. All eyes were still on him.

"So that's it," he finished and looked back at the ground.

"Well that's a fine explanation, Charlie. Thank you," Zack said. "Okay, gang. Let's head inside." Zack looked at Amy and instructed her to get the kids set up in a semicircle in the doorway. He had already put Mozart, the horse he was going to brand, on the cross ties. "Make sure you get the little ones in front so they can see what's going on," Zack added and walked toward Mozart to get things started.

The branding demonstration was a complete hit with the campers, who were enthralled with the process. Dani could tell that Charlie was grateful and much more comfortable to fade into the background and be part of the group after his moment in the spotlight. After the demonstration was over, it was time for lunch. A canopy had been set up on the flat along the outside fence line of the paddock. A series of tables and a big barrel drum barbeque had been set up on the far end. A stream of smoke billowed from the top of the barbeque.

After lunch, the afternoon was devoted to games, exploring, lazing in the afternoon sun, or whatever else the campers wanted to do. Dani joined a volleyball game. Periodically, she checked the far field to see if Charlie was still nearby. He had chosen a lone grove of aspens farther down the fence line toward the mountains. He had succeeded in finding what looked like a perfect place of solitude. Once the game was over, Dani opted out of the rematch. She went back up to the lunch pavilion and grabbed a bottle of water and looked out toward the aspens.

Charlie was still there. She reached into the cooler and grabbed another bottle of water and decided to give another shot at getting to know him.

"Hey," Dani said and smiled. "It's hot out here, and I thought you might want something cold to drink." She offered Charlie one of the water bottles.

Charlie reached up and took the bottle. "Thanks," he muttered as he twisted the cap off and swallowed nearly half of the contents in one gulp.

Dani looked up at the sky and could see the hawks that always seemed to circle near one particular peak. She watched them trace their invisible patterns across the azure sky and let out a sigh. "I said, it's hot today, huh?"

"Not really," Charlie said.

She looked down at him and shaded her eyes from the sun. "Well I didn't mean hot like 'I can't stand it' hot. I meant hot like 'it's a nice day' hot," Dani explained.

"Sure," Charlie said and took another gulp of his water.

"Charlie, why are you so angry all the time?" Dani asked.

Charlie ignored her. He looked out across the valley intent on making her feel like she was nonexistent.

Frustrated, Dani huffed, "Hello? Anybody in there?"

"What's with you? Don't you get that I don't want to be around anybody? Are you stupid or something?" he snapped.

"You're so—I came over here because it was nice to talk with you yesterday. Then I tried to be nice to you this morning, and you treated me like crap. Now I'm trying to be nice again, and you're even meaner and ruder than you were this morning. You don't even know me." She grabbed the remnants of wheatgrass she'd been chewing from her mouth and threw it to the ground. "No wonder nobody wants to be around you." She spun around and walked away.

"Wait," Charlie said.

Dani stopped but didn't turn around. "Why? Do you want to pretend to be nice to me?" She turned around, and in a slow and controlled tone, she said, "I don't need you, Charlie—seems like you don't care if anybody needs you. I wasn't coming over here because I felt sorry for you. I came because I wanted to talk. But you obviously don't

171

know how to do that. What are you so afraid of? Wait! Maybe you'll make a friend, and wouldn't that suck?" she said sarcastically.

When Charlie didn't respond, Dani shook her head. "Whatever. I'm out of here."

30

Later that night after Dani climbed into bed, she lay there staring into darkness. It was nearly ten, and again she was having trouble falling asleep. She reached over and turned her light on. She lay there for a few moments thinking about the day. She threw her covers back and climbed out of bed. She went down the hall toward her mother's room and saw the light coming out from underneath the door. She tapped lightly and waited for a response.

"Yep?" Lou answered.

"Mom?"

"Punk?"

"Yeah," Dani answered.

"Come in, honey."

Dani opened the door and stepped inside. She reached behind her and closed the door and leaned against it. Lou looked at her daughter and could tell by her troubled expression that something was wrong.

"What is it, Punk?" Lou set her book down on the nightstand.

"I don't know. I just wanted to ask you something." Dani looked down at the carpet and concentrated on making circle patterns with her big toe.

"Are you okay?" Lou asked.

"Hmm? Yeah. I'm fine. It's just that—well I don't know what to do—there's this kid in our group—"

"Come sit down, Dani." Lou patted the bed.

Dani looked at her mother and walked over to the bed. She climbed up and crisscrossed her legs. She let out a deep sigh and looked down at the blankets. She grabbed a lint ball and twirled it in her fingers. After another moment's silence, Dani mumbled, "Charlie."

"I didn't hear you, honey," Lou said.

"Charlie—his name is Charlie." Dani looked up at her mother.

"Okay. What about Charlie?" Lou asked.

"He's a jerk!" Dani said.

"Why don't you tell me what happened," Lou encouraged.

Dani flicked the lint ball from her fingers and smoothed her hands on her pant legs.

"It's not what happened. It's how he acts," Dani said. "Yesterday was so great. I mean, you know he was stupid when I told you what happened—"

"Dani, I never thought he was stupid and certainly never said that," Lou interjected.

"Mom, I know that. Can you please let me finish?" Dani demanded.

"Okay, Punk, no more interruptions." Lou reached her hand up to her lips and pretended to zip them closed.

Dani rolled her eyes and continued. "Anyway, maybe he wasn't stupid, but he definitely was an idiot—not the whole day. After we all went down to the lake, on the way back it seemed like he was sort of nice and wanted to be friends. Then this morning was a disaster. Amy and I went to breakfast, and he acted meaner and ruder than he was the first day. When I saw him, I told him 'good morning,' and he totally ignored me. When we were eating breakfast, I asked him what was wrong, and he said I was the one who had something wrong!"

Lou remained quiet and listened to Dani.

"So when we went to the barns," Dani continued. "Zack and Bobby were getting ready to do a branding demonstration, and Charlie yelled out some question. The next thing you know, he's telling everyone his story about when he worked at race tracks and why tattoos were better than freeze brands for horses." Dani shook her head at the memory. "Anyway, Zack asked him to tell us about that and the more Charlie talked, the more I could tell he was getting mad."

They sat quietly on the bed together. After a few more moments, Dani looked at her mother. Exasperated she asked, "Well aren't you going to say something?"

"Dani, I'm sorry. I didn't know I was supposed to say something. I was trying to respect—"

"Mom!" Dani snapped, "I thought I could come in here and talk to you." Dani uncrossed her legs and was about to get off the bed.

Lou grabbed Dani's arm. "Dani wait. You can come and talk with me anytime. I just thought you wanted me to be quiet and listen. That's what I was doing," Lou explained. "If you're asking me for some feedback, I am happy to give it. You just need to ask. I am not a mind reader, honey."

Dani thought about this and relaxed back on the bed. She lay down on her stomach and propped her head in her hands. "Sorry." She looked at her mom and forced a grin. "Anyway, after Charlie told his story when we did the tour and stuff, the whole time he acted like he didn't even want to talk to me. I tried to tell him how cool I thought it was that he knew about race horses and the track and stuff, and he made me feel like I was some stupid girl. So when we got to lunch, I ignored him and hung out with other people. He pretty much kept to himself. But I still decided to try one more time to talk to him. So after the volleyball game, I grabbed some water and went to where he was sitting—alone— again." Dani shook her head. "And when I tried to talk to him, he totally dissed me. He was mean and nasty and didn't even give me a chance to be nice. So I told him the reason nobody wanted to be around him was because he was so rude and mean, and I left," Dani finished and looked up at her mother.

"Wow," Lou said. "It sounds like you two are trying to get to know each other but are struggling with how to do that."

"I think I'm trying harder than he is," Dani mumbled.

"First off, Dani," Lou began, "I'm very proud of you for trying. But—"

"Here we go again. I tell—"

"Wait a second please," Lou said patiently, "You wanted me to listen to you. All I'm asking is that you listen to me now. Fair enough?"

Dani looked at her mom again. "Okay."

"Great. What I was going to say is that it sounds like Charlie struggles with trusting people. Based on his childhood, this is understandable. I don't think he wants to hurt you, Dani. I think he's trying to figure out why somebody wants to take the time to get to know him. He's afraid, Dani," Lou explained. "It's not that you scare him. I mean he is afraid because everything that he thought was constant in his life is gone—his parents, his grandfather; even his brothers are gone. It is a blessing for him that he was able to come out here. I would even venture to guess deep down inside, he is happy to be here, and I think he

175

does like you. His struggle is he is afraid to get close to you because he knows he will be leaving at the end of the week."

"Yeah, but, why can't he just be happy to be here now and have fun? I am trying, Mom," Dani insisted.

"Honey, I believe you are trying, and, again, that makes me very proud. Maybe Charlie is being overly cautious because he hasn't had somebody like you in his life for a very long time. He doesn't understand how to accept the kindness without thinking there is something he must give in return only to have it taken away. He is vulnerable, Dani. Does that make any sense?" Lou asked.

"Maybe," Dani said. "I mean, the bad things that happened in his life aren't my fault. He even told me the first day that he hated it when people felt sorry for him. So I have been trying real hard not to do that."

"I believe you, honey," Lou said, comforting Dani. They grew silent again. "Dani?" Lou asked.

Dani looked up at her mother. "Hmmm?"

"It sounds like the approach you have been taking up to now doesn't work. How about you try something different tomorrow?" Lou offered.

"Like what?" Dani asked.

"Maybe instead of seeking Charlie out tomorrow, you give him some space and let him come to you. If he does, let him attempt friendship instead of you taking charge."

"Geez, Mom, I'm not a bully. I haven't been forcing myself on him."

"I know that, Punk, I'm just thinking that if you let him come to you and you accept his invitation to talk, maybe he will open up and trust more. It may provide some assurance to him that friendship between the two of you isn't a threat. What do you think?"

Dani considered her mother's suggestion and asked, "What if he doesn't?"

Lou grinned. "Oh, Punk, ever my little negotiator." She reached over and gave her daughter a hug. They sat quietly together on her bed, allowing the silence to comfort them.

After another moment, Dani pulled away. She sat up and ran her fingers through her hair. She climbed down off the bed and looked at her mom. "I'm getting tired. Tomorrow is the rodeo, and Amy said we have a lot of work ahead of us. I should get to bed." Dani turned and walked toward the door. She reached down to open it and turned back to her mother. "Mom?"

"Yeah, Punk?"

"Thanks. I get it." Dani smiled and left.

31

When Dani awoke the next morning, she thought about the talk with her mother. Maybe her mom was right in suggesting a different approach with Charlie. Dani decided to give Lou's suggestion a try. At breakfast, the general excitement among all the kids was palpable. The rodeo would mark the halfway point to their time at Echo Ranch. A slight high-pressure system was moving through the area, which made for spectacular weather. The sky was a flawless, deep blue, and the hint of a cool breeze caressed the valley enough to temper the heat.

When Carla planned the event this year, she had included straw cowboy hats in each care package with the rodeo in mind. As the campers filed out of the tent onto the wagons, they looked like a procession of the next generation of cowboys and cowgirls.

As the wagons pulled up to the makeshift arena, the air was energized with excitement and anticipation. A large round pen had been set up to serve as a rodeo ring. Surrounding the ring were bleachers, and crowds of people were already filling the seats. In addition to all the youngsters and counselors many townspeople were there to show their support. Kiosks were set up outside the arena with stations of carnival games, cotton candy, and popcorn. Rodeo clowns canvassed the grounds, entertaining passersby as they blew their bicycle horns and performed slapstick antics. Men dressed in candy-striped shirts walked the bleachers selling hotdogs and cold drinks. A stage was erected farther beyond the arena with a makeshift wooden dance floor installed in front of it. A popular local country band would kick off the evening activities with live music and dancing after dinner.

Dani was in awe. Each time she thought she had seen it all, something else would catch her attention. She saw her mom across the way with Tessa and Carla and felt a moment of absolute love for her when she saw the smile on Lou's face. Her mom looked so happy and pretty in her cowboy hat, jeans, and boots. She liked to see her mom smile and be truly happy. She continued to scan the crowds and saw Charlie standing by the cotton candy kiosk. His back was slightly turned to her, and she could see he still had his canvas bag with him. The fact that he was wearing the cowboy hat distracted Dani because she honestly thought he would be the last person who would wear the hat. She wanted to go over and say hi but thought about the talk with her mother. She looked beyond him and saw some other campers who were heading into the arena behind some of the other kids and decided to catch up with them to be sure they knew where they were going.

Announcements were being made over the loudspeaker for everyone to take their seats. The show would begin in less than fifteen minutes. Dani quickened her pace as she made her way through the crowd to catch up with her group; she made the climb up the bleachers and sat down. She looked around, took a mental headcount, and saw that Charlie wasn't there. She started to get up to go look for him, and as she turned, he was standing beside her.

"Hey," Dani said.

"Hey," Charlie said.

"Listen, the show is—" Dani started to say.

"Yeah, I know. Is it okay if I sit here?" Charlie pointed to the empty seat next to her.

Dani looked down at the bleacher and back at Charlie. "Sure," she said, smiling; she could feel her face flush. She sat back down and picked up her program to fan herself.

Zack's voice came booming through the loudspeakers from center arena. "Ladies and gentlemen! Welcome to the Echo Ranch rodeo!"

The crowd got on its feet and cheered. He gave them a minute to settle down and continued. "I know you didn't come here today to listen to me, so I'll keep this short. I just want to take a moment to thank everyone for coming out today. It's a beautiful day, we've got lots of fun planned, and we couldn't ask for much more."

The crowd boomed again, and he gave them a moment to settle. "I want to finish by giving special thanks to a couple of people." He looked to the bleachers and asked, "Where are Carla and Frank Preston? Could you please stand up for a minute?" He looked around the arena, and when his eyes stopped near the entrance down toward the bottom, he saw them. "C'mon out here for a minute, you two."

Carla joined hands with Frank, and they walked to the center of the arena. When they got next to Zack, he said, "There's not a whole lot more I can say about how great I think you two people are. We have been

179

doing this camp thing for a few years now, and by God, Carla, you outdo yourself with each passing year." Zack chuckled.

The crowd began to cheer again, and a wave of whistles, hoots, and claps filled the air. Zack held his hand up to the crowd, and slowly they quieted down.

"I just want to say thank you again for all you do for so many people. More importantly, I want to say God bless you both for the way you honor your beautiful child, Justin, and so many other outstanding kids." Zack put the microphone down by his side and gave them both a hug.

Frank put his arm around Carla's shoulder, and they walked back to their seats. Dani could feel tears in her own eyes after Zack's speech. She looked at Charlie and could see what Zack had said moved him as well. He looked back at her, and for the first time since she had met him, the smile he gave her felt genuine.

"Let's get this show going," Zack yelled and the crowd started stomping its feet.

As the day progressed, there was no question the rodeo was a huge success. When the country band finished its last song and the crowds began to thin, the counselors began ushering their kids back to the wagons. Dani and Charlie were some of the last to climb in. Charlie asked Dani if she wanted to sit next to him for the ride back. She looked down at the bench and back at him.

"Sure," she said.

Once underway, some of the kids had drifted off to sleep, slumping next to each other, and stirred intermittently when the wagon hit a rut or bump in the road. The moon was three-quarters full; by the end of the week it would be full for the farewell bonfire. Dani looked across the valley and noticed that, in the moonlight, the brush and scrub looked like a community of gremlins granting passage to their wagon.

"It's pretty quiet compared to today," Charlie commented.

Dani looked at him and smiled. "Right? Wasn't that amazing today?" She looked at Charlie. "I mean, some of those bulls were huge when they were doing the bull riding competition."

"Ah, yeah," Charlie said.

"I thought for sure that one guy would get stabbed. That bull was so mad. Remember?" Dani asked, "That big white bull with the brown spots?"

"Oh yeah," Charlie agreed. "He was so pissed when that clown ran away from him."

They slipped into silence again.

"Dani?" Charlie asked.

"Hmmm?"

Charlie looked at her and struggled for words.

"I wanted to tell you that—it's just yesterday made me think about a lot of stuff— and, well, what I'm trying to say is I'm sorry for the way I treated you." Charlie looked down at his hands.

Dani's heart began to race. She looked at Charlie and said, "Thanks for apologizing. Can I say something?" she asked.

"Sure." Charlie said.

"I just want you to know that I think it would be nice if we could be friends. I get where you're coming from—really," Dani said. "You also need to know that I never wanted you to think I felt sorry for you because I didn't."

"I guess," Charlie said.

"Well it's true. Let's just keep going from here. There are a ton of fun things left to do, and I think it would be great if you joined in on some of the fun." Dani smiled at him. "Like today. You have to admit today was awesome."

"Yeah, I guess," Charlie agreed.

"Good. Then let's leave it at that."

The wagon pulled up to the tent, and the riders began to stir. They groggily made their way back inside. Amy, Dani, and the other counselors got their groups settled and wearily walked back out to the Gators. Another full day would be upon them soon enough.

32

Throughout the remainder of the week activities were nonstop. Except for the rodeo, Zack closed his operations to the public. His gift to the children was to give them free rein of the ranch and everything it had to offer soley for them. The only exposure some of them had ever had to a horse and a mountain was something they may have seen in a photograph. To give them the reality of touching a horse and the experience of climbing a real mountain was a wonder to behold. Dani had naturally assumed her role of leader with some of those kids. She was patient and gentle, but took her job very seriously when explaining the importance of treating the horses with kindness and respect. She was in her element, and while it was work, she made it look like just another glorious day to be able to be among such majestic creatures.

On the last night, everyone gathered down valley at the lake for the final cookout. Some of the ranch hands had spent the week gathering brush and scrub and built a massive burn pile for the grand finale bonfire that would follow the closing ceremony and barbeque. The next day would mark the end of another successful year. The tour bus would arrive, and the children would gather up their belongings. They would tuck them into their new duffel bags and solemnly file back onto the bus. When the last child was seated, the doors would close, and the bus would slowly pull away. The departure would be far different than the arrival.

As the group of campers rode in the hay wagon to the bonfire that night, Dani felt that first sting of something good nearing an end. By this time tomorrow, Charlie would be on the bus with all the other kids and headed back to Kentucky. They had promised to keep in touch with letters. She told him that the only letters she had ever written were thank-you cards to aunts and uncles she didn't really know; usually she just texted everyone. When Charlie told her that he had never even owned a cell phone, it was another reality of some of the things she took for granted.

"So what're you going to do when you get back to Kentucky?" she asked.

"I don't know," he said. "Go back to work, I guess."

"I hope I'm going to be coming out here next summer again for a few weeks' vacation with my family. Maybe you can come out then too. I can ask Zack."

"Yeah, right," he interrupted with a grumble. "I won't have money to come back here. Besides, the only reason I came this year is because my aunt made me, and it didn't cost anything."

"You didn't even let me finish," she insisted.

"What?" he asked.

"Like I was saying, maybe you can come out here next summer and work. Zack has lots of people he hires just for the summers. I mean, look around this place." She gestured to the ranch. "You don't think it looks like this with just a few people taking care of it, do you?"

"Yeah, well, I'd still have to be able to get here. Besides, you don't even know if that guy would—"

"Zack," Dani said firmly. "His name is Zack, and, yes, he would."

"Knock it off, Dani," Charlie said. "Listen, it's been great meeting you, and maybe I'll see you again sometime. Let's just have fun tonight and forget about the rest of the stuff." He looked down at his hands.

The wagons pulled up near the grove of Aspens by the lake and stopped. Everyone began to pile off and head toward the burn pile, but Charlie and Dani stayed behind. They sat side by side watching everyone join in with the activities. Frustrated by Charlie's self-inflicted pity party, Dani was annoyed.

"You're so stupid sometimes," she said.

He whipped his head around and frowned. "Oh, that's brilliant. You're acting like the spoiled little brat you were when I first met you." he challenged.

"What? Brat? You're a jerk. I'm not a brat. All I was saying is if you'd stop being such a crybaby and feeling sorry for yourself all the time, maybe there'd be some awesome stuff you could do. I thought you'd be excited if I talked to Zack for you and asked if you could come back, but forget it." She slumped back against a bale of hay and crossed her arms.

Charlie looked at her and grinned. "You are a brat." He chuckled and reached over and poked her shoulder.

Dani swatted at his hand, but he yanked it away too quick, and she smacked it into the hay instead.

"Ouch." She pulled her hand back to inspect it and plucked a piece of hay that was stuck in her palm.

"Here. Let me see." Charlie reached out and took her hand. She let him hold it and stared at him while he inspected her hand. He looked back up at her and then reached in and kissed her. She started to kiss him back, but then jerked away quickly. She took her forearm and wiped it across her mouth. She'd kissed other boys, but she usually knew when it was going to happen. Charlie's kiss caught her completely off guard, and it made her feel awkward because she didn't feel like she knew him long enough to kiss him.

"What'd you do that for?" she demanded, feeling her face flush. "Geez." She scooted over to the edge of the wagon and jumped off. As she started to walk away, Charlie jumped off the wagon and caught up with her and grabbed her arm. She flinched and tried to yank her arm out of his grip. He eased his hold and dropped his hand away. He took a few steps back and held his hands up.

"Dani," he said, "I didn't mean—wow—I mean—"

She started to giggle, which made him visibly angry.

"What's so funny?" he asked.

"You," she said, giggling. "I honestly think this is the first time all week you couldn't think of something to say."

"Forget it," he said, then turned and started to walk away.

"Charlie," she said.

He stopped and turned. "What?"

"Can we just have a nice time tonight and not get into all this stupid stuff?" she asked. "It was really great getting to know you this week, and I think we will see each other again sometime. Let's not worry about that now. Let's do like you said and go up there, enjoy tonight, and remember this week as one of the best weeks we've ever had. I mean, that's what I want to do." She smiled and held out her hand to him.

He walked back up to her and folded his arms around her. They stood there for what felt like an eternity to Dani. It was exactly the moment what she wanted at that very second in time. She didn't care if Charlie's reasons were light-years apart from her own; it didn't matter.

184

She had found something new in herself through meeting Charlie and knew that tomorrow and the next day would be okay because of it.

They joined the rest of the campers and laughed well into the night as they roasted marshmallows and sang along with the hokey, lonesome cowboy songs Bobby and some of the other hired hands played. They even went so far as to join some of the other kids in a serious game of flashlight tag, and together, they were unstoppable. Dani saw her mom, Zack, and some of the other counselors through the night, but didn't stray too far from Charlie. She was afraid if they got separated, she'd never see him again before she was able to tell him just how awesome she really thought he was.

33

Dani got up extra early the next morning and walked down the hall to the spare room where Amy was sleeping. She quietly tapped on the door and could see the light coming out from underneath it indicating Amy was up.

"The bus should be here in a little while. Let's head over to the tents and help with the pack up before breakfast."

"Okay," Dani said.

As they approached the tents, the shadows of campers inside gathering their belongings became visible. They walked inside and met up with the other counselors. Amy pulled the whistle from around her neck and gave it a couple of short blows.

"Okay, everybody, listen up," she said. "Breakfast will be ready in about ten minutes. Before we head over to the mess tent, we're going to do a walk through to be sure everybody has everything packed up. We also want to make sure that any trash or junk is picked up and put in its proper place before we head out because we won't have time to do that after breakfast. You'll have just enough time to come back and grab your stuff before you have to leave." She glanced across the group and asked, "Any questions?"

With no response, they finished the cleanup and went to breakfast. Unlike the first day, Dani made a point of securing her seat next to Charlie. He came back to the table with a plate full of food, smiled at her, and sat down.

"Hey," he said. "Last day."

"Yeah." Dani looked down at her plate.

They ate in silence, and as he got up to throw his plate away, a folded piece of paper fell on the bench next to Dani. She reached down to pick it up, and Charlie swooped in and grabbed it.

"Geez. Relax. I was giving it back to you," she said, shaking her head.

"Sorry. I just didn't want you to have it until I was leaving."

He stuffed the paper into his pocket and walked away. Dani watched him go and picked at her food a little more before she surrendered to the fact that she wasn't hungry anymore. She picked her plate up and caught up with him by the buffet. She heard the distant hiss of the air breaks from the bus and knew he would be leaving soon. She

186

felt like she was going to start crying and pretended she had something in her eye. Charlie looked at her and grinned.

"There you go again, doing something girly."

She looked at him and smiled. "Yeah. Shoot me. I'm a girl, stupid. That's what girls do."

They walked back to the tent together to go get his things. He had come with nothing more than a grimy, canvas bag, and, although he still carried it with him everywhere he went, he would leave with a bigger, newer, and much cleaner bag in which to carry his prized photo of his family. Most of the kids had already loaded the bus, and, aside from a few stragglers, Charlie was the last to board.

He turned to Dani and reached in his pocket. "Here." He handed the folded paper to her.

"What is it?"

"It's my address, but it's a letter too. I figured I'd start by writing you so you can see what a letter looks like so you know how to write one back." He grinned.

She giggled and punched his arm. "Very funny. I know what a letter looks like."

She looked down at the paper and back at him. He reached down and gave her a gentle kiss on her cheek. He stood back and shifted his duffel bag on his shoulder and gave a slight wave. "See you around, Dani, it's been real."

He turned to walk away, and she grabbed his shirt. He turned back to her, and she threw her arms around his neck and planted a hard kiss on his cheek. When she stepped back, she could feel a tear running down her own cheek and quickly brushed it away. "See you, creep."

"Yeah. You too."

She watched him climb up the stairs onto the bus, and never once did he turn around. She could see him making his way to the back of the bus to the same seat where he had come from on the first day of camp when she genuinely thought he was a creep. She watched him scoot into the booth, settle himself and reach up to open the window. He leanded out and motioned for her to come over.

She jogged over beneath the window and looked up at him. He smiled down at her and said, "You're the best person I've met in a long time, Dani. Take care of yourself, and we'll see each other again sometime. Okay?"

He didn't wait for her to answer and as the bus slowly started its roll forward, he continued to look straight ahead.

Amy came up to Dani and put her arm around her shoulder. Knowing it was safe to do so now, Dani let the tears stream down her face. She looked up at Amy and didn't care that she was crying. She had made a new friend, and, just like everything else she held dearly in her life, it was hard when the time had come for her to let it go.

"C'mon, Dani," Amy said. "We've got a full day of work ahead of us. Let's go find the other counselors and get started on the cleanup."

34

It was late afternoon on Sunday. A blanket of peace and tranquility had returned to the ranch. Sitting on the porch with nothing more to do than watch the sun make its trek across the western sky felt good to Lou. She thought about her journey through the days since she and Dani had arrived. She thought about the angry child who came with her and how Dani had insisted she didn't want to be at the ranch. A lot of healing had happened. She knew there was work left to be done, but right at that moment it didn't matter. Rather, she wanted to revel in the strides they had made together as well as individually to get to this point. She heard the door creak and turned. Zack walked out holding a couple of glasses and a bottle of wine tucked under his arm.

"What you got there?" she asked, smiling.

"I thought since we survived this past week, a celebration was in order." He set the glasses and bottle down on the table next to her. "Where's Tessa?" he asked.

"She and Dani went into town to meet Carla and Amy. They had some final details to settle about the books, and they were going to grab a bite to eat afterward."

"Well then, I suppose we'll have to fend for ourselves," Zack said.

He popped the cork on the wine bottle and poured two glasses, then settled into the seat across from Lou. They raised their glasses toward each other. "Another great year," he said.

They sat quietly and watched the sun go down. The sky was in its holding pattern between daylight and dusk. Lou let out a deep sigh.

"How do you do it, Zack?" she asked.

"Do what?"

"This," she said and waved her arms toward the scenery.

"Hell, honey, I didn't do that," he said. "I'm just here for the ride. All that is what was left for me to take care of."

"I know that, but that's not what I meant." She looked at him. "I mean, how do you live in the moment and be thankful for what's happening in each moment?"

He considered her question as he reached for his glass, then took a sip.

"Well, I'll tell you," he said. "I can assure you it hasn't always been like this. When my daddy first turned the responsibility of this ranch over to Tessa and me, I was more than a little scared. Hell, he had run this place like a fine-tuned machine for so many years; a part of me didn't know if I was ready to take the lead." He paused and shook his head over the memory.

"Something must have happened for you to get over your fears," Lou said. "I look around this place, and all I see is perfection. I've watched you and Tessa and your hired help over this past chaotic week. It's as though there was never a time when any of you doubted what you needed to do to make the magic happen all day every day."

"Thanks, Lou. That makes me feel real proud," Zack said, smiling at her. "But I don't think you're interested in hearing the ups and downs of Echo Ranch. What I think is that there's something on your mind and you don't know how to get it out, so you're stalling with this idle chitchat until the words find their way."

Lou picked up her glass, took a sip, and thought about his words. "You know me too well," she admitted.

Stars began to pop one by one across the distant sky. Dusk and night may have been vying for first place, but it was nightfall that was clearly gaining momentum.

"I was thinking about when we first got here. I had spent most of the drive obsessing over what I would do each day to make sure I came up with the perfect plan toward creating my new-and-improved Dani who I would take back home with me. Then we got here. As soon as we pulled up to the house, I panicked because I didn't have a clue where to start."

Zack looked over at her and smiled. "You know, Lou, that's the problem most people have, including myself," Zack said. "We get so darn caught up in worrying about what's going to happen and when. Hell, we spend a good part of our lives forgetting how to just live in the moment. Tessa and I don't have kids. So for me to sit here and give you all the answers just isn't something I can do. What I can do, though, is tell you what I do with my horses because I treat them like they're my kids."

He took another sip of wine and said, "Early on, most of the horses that were here—when I first took over—were push-button. We sprinkled a couple of newbies into the herd here and there, but for the

190

most part, every one of those horses knew who they were and what their job was thanks to my daddy."

She listened.

"My point is," Zack said. "I didn't have the faith that I was ready to step in when my daddy stepped aside. He saw I had it in me, but I couldn't see it. That first year he spent a fair amount of his time pointing me in directions and teaching me things I had no idea about. All the while he refused to do anything for me, even if I needed the help." Zack smiled over the memory and said, "I'd get so darn mad at him. I was a grown-ass man, and there I'd be throwing a temper tantrum."

"I would have loved to have seen that," Lou said.

"Bottom line, Lou," Zack said. "He was turning me out into the world, and it was up to me to sink or swim. Looking back now, I know he had way too much invested in what he'd made around here to let it all fall by the wayside. What's more important is he knew he couldn't keep doing everything for me. It was high time I took on all the responsibilities because he'd earned the right to rest comfortably for the balance of his life. He and my momma had places to go and things to do. It was their time to take it easy."

Zack sat back in his chair and looked up to the sky. "Yeah, you old son of a gun," Zack said, smiling. "You knew it was going to work out."

"So do you think I suffocate Dani?" Lou asked.

"Not exactly," Zack said. "Hell, she's still just a kid; she needs you to be there for her. I'm saying I see two very different people today than the two ladies who showed up at the beginning of summer. Dani's still a wild child, but she's learning how to manage herself better. I think one of the best things that has happened to her since she's gotten here is to be paired up with Poet. He's a big boy and a hell of a lot stronger than she'll ever be. She's a strong-willed kid. Between the two of them, they're working it out. What's even more important, and what you need to do," he said, looking over at Lou, "is take a step back and let her figure out what it means to fall and have to pick herself up instead of you rushing in with the cavalry to do it for her."

Lou could tell Zack was looking at her for a reaction.

She sat quietly, processing his words. She took another sip of wine and set her glass down.

"I'm trying, Zack. I really am," she said.

"I know you are," Zack said. "I'm just saying stop expecting instant miracles and spend more time enjoying the moment. Don't wait until your babies have flown the coop to start enjoying your own life. Learn from what's going on now and embrace the little gifts along the way."

He tipped his glass to her and finished the last sip then set the glass down on the table and stood up for a stretch. He picked up the empty bottle and turned back to her.

"You want another?"

"Why not? I've earned it."

"That's what I'm talking about," he said, smiling. "I'll be right back."

She watched him go into the house, took the blanket from the back of her chair, opened it up, and wrapped it around her shoulders. The sky was completely dark, and an army of stars twinkled down upon her. The night air was cool, a reminder that summer had passed its crescendo. In the few short months ahead, fall would step in and lead the way to another winter.

Lou knew Zack was right. She didn't take time for herself. Changing that pattern would be much easier to say than do. She couldn't remember the last time she had thought about anything that didn't incorporate either Kylie or Dani. Kylie's teen years and preparing for college had dominated Lou's life. Right on the heels of Kylie leaving home, Dani entered her teen years. With them came a whole new set of challenges that redefined their job and what would be needed to see Dani through the same stressful years. Many times, they had been completely equipped to take on a challenge, but just as often they hadn't known what to do. Sitting here and reflecting on the past months gave her more strength than she thought she would ever have to be able to go forward with the next couple of years. She felt as though things would be okay, and for once, she decided not to question the feeling.

Zack came back out with another bottle of red wine. He pulled the cork and filled her glass. He refilled his own and settled back down. "Nice night, huh?"

"It is," she agreed. "I was just thinking about how quickly this summer has passed."

"Yeah? Wait 'til you get to be my age." He laughed. "It goes by a lot quicker."

"If I arrive at a place half as good as where you've arrived, Zack, I'll count myself a lucky lady."

He looked over at her and put his glass to his mouth. Before he took a sip, he said, "You have no idea, Lou, no idea."

They finished the second bottle and were content to sit and enjoy the peace nighttime brought. They could see the headlights from the car pulling around the last bend as it made its way up to the house. Once the car pulled up to the house, Tessa and Dani joined them on the porch.

"I didn't think you two would still be up," Tessa said.

"We've just been sitting here solving the problems of the world," Zack said.

"Well I'm glad to hear it." She reached over and patted his leg. "I think I'm going to head inside. It's been a long day." She turned to Dani and said, "Thanks for going into town with me, Danielle. I had a lovely dinner with you."

"Thanks, Tessa. Me too." Dani smiled, stood up, and gave Tessa a hug.

"Good night, all," Tessa said then turned to Zack and said, "Honey, don't forget you have that meeting in town tomorrow."

"Yeah, I know," he grumbled. "Lawyers. I don't like spending much time with them, but they have some paperwork I need to sign. That's the part of this place I don't like." He stood up. "I think I'll call it a night too."

He turned to Dani and said, "Don't you stay up too late. You and Bobby are working in the front fields tomorrow."

"Okay," Dani said to Zack then turned to Lou. "Are you coming, Mom?"

"Sure, Punk, help me with these glasses. I'm right behind you."

193

35

The weeks after the event passed quickly. Summer began to show subtle signs of making way for the fall at Echo Ranch. The last push of summer groups and a constant flow of horses climbing up and down the mountainsides kept Zack busy. Apparently, everyone wanted to get that final summer adventure in before life forced them back into the reality of school and work. Dani had long since become Zack's right-hand gal. If she wasn't going on trail rides with him and his groups, they were down in the barn side by side grooming horses, cleaning tack, mucking stalls, or assisting the farrier. She had even learned a lot about the day-to-day functions of a working ranch and the inherent need to make constant tweaks and repairs. She worked hard at doing her job the right way, whatever the assignment. The one job she had managed beautifully throughout the summer was training Poet. The love and trust that had grown and developed between the two of them truly was poetry in motion, further affirming the name he owned. Through patience and long hours, they had graduated together; successfully completing his backing process.

Lou believed the reason her daughter worked consistently hard with all the chores and jobs given to her was because of the dangling carrot of Poet on the other side of those jobs. Gone was her hardness, and in its place, a sweet young girl full of hopes and dreams of what she and that magical horse would do together. Lou knew that Dani was riding him right that moment. Dani still wasn't permitted to take him across open land, but most of the paddocks could have easily been considered wide open space due to their size. Bobby still maintained close contact. Zack's rule was that if Dani was riding Poet, Bobby was riding with her. Bobby had his favorite mounts, and Poet seemed to have his favorite companions. Bobby was very particular about which mount he chose, and together he and Dani would saddle up their horses and do maneuvers in whichever paddock was the arena of choice for their lesson.

Many nights Dani would come back up to the house and collapse into bed immediately after dinner so she could rise early the next morning, anxious and excited to put in another day of work. Lou stood back and watched her daughter's transformation with great pride. The teenage moments still had a way of making their presence known, but they weren't as volatile. Lou noticed when Dani got to a certain point, instead of becoming angry and lashing out, she caught herself and told her mother she needed some time alone. Lou was also learning how to recognize and respect those moments. The fact that her daughter was maturing enough to know when she crossed a line and how to manage that situation was admirable.

One morning in early August, Lou sat at the breakfast bar with Tessa. All through breakfast, Lou could barely contain herself.

Once Zack and Dani left for the barn, Lou exclaimed, "Tessa, I cannot wait to see the look on Dani's face when we get back from the airport!"

Lou was going into Grand Junction to pick up Kylie. As promised, Jake had made all the arrangements for Kylie to fly out the day after she returned from her summer job. Kylie hadn't hesitated when the proposition had been presented to her. The fact that she would be able to extend her time with horses and see her sister had been an easy choice as far as she was concerned. Lou couldn't wait to have the two of them together, even if it was only for a few fleeting weeks.

"What time does her flight get in?"

Lou looked up at the clock on the stove. It was nearly ten.

"At eleven. I should get moving."

"Okay, dear, you go on. Carla is coming by in a while. We were thinking about taking a trail ride down to the lake because it's such a lovely day. We probably won't be here when you get back but should be back around four," Tessa said.

"I think that's wonderful, Tessa," Lou said. "Carla is such a lovely person. That woman has been through some tragedy in her life. The fact that she has come through it to the other side is a miracle."

"That she has," Tessa said, sighing. "I think the main reason we're going for a trail ride today is because she and Frank have come to a decision concerning Justin's future. She hasn't come out and said that, but I know her well enough to know she has something she wants to talk about. I could hear it in her voice when we made our plans the other day."

Lou looked at her in horror. "What does that mean?"

"It means he's been on life support for a very long time. They both know it's time to think about the future—all of their futures."

195

"Oh, Tessa," Lou walked around the counter to put her arms around Tessa. "I'm so sorry. I know how much you love Carla. I'm sure this is very difficult for you too." Lou hugged her. "I should get going; otherwise my daughter is going to be standing in the airport terminal wondering if she landed in the wrong place."

"Okay, dear. I'll see you later this afternoon. I cannot wait to meet Kylie."

"Please give Carla a big hug for me. Know I'm thinking about you both today," Lou assured her.

"I will, dear."

Lou set out for the airport. The Colorado sky was deep blue against the magnificent, rugged mountains. She couldn't determine what she was more thrilled about: the prospect of seeing Kylie, or the moment when both daughters would be reunited.

Once at the airport, Lou pulled into short-term parking and made her way to the Southwest baggage terminal just in time to see the red light flip on, indicating Kylie's flight had arrived. She watched the carousel as bags started sliding down. She was lost in her thoughts when she felt a tap on her shoulder. She turned around, and standing before her was a man with a warm smile.

"Oh my God, Jake!" she exclaimed.

She practically jumped into his arms as she wrapped her own arms tightly around him.

"What are you doing here?"

"Hey, Mom," Kylie said, coming up behind him.

Lou released her grip from Jake. She started to cry and pulled Kylie to her.

"Hi, baby," she whispered.

"Mom, it's okay."

Kylie gently pushed her away. "Are you surprised?" she asked, grinning.

Lou took a moment to compose herself and wiped her tears away. She looked back and forth between her husband and daughter.

"What are you doing here?" she asked Jake. "I had no idea."

"I know. When I called Kylie to ask her if she wanted to come out, of course you knew what the answer was going to be. Anyway, I made some arrangements at the boatyard and decided I needed to be with my family. I have to head back in a couple of days," he said. "There's a transport I couldn't get out of, but let's not worry about that now. Let's get our things and get out of here."

"This is wonderful," Lou said. "Dani is going to be so surprised. Oh, Kylie! Wait until you see her. She misses you so much. I missed you."

"Me too, Mom," Kylie said.

Kylie pointed to a bag that was sliding down the chute and said, "That one's mine."

Jake reached over and retrieved the bag, then his own when it came through.

On the drive back to the ranch, the car was filled with the warmth and energy Lou had been feeling more and more with each passing day. Conversation never lagged, particularly from Kylie as she shared many of the events she had experienced over the summer.

Lou slowed the car and made the turn into Echo Ranch.

"Wow. This is like something right out of a movie," Kylie exclaimed.

"Wait until you see the rest of the property," Lou said.

Jake looked around as they made their drive up to the house and asked, "How many acres did you say Zack and Tessa have?"

"About 4,600."

"Wow," he responded. "I didn't think there were places left like this anymore."

"I know. I can't even begin to tell you how good this has been for us, Jake. I think I needed this trip as much as Dani."

"I know. I'm glad you did this. The proof is written all over your face." He reached over and rested his hand on her shoulder.

They rounded the last bend on the drive and came into the opening by the house. Lou was reminded of the day she and Dani arrived. She also felt an incredible amount of pride getting to show the rest of her family how very impressive Echo Ranch was and why it was still so important in her life.

"Whoa, that's some house," Kylie exclaimed. "Where's the barn?"

"Oh my gosh, Kylie," Lou said, laughing. "Your sister said the same thing the first time she saw the house."

Lou parked the car, and they got out. Kylie came around to the driver's side and saw the horses in the paddock beyond the house.

Jake followed Lou through the great room and up the stairs. Lou could tell that Jake felt at ease because of the familiarity with the house she was projecting. The constant, tense vibes of electricity pinging back and forth between them had all but disappeared. Lou felt relaxed and genuinely happy and couldn't wait for Jake and Kylie to meet Zack and Tessa.

"Dani's room is in there," Lou nodded as they passed it.

Jake stopped and peeked inside. When he pushed the door open, he saw beyond the bed to the large window that framed the view of the south-facing valley.

"Some view," he said and shook his head.

"Right? C'mon. We're down here."

Lou led Jake down the hall to her room where the view was just as spectacular. He set his bag down, came up behind her, and wrapped his arms around her.

"This is fantastic, Lou," he said, then reached down and gave her a kiss.

"Thank you, Jake," Lou said. "Thank you for having the faith in my decision. I knew it was the right decision, but the fact that you agreed meant so much. I must tell you it's going to be a hard pill to swallow when we have to leave. Don't get me wrong, I'm looking forward to getting home and back into some sort of routine, but it's going to be very hard to say good-bye to Zack and Tessa and Echo Ranch when the day comes."

"I get that, honey," Jake assured her. "But, hey, it's not like this place is going anywhere. I'd love to be able to come back with all of us— like a summer vacation maybe."

"I'd like that too. Let's go get Kylie. I want to take you guys down to the barns."

36

They hopped into the Gator and headed down to the barn. Just like she had done the first day with Dani, Lou paused at the top of the hill before making the final descent. The pristine beauty consumed them as they sat quietly and admired the majestic mountains and valleys creating the landscape surrounding them.

"This is so unbelievable. Dani is so lucky," Kylie sighed.

They pulled up to the barn, and Lou cut the engine on the Gator. When they got inside, there were no signs of life. Most of the horses were still out.

"Dani is probably out in one of the paddocks," Lou said and motioned for Kylie and Jake to follow her.

They continued down the center aisle of the barn. Kylie read the names on the stalls as she passed each one.

"I love some of the names these horses have," she said, giggling. "I can't wait to match the horse up with the name."

"Zack holds title of official name giver for the horses," Lou told Kylie. "He says it comes to him the first time he meets them. Sometimes he's inspired by a marking or mannerism, but each one is unique. He says that's what gives him the inspiration to give them their names."

"Cool. How many horses are there?"

"I think there are sixty—maybe a few more."

"Get out!" Kylie said and stopped. "Sixty?"

"At least."

"Okay. Now I'm jealous. I can't believe Dani has had this at her fingertips all summer. She probably hasn't ridden the same horse two days in a row."

"Sort of," Lou said. "She's been working pretty closely with one particular horse. His name is Poet. He's been her project most of the summer. He's a three-year-old, and a couple of weeks ago they finished backing him. Since then, she's been working on riding him."

"Seriously? My sister trained a horse."

"Not only has she been training him," Lou said, "but wait until you see how he responds to her. It's been wonderful to watch them both come along." Lou smiled with pride.

"Are we going to get a chance to see her riding him?" Jake asked.

199

"Absolutely," Lou said. "As a matter of fact, she's probably out in the pasture right now working him with Bobby. If she is, let's try not to let her see us until she's done. I don't want to distract her because, like I said, she's just started riding him. I don't want to spook them."

"Lead the way," Jake said.

When they came out the other side of the barn, Lou saw Bobby and Dani at the far end of the paddock. They were working on direction changes, and from what Lou could tell, it seemed to be going well. She could hear the muffled commands Bobby periodically called to Dani as he sat in the corner on Lucy. Poet responded beautifully. Dani gave him a couple of kicks, and he would take off on whatever lead she directed him to take. They trotted along, then she stopped at the halfway mark to where Bobby stood. Dani took a moment to collect her reins, gave Poet another kick, and they continued.

"That's something else." Jake smiled as he watched his daughter.

"She's doing great," Kylie agreed. "He's gorgeous."

Lou beamed. She intently watched Dani and felt happier than she could remember, having her family by her side to witness this experience.

"Let's go back into the office and grab something to drink," Lou suggested. "They'll probably be finishing up soon. I know they'll bring him in for Dani to groom him down before she turns him back out. We'll let her finish that up before we surprise her. She is going to die when she sees you two."

Lou led the way back to the office. They were catching up on the summer when she heard Zack's truck pull up and heard him coming toward the office. When he came through the doorway and saw the three of them sitting there, he did a double take.

"Well look at this," he exclaimed.

He reached his hand out to Jake.

"You must be Jake. It's a pleasure to finally meet you," Zack said. "Lou has been talking about you all summer long. She didn't tell me you were coming out too." He smiled and gave Jake a hearty handshake.

"That's because I didn't know. I was as surprised as you are," Lou said, smiling.

"Well now. Isn't that something," Zack chuckled.

"And I suppose this must be Kylie," Zack said.

"She is indeed," Lou said, smiling.

Zack reached past Jake and extended his hand.

"It's real fine to meet you, Kylie. Your momma tells me you're just as horse crazy as your little sister."

Kylie giggled and said, "Definitely. I'm so jealous she's been here all summer. You have an amazing ranch, Mister—"

"Okay, Lou." He looked over at her. "Can you explain to Kylie that I'm not Mister anybody? I'm just Zack."

She smiled at her daughter. "Honey, you can call him Zack."

"Okay, Zack," Kylie said.

"That's better," Zack said. "Now where's Dani? Does she know you guys are here?"

"Not yet. She's out in the paddock finishing up with Poet and Bobby. I didn't want to distract her, so we thought we'd wait in here and surprise her."

"That's a good idea. That boy can still be a knothead when he wants to," Zack smiled, shaking his head.

They heard the clip-clop of a horse along with muffled voices coming from the far end of the barn.

"Shhh," Lou said, putting her finger up to her mouth.

They waited patiently in the office. Zack and Jake had settled into conversation. Lou decided to take Kylie out to the front paddock to meet Cheetah and Gandy Dancer. When the horses saw them approach, they trotted up to the gate, certain there were treats in it for them. Lou and Kylie fed them some carrots and petted them for a few minutes.

They got back into the office seconds before Dani came around the corner. They could barely contain themselves as they anticipated her reaction once she saw them. They squished themselves up behind the door so when she first walked in the only person she would see would be Zack. He was sitting at his desk pretending to be doing some paperwork.

"Zack, I was just—"

"Surprise!" they yelled in unison.

Dani jumped and spun around. She froze when she saw her family standing there. The expression on her face was confirmation that she hadn't quite connected the image with the reality.

"Shut up!" she screamed and jumped into her sister's arms.

They stumbled and nearly fell to the floor.

"Oh my god! Kylie! What the heck!"

Jake and Lou stood back and watched their daughters' reunion. Jake placed his arm around her shoulder and pulled her closer to him.

"Hey, Punk, don't I get a hug too?" Jake held his arms out to her.

Dani ran, jumped into his arms, and buried her head in his shoulders.

"Daddy, I can't believe you guys are here. This is so great!"

She gave him a big kiss on his cheek and squeezed her arms around his neck. She looked over her father's shoulder toward her mother and smiled at her.

"You knew about this, didn't you?" she said

"Guilty as charged," Lou said, held up her hands, then wiped a tear away. "Are you surprised?"

"Yes!" Dani laughed and slipped out of her dad's arms. "This is so awesome."

"Are you surprised?" Zack asked, teasing.

"Totally!" she exclaimed. "I mean, when I came into the office, these guys were the last people I expected to see. When they yelled surprise, it freaked me out for a second because I was totally shocked." She turned to Kylie and said, "Wait until you see some of the horses. You are not going to believe it." She turned back to Zack. "Do you think it would be all right if I took her to meet some of the horses?"

"I was wondering how long it would take you to ask that question," Zack said, grinning.

"Cool," Dani said, then turned back to Kylie. "C'mon, there's this one horse that I know you are going to absolutely love. His name is Sitting Bull. Zack calls him Bull."

The girls left the office together.

37

The girls settled down on a couple of hay bales outside the front paddock gate.

"What was the place like where you were this summer?" Dani asked.

"It was pretty cool. It wasn't anything like this. They definitely had a few barns and riding rings and junk like that, but most of the stuff I was doing was class work."

"You had to go to school every day? Yuck!" Dani scrunched her nose.

"Well it wasn't all school. They took us around on rotations to teach us how the different parts of an equestrian business work and junk like that. It was fun. I learned a lot. Besides," she said, giving her sister a smug look. "If I want to, I can go back again next summer." Kylie got serious and looked over at her sister. "Remember how we used to always say we were going to own a ranch some day and have a lesson program and lots of horses?"

"Yeah. We still are, you know," Dani said, giving Kylie a worried look and asked, "Why? Don't you want to do that anymore?"

"Of course, I do," Kylie said. "It's just that looking at this place makes me think it will cost a lot of money to get started."

Dani thought about what her sister said and remembered the drive out. She had been very angry at her parents. She remembered promising herself that no matter what happened, she was going to make her mom miserable every single day. Then she got here and met Zack, Tessa, Bobby, and the many other people who made Echo Ranch come alive. It wasn't until she met Poet, however, that she realized no matter how hard she tried, she couldn't maintain her anger.

"Yeah, well, it wasn't like that before we got here," Dani said. "So"—she picked a piece of hay up and twirled it in her fingers— "Did you see me on Poet before?"

Kylie looked at her sister and smiled. "Yes, I did. You looked great on him."

Dani relaxed. They had always been in fierce competition with each other where their riding was concerned. Back in the days when they both competed, Kylie always seemed to pin the blue ribbons and pick up a champion while Dani would pull up the reserved champion or lower. Dani was proud of her sister but always wanted the opportunity to show Kylie and the world that she could take the blue-ribbon home. Dani remembered many fights with her mother when she would insinuate that Lou was more proud of Kylie than Dani.

"Yeah?"

"Yeah." Kylie nudged her. "When we first got here, we were hanging back over there," she said and pointed to the open barn doors. "You couldn't see me, but I definitely saw you. You looked like a natural. I mean, Zack was telling us that Poet is barely three, and you were training him this summer. My sister"—Kylie shook her head— "a horse trainer. Geez, Dani, I've never trained a horse."

"Well it hasn't been all easy you know," she said humbly.

"Whatever! C'mon, let's go see where—"

Kylie looked at Dani, "What's the guy's name that works the barns?"

"Bobby," Dani said.

"Let's go see where he is. He's supposed to take us back up to the house."

They got up and brushed off their pants. Bobby was coming from the other direction as they approached the barn.

"Hey, girls," he said and tipped his hat.

"This is my sister, Kylie," Dani said, introducing Kylie to Bobby. "This is Bobby. He knows everything about Echo Ranch."

"I can probably run you guys up to the house now if you're ready."

Dani stopped by the office to grab her backpack. They climbed up into the pickup and headed toward the main house. Kylie took the window seat. Dani could tell Kylie still couldn't get over the land that spread out beyond the window. The sun had made her final descent over the southern ridge. The night sky was settling in with a glorious explosion of reds and pinks.

"Wow," Kylie exclaimed. "This place is so beautiful."

Dani watched her sister and realized that her reaction had been similar the first time she had seen a sunset on Echo Ranch. Life was so different here than it was at home. No traffic lights or malls or cars driving through the neighborhood at Echo Ranch. The first couple of weeks had been an incredible adjustment for her. On more than one occasion she had pined for the mall or to hang out with her friends. But once she settled into the rhythm of ranch life, it hadn't been so bad. She missed her friends, but the more time she spent on the ranch, the more she realized how much she loved being around horses from the time she rose to the time she went to bed.

"Look!" Dani said and pointed down valley.

"That's cool. I'm blown away by how massive this place is. I mean everywhere I look there's either mountains or valleys and horses."

"Yeah, I'm sad that we'll be leaving soon," Dani admitted.

When they pulled up to the house, they saw everyone sitting on the porch. Tessa came to the head of the stairs to greet them. They scrambled down out of the truck and ran to the stairs. Bobby backed out and gave a toot and a wave as he pulled away.

"Hello, girls," Tessa said and smiled. She held her hand out to Kylie. "You must be Kylie."

She reached for Tessa's hand. "Yes, ma'am."

Tessa laughed. "Call me Tessa, dear. It's very nice to meet you. Danielle and your mom have told me so much about you. I understand you love horses too?" she asked.

"Definitely. You have a beautiful ranch and amazing horses."

Dani added, "Yeah, and they all saw me riding Poet when they got here."

"I'm sure that was an impressive sight to see," Tessa said, smiling. "Are you two hungry?"

"Starving," the girls said in unison.

"Do you think it would be okay if we went up and took our showers before dinner?" Dani asked.

"Of course. I was going to put Kylie in the back bedroom down the hall from your mom's room. C'mon, I'll help you get settled," Tessa said.

Tessa looked at Zack. "Are you guys okay out here? There's more wine in the bar and some more fruit and snacks cut up on the counter in the kitchen. I shouldn't be very long. Louisa, maybe you and I can set up dinner when I get back."

The sky had turned to night, and they could see thousands of stars in the heavens. The stars looked like perfect sugar crystals against the black backdrop of night. The crescent moon was high above the southern ridge and projected just enough light for them to see the traces of the jagged peaks against the darkness. They could hear the random calls from crickets and night bugs. A hoot from a night owl broke the silence. Pearl was in the front paddock, and Beau was next to the front gate. A snuffle or sigh would sound and remind them the horses were nearby just in case somebody wanted to bring over a carrot. Jake and Lou sat on the porch swing, gently rocking. She rested her head on her husband's shoulder, content to have her family together again.

"You okay?" Jake whispered.

"I'm fine. I was just thinking how lucky we all are."

Tessa returned, let the screen door close behind her, and settled into a seat next to her husband.

"Louisa, do you want to help me in the kitchen? I thought since it's such a lovely night, we could eat out here tonight."

"Absolutely!"

Lou got up and followed Tessa back into the house.

38

Tessa and Lou had finished setting the dinner up as the girls joined them.

"Hey, you two," Zack said, taking a plate. "I was just telling your daddy I was thinking about all of us taking a trail down to the lake tomorrow. What do you think?"

"Seriously?" Dani asked, looking at him and back at her sister. "The lake is so cool. There's this giant rope swing that swings so far up in the air that when you drop it feels like forever until you land in the water."

"Cool," Kylie said, smiling.

"But don't we have a couple of groups coming in tomorrow?" Dani asked Zack.

"Of course, we do, but I'm the boss, and since I'm the boss, I can decide when I want to delegate responsibility." He winked.

She put a piece of chicken on her plate and began chattering away her ideas of horse assignments for her family. "I think you should put Daddy on Bull and Kylie on Cheetah and—"

"You got it all figured out, do you?" Zack asked, interrupting then laughing.

"I think Mom should ride Lucy," Dani turned to Tessa. "Tessa, you'll ride Black."

"Well I suppose it's settled," Zack said, laughing. "Let's eat! This is a real fine meal you've made again, Tessa."

Later that evening when Jake climbed into bed, Lou took off her reading glasses, closed her book, and set them on the nightstand next to the bed. She snuggled up next to him and rested her head on his shoulder.

"This is nice," Lou sighed. "I'm so glad you're here."

"Me too," he said as he stroked her hair. "You're happy, aren't you?"

"Mhmm," she said, smiling. "I'm happy my family is together again."

"I think it's more than that."

Lou pulled away from him and propped herself up on her elbow. "What do you mean?" she asked.

"Relax," he said. "What I meant by it being more than that is this house, this place, Zack and Tessa—the whole package."

Lou settled back down. "It's pretty amazing, huh?"

"That's an understatement," Jake said. "I think this is one of the best decisions we've ever made for all of us."

"I'm glad we were able to bring Dani here this summer," Lou said. "I think it's done her a world of good, and it's been extremely important for me too. These past months have given me an opportunity to take a step back and see what's been going on in my life and how I've been living."

"Yeah? How's that?" Jake asked.

"It's made me realize that Dani is her own person too. She's not somebody I can mold into the person I think she should be. My job is to teach her how to manage her life and expose her to situations so that she can determine how she should go forward. It doesn't mean that she's going to make the right choice every time. What it means is she needs to practice her way of doing it, and if I think it's not the right way, that's how I think, not her."

"Okay, you're starting to lose me."

Lou sighed and continued. "It means that I realize now there were times when I was suffocating our daughter. The angrier she became, the more I thought it was best that I lock her down and not even give her the chance to make a mistake. Trust me, Jake, there have been a few times this summer when I thought I'd bite my tongue in half, but I had to do it anyway just to see where she'd take it. What it has done, for me, anyway, has shown me that we have a child who is still on her journey toward becoming a young lady. It's taught me that there are many bumps in the road along the way, and if we want to see her make it, we needed this. More importantly, though, I needed to take a step back and watch her fall a few times. She still demonstrates the fact that she's a teenager and is a master at that, but she's learning how to channel that strong will and is starting to recognize good versus bad choices."

"Our kid isn't bad, Lou," Jake defended Dani.

"Of course, she isn't," Lou said. "I just think that when we pull out of here, I'll be driving home with a much more enjoyable travel companion. Truth be known, I'm looking forward to having someone in the car who will actually talk to me instead of listening to the voice inside my head."

Lou reached over and turned the light out on her nightstand. She bent over, kissed Jake's forehead, and settled back into his shoulder. She let out a deep sigh.

39

Everyone met down at the barn the next morning before eight. Zack and the girls had already pulled out the horses they planned to ride to the lake. Lou walked up to Lucy and rubbed her nose.

"Hello, pretty girl. Are you ready to ride today?" She kissed Lucy's nose. She turned to Jake. "Honey, that's Bull," she said, pointing to the paint on the cross ties. "He's one of the most comfortable rides on this ranch; he's a real sweetheart. He's got a soft mouth, but you'll figure that out once we get underway."

"Hey, Bull," Jake said, holding his hand under Bull's nose and allowing him to sniff. "Looks like it's you and me today." He stroked Bull's neck.

"How are doing there, Jake?" Zack asked, as he walked into the barn.

Lou and Jake turned around.

"I think I'm just about set," Jake said. "Maybe you should check that girth. It's been a while since I've tacked up a horse; last thing I want is to lose my saddle."

"That would be a problem."

Lou watched as Zack stepped up to Bull and lifted the saddle flap. He made a few minor adjustments.

"I think you're good. Go ahead and lead him out. I'll finish up with these two and see you in a minute."

"Sounds good," Jake said and gathered Bull's reins. He gave a slight tug, and Bull responded quickly to his command.

They saddled up and headed out.

Lou and Tessa eased into a comfortable stride alongside Zack and Jake. The girls were well ahead of them.

"Dani," Zack called out.

She stopped her horse and turned around.

"Yeah?"

"Just remember to stay on the trail along the fence line. Bobby has some repairs he needs to do to some of the footing this side of that opening there. I don't want anyone getting hurt today. Got it?"

"Okay." She turned back around, gave Duck a kick, and she and her sister cantered off together.

"Will you look at that?" Zack said to the group, "Tell me that isn't a sight to behold."

"Those are my girls," Jake and Lou said simultaneously then laughed.

"Zack, Jake and I were talking last night about how much we thought this was a wonderful experience for Dani and me. We were wondering if you and Tessa would mind if we came back out again next summer."

Zack stopped Jasper. He took his hat off, smoothed his hair back, and placed it back on his head. He looked around his property and back at Lou.

"Lou, I can't think of anything we'd like more. If you haven't figured it out by now, you never will; you're family. You always have been. It's been a gift to have you two here this summer. The prospect of having all of you come back next year is great. We'd love to have you. Besides, I was expecting to have at least Dani back because Poet sure is going to miss her once she's gone."

"Poet," Lou whispered. "I'm not looking forward to that good-bye." She looked over at Zack and Tessa. "It's going to break her heart to have to leave him, you know."

"I know it is," Zack said, reaching down and giving Jasper a couple of pats on his neck. "But that's part of life. It's downright miserable when you have to say good-bye to something or someone you love so much, but sometimes that's just how the cards play out." He gave Lou a serious look. "But I'll tell you something right now."

"What's that?" she asked.

"If you ever let another twenty years go by before we see your face again," he warned, "well, you'll have some serious explaining is all. Besides, who knows if I have another twenty years left?"

"Don't talk like that," Lou said.

"Ah, hell, I'm not going anywhere," Zack said, laughing, "I'm just making a point. You've treated Tessa and me to the family we always knew we wanted. The thought of it being taken away now is something we just don't want to happen."

"I know. I promise we'll be back next summer. As a matter of fact, we'd love it if you guys would come back East and spend Christmas with us. Do you think that's a possibility?" she asked.

Tessa and Zack looked at each other.

"I'm not real fond of cities and traffic, but I'd definitely make an exception if it means spending more time with you guys," Zack answered then turned to Tessa. "Honey, what do you think about that?"

"I think it's a marvelous idea. Louisa, we'd be thrilled to be a part of your holidays this year."

"Then it's settled," Lou said, smiling as she watched the girls. "I think we should get moving. Look at those two."

Kylie and Dani had long since passed the last part of fence line and were in a full canter side by side. Dani's ponytail swished back and forth in cadence with her horse's strides. Kylie was right beside her with her long blonde hair flowing in the warm summer breeze.

Lou saw Zack and Jake pick up speed also and wasn't surprised when the men caught up with the girls then passed them by. Dani had become a part of the ranch and its terrain; she knew the way to the lake. Lou sighed and relished the thought that today they all had plenty of time to enjoy a lazy lunch with an afternoon ahead of it with nothing more to do than be together.

By the time they got to the lake, the day was picture-perfect. The sky was completely clear, and the summer breeze was warm. The lake gently rippled; the rope swing was tethered to its tree and seemed to beg a girl to take it down for a ride. After the girls finished eating, they disappeared into a grove of trees and changed into their swimsuits. They came back out and ran to the rope.

"Hey, Mom," Dani yelled. "Watch this!"

She unwound the rope and pulled it back until it was tight. She settled onto the giant knot and ran until her feet left the ground. She careened into the air, and, when she was practically parallel with the water below, she opened her legs, threw her hands away from the rope, and squealed as she flew. She crashed into the water and seconds later surfaced.

"Did you see that?" she yelled.

"Every minute, Punk, that was cool."

"Hey, Punk, I think I might have to try that," Jake called.

"C'mon, the water is great!" Dani called back. "Kylie, do it!" She cheered her sister on.

Kylie pulled back on the rope and took a running start. As soon as her feet left the ground, she screamed. Once she was fully airborne, she let go of the rope and plummeted into the water a few feet from her sister. She surfaced with a gasp.

"Oh my god," Kylie sputtered. "This water is freezing."

Dani was laughing hysterically. "I know!"

Kylie started to swim back to the shore.

"Let's do it again," Dani called as she swam.

"You are so in trouble," Kylie said and tried to catch up with her sister. "You told me this water was warm. Hey, Daddy, come in."

"I don't know," Jake said. "Sounds like the water is a little cold."

"It's not that bad."

Jake looked at Lou. "You coming?"

"Are you crazy? I'm not getting in that water. It is freezing. I don't care what they say. I'm not going in." She shook her head.

"Chicken," Jake said over his shoulder as he trotted off toward the girls. "Okay, you two. Tell me what I need to do." He grabbed the rope and brought it into him. Dani stood by his side and helped him arrange the rope.

"Make sure you have that knot like a chair between your legs," Dani instructed. "Yeah, like that. Now take a couple of steps back until the line gets tight."

She stood back a little. "Perfect. Now just run as fast as you can. Remember to lift your feet up when you get to the edge and swing yourself out over the water."

The girls stood back and watched their father take off. They cringed when he got to the edge and lost his footing, nearly falling from the rope. He managed to hang on, and once he was airborne, he let go. He torpedoed into the water, and when he surfaced, he was gasping for air.

"Oh my god! This water isn't freezing, it's frozen!" he exclaimed.

He threw his hair back from his forehead and began to swim to the shoreline.

213

"Thanks a lot, you two," he said, laughing as he climbed up the bank. "Have fun with that because I'm done swimming for today."

"Aw, come on, Daddy," they pleaded. "Try it again. Isn't it a blast?"

He looked at his daughters and couldn't resist their pleas.

"Okay, but this is the last time."

He ran back over to the rope and took off in a run. He leapt off the bank. Once he was airborne, he managed enough distance off the water to do a somersault before he plunged into the lake headfirst. When he surfaced, the girls were clapping and cheering him on.

"Whoo-hoo! Awesome job," Kylie said, laughing.

"That's it for me. This water is way too cold." He shook his hair out, spraying them both. He walked back over to the picnic blanket and grabbed a towel. He wrapped it around his shoulders and shook his head again. A few drops hit Lou, and she jumped up from the blanket.

"Like I said," she laughed. "I am not going in that water."

Tessa and Lou set out on a walk. They passed by the grazing horses, leaving Zack and Jake to settle into conversation. The girls were oblivious to what the grownups did; they were completely happy to have each other.

After a fun but exhausting day at the lake, the got back to the barn late afternoon. Dani and Kylie finished grooming Cheetah and Duck and were leading them out to the back field.

"Hey, guys," Dani called. "Kylie is coming with me while I work Poet. Is that okay, Zack?"

"It's fine with me as long as it's fine with your momma and daddy," Zack told her.

"Is it okay, guys?"

"Sure, Punk, we'll see you back up at the house later," Lou answered.

"Cool. C'mon," she said, grabbing her sister's arm and pulling her off toward Poet's paddock.

40

The next day, Tessa, Lou, and the girls went into town. They had arranged to meet Carla and Amy for lunch.

After lunch, Lou wrapped her arms around Carla one last time. "You are truly a magnificent human being. Remember what I said. Call me," she reminded Carla.

"Thanks, Lou, I will." Carla called Amy, "Hey, kiddo, it's time to go."

"You know, if you'd like, we can take Amy back to the ranch with us," Tessa offered. "I'm sure she'd love to spend some time with the girls."

"Amy, Tessa and Zack are going to do a night trail ride and bonfire tonight. Do you want to go back to the ranch with these guys?" Carla asked Amy.

"That would be great. I have to call my mom and ask her, though."

After all arrangements had been made, they were off to the ranch.

That evening, the group set out on the trail toward the north valley around six o'clock. The late afternoon sky was pure. As far as the eye could see, no clouds interrupted its flawless perfection. After thirty minutes of riding, they crossed over the north branch of the creek and began a slight climb into the foothills at the base of the trail that lead to Final Fall. Dani rode between Amy and Kylie.

"Look." She pointed to the ridge high beyond them. "That's a really cool place up there. Zack took me up there about a week before you got here, Kylie."

Kylie looked straight up. "Wow, that looks pretty steep. Were you scared?"

"Sort of at first. It looks like that trail is really narrow, but once you're on it, it's not so bad."

"Maybe we can go there before we leave," Kylie suggested.

As they continued down the trail, Kylie and Dani shared stories with Amy about their lives back East. Kylie and Amy hit it off instantly. Dani listened intently to their college-life tales and realized she couldn't wait to experience some herself. The mere notion of being able to come and go as she pleased without having to ask a parent was beyond appealing.

They rode on for a while in silence. Zack had explained to the group before they left that it would take about an hour to get to the site, depending upon how fast or slow the pace was. It didn't matter to the girls. They were riding, and that's all they cared about.

A trace of the three-quarter moon was barely visible on the horizon. Dani and Kylie had never ridden at night. They were excited over the notion of riding by the light of the moon.

"You know, Bobby and a bunch of the guys are camping out by the bonfire tonight," Dani said. "Zack told me the reason they do that is to make sure the fire doesn't spread after we leave. I think that's a good idea."

Kylie hesitated. "I don't know if I'd want to camp out here."

"Why not?" Amy asked.

"Dani was telling me there are wild animals in the mountains. I've seen some of those TV shows when people are attacked by mountain lions and junk like that. I just think since we know there's that kind of stuff here, it would be stupid to risk it," she said.

"Of course, there're wild animals," Amy said. "They're all over the place in the mountains. The thing is, they're more scared of us than we are of them. We've got so many people with us they're not even going to try coming around us."

"Yeah, well, I don't want to be that one statistic that proves your theory wrong," Kylie argued.

"Geez, Kylie, I've ridden over tons of places around here and haven't seen a bear or anything," Dani said. "Besides, Zack said if there was a big cat or something like that, it's more likely to be down by the south valley because of the way the mountains are situated. He said that's the main migration path for deer and elk. He told me in the late fall you can see tons of deer and elk coming down out of the mountains and going across that valley on their way to their winter homes. Another reason they cross down there is because that's where there's a lot of the stuff they like to eat."

Kylie looked at her sister in amazement. "Dani, I am so impressed. You sound like a little history book. Who would have thought

216

my little sister would actually pay attention and learn something this summer?"

"That's not very nice. I've learned a lot of stuff this summer, and the reason I was telling you about it is because you sounded like you were scared about wild animals. I was just trying to make you feel better," Dani retorted.

She gave Duck a slight kick and trotted off to catch up with the adults.

Dani eased into the trail beside her father. "Hey, Daddy."

"Hey, Punk, are you having fun?" He smiled at her.

"Yeah, I guess," she said.

"What's up?"

"I don't know."

"Okay," Jake said.

They rode quietly for a few moments, and then Dani said, "It's just that sometimes Kylie treats me like a baby."

"Why's that?"

"I don't know. She just does," Dani insisted. "It's just that she was saying she was afraid to have a camp out in these mountains because she didn't want to get eaten by a mountain lion or bear."

"Neither would I," he said, laughing.

Dani looked at her dad and rolled her eyes. "Nobody's going to get eaten by anything out here. Zack would never let that happen."

"So why do you think Kylie thinks it will?"

"I was telling her about some of the wild animals up in the mountains," Dani said. "She's the one that asked about it."

"What brought it up?"

"I don't know. We were talking about college and sororities and junk like that, and the next thing I know, we're talking about mountain lions and bears, and she just thought it sounded dangerous."

"Dani, I'm not sure I know where this is going."

"I told her about some of the animals that live in the mountains down by the southern range. When Mom and I first got here, Zack told us he never turned horses out overnight down there in the summer because it was too risky. He said that area was part of the wildlife refuge, and the animals were protected because of it. He lost a horse once to a mountain

217

lion, and they had to track the mountain lion for a couple of days and kill it because it was a threat to his livestock. They had to do it because if they didn't catch it and kill it, maybe more of his horses would be killed." Dani paused and shook her head. "I was trying to tell Kylie about that, and the next thing I know she's laughing at me. She told me I sounded like some stupid history book."

"How about this?" Jake asked.

"What?"

"Why don't you just ride up here with me for a while and tell me a little more about those wild animals. I don't care if you sound like a history book. As a matter of fact, I think it's impressive that you've learned so much about this place in such a short time. Maybe once we get to the campsite, you and Kylie can sit and talk things out. You can tell her how it made you feel when she said those things to you," he suggested. "Sometimes, Punk, people say things, and they have no idea how it hurts the other person. Maybe that's what's going on with you and Kylie."

Dani thought about that for a moment and could see what her dad was suggesting, but only felt a little bit better about the whole situation.

"I guess. I don't know. Besides, she and Amy are talking about college stuff, and it's boring. Maybe I'll just ride with you until we get there."

"That's fine with me, honey. Think about what I said, though."

She looked at her dad and said, "Sure."

By the time the group made it to the north valley, the moon had made progress in its journey into night. Dusk had blanketed the heavens and earth, and stars were already springing up. The burn pile was round and tall. From a distance, it looked like an African mud hut from a *National Geographic* special. Most of the debris was scrub brush and fallen trees, but there was also some old fencing boards and other odds and ends thrown on.

A water truck was parked off in the distance. Dani recognized it from some of the chores she'd done with Zack. On a few occasions during the summer they had driven the water truck to the outlying pastures where some of his herd roamed. Those work days had been fun because when they had pulled up to the troughs to replenish the water, the horses would come thundering down over the hills. She remembered how thrilled she had been the first time she had witnessed something like that. She felt like she was living in a time before modern civilization. In her mind, she pretended to be a prairie girl doing her chores. It also made her think about those prairie stories she used to read when she was in elementary school.

The camp was a sight to behold. A mess area was covered with a canopy, and underneath it was a giant oil drum barbeque. A constant stream of smoke came from its stack, and the aroma smelled delicious. Two long banquet tables were covered with checkerboard tablecloths and an assortment of covered dishes. Stashed under a few tables were coolers filled with drinks. Out near the water truck was a makeshift corral, a circular pen fashioned with ropes and stakes, and Dani could see that some of the ranch hands' mounts were already inside. Organized around the burn pile were a series of collapsible chairs and some box crates for seats and stools. A guitar leaned against one of the crates.

Dani hopped off Duck and led him over to Bobby.

"Hey, Bobby," she said, smiling.

"Hey, Miss Dani, how was your ride?"

"Fine," she said, looking around. "Are we supposed to put our horses over there?" She pointed to the temporary corral.

"Yes, ma'am, go ahead and take his tack off. Make sure you put his halter on him, then you can turn him out with the horses already in there. Put your tack over there." He pointed to another canopy that had been set up with a bunch of saddle stands beneath it. "It'll be pretty dark when you guys head out later, and it will be a lot easier if all the tack is in one place."

"That's a great idea. This is so cool. This is like being at a mountain barn. You guys have everything here."

"Yes, ma'am, we've done a lot of overnights and this is a lot like what those riders get to experience."

"I've never ridden at night."

"Well we all have, so don't worry," he assured her, "you're in good hands. Wait until you see the burn later. It's a great pile."

Dani looked beyond the corral and saw a couple of tents erected. They were bigger than the ones her family had used for camping when

219

she and Kylie were little. They looked like the big community tent that was set up when a bunch of families camped together.

"Is that where you guys will sleep tonight?"

"Yes, ma'am, we'll be out here all night. We won't leave tomorrow until we're sure the burn is completely out. We've done a lot of burns over the years. By the grace of God, we've never had any problems. We don't want this one to be the first."

"I'm going to go find my sister and Amy. I'll see you later."

She continued to lead Duck to the corral and could see Amy and Kylie ahead of her. A part of her wanted to drop into formation with them, but she had a stronger urge to ignore them. As she was trying to determine what course to take, Kylie turned around.

"There you are. Come up here with us. We're not sure what we're supposed to do here."

Dani stifled her anger for the moment because suddenly her big sister needed her help.

"I'll show you," Dani said then turned to Duck and gave a little tug on his reins. "C'mon, boy, let's show these guys what they need to do. Bobby said we need to put our tack over there. See where all the saddle racks are under that canopy?" She pointed.

"Yeah."

"Make sure you put a halter on Cheetah." She leaned forward so she could see Amy. "And you too, Amy."

"Got it," Amy said.

"And once you have the halter on, turn them out with the horses already in the pen. Bobby said it'll be get pretty dark by the time we leave, and that's why we have to do things like this."

"Then what?" Kylie asked.

"What do you mean?"

"What do we do after we turn our horses out?"

"I don't know. Just go back to where everybody else is. Why are you asking me?"

"I was just asking," Kylie said defensively.

"Yeah, well, I'm not the boss of everything and don't have that information in my history book."

Kylie stopped, but Dani continued to walk toward the corral. When she realized her sister had stopped, she stopped and turned around. "Are you coming?"

"Go ahead. I'll be there when I get there," Kylie said.

Dani rolled her eyes. "Suit yourself."

"Uh, guys?" Amy interrupted. "I think I'll see you up there." Without waiting for a response, she led her horse around Kylie and continued past Dani.

The two girls held their ground, each daring the other to speak. The silence became too awkward for Kylie, and she spoke. "Dani, I know you're mad at me. I'm sorry if I pissed you off. Relax. It's no big deal."

"It is a big deal, Kylie. You always do that," Dani said. "Every time you say something, like what you said back there, it makes me feel like you think I'm stupid. Well, I'm not stupid, and you shouldn't have said the things you did." Dani kicked at the dirt. "Besides, you embarrassed me in front of Amy."

Kylie gave Cheetah's reins a tug. She came up next to Dani and dropped the reins. She reached out to her sister and put her arms around her. Dani stiffened because she was still angry.

"I didn't mean to hurt you. I didn't mean to embarrass you. I guess I was sort of jealous because I really was kind of freaked out about wild animals and the thought of being attacked. When you started telling me all that stuff, it sounded like you knew what you were talking about. It made me feel dumb because I'm the older sister."

Dani pushed away.

"I wasn't trying to sound like a know-it-all," Dani said. "I was trying to tell you that you're safe here. Zack and his guys know this entire place like the backs of their hands. If there was any chance of danger, do you honestly think they'd bring us out here?"

"Probably not," Kylie said, grinning.

"What's so funny?" Dani said, glaring at her sister.

"I was just thinking that if there was mountain lion ten miles from here, Mom would never come out here."

Dani looked back down at the dirt and kicked it some more. When she conjured the image of her mother coming face-to-face with a mountain lion, she started to giggle too. She looked up at her sister and giggled a little harder.

"Seriously, Mom would probably run back to the house faster than her horse could get her there."

They burst into laughter. Kylie reached back down and gathered up Cheetah's reins.

"C'mon, let's go catch up with Amy. It'll be a blast tonight. I can't wait to see the bonfire all lit up."

She walked off knowing her sister would follow.

They feasted on an enormous bounty of food: pulled pork, beef, and chicken in a savory barbeque sauce; every imaginable salad, from potato to coleslaw, macaroni to fresh beet; and desserts, from rich chocolate cake, brownies, to chocolate chip cookies the size of a grown man's hand. Fresh fruit and vegetables from Tessa's garden had been used in everything possible. It was a celebratory feast and homage to the notion that summer was gracefully departing.

The girls pulled up a couple of chairs on the far side of the burn pile. The night was cool, another indicator that summer's end neared. Dani had a saddle blanket wrapped around her shoulders. It had vibrant colors and Native American symbols.

"When will they light the burn pile?" Kylie asked.

Amy looked back toward the food tent. "I don't know. Looks like all the adults are still eating. Maybe we should go ask Bobby."

Kylie popped up out of her chair and looked back at her sister. "Hey, Pocahontas?" she asked, giggling. "Want to come?"

Dani grinned up at her sister. "Very funny," she mumbled, unwrapped herself, and tossed the blanket back on her chair.

They headed off toward the horse pens and sleeping quarters. They could see lights coming from the tents. Bobby was walking their way with a couple of the other ranch hands.

"Hey, Bobby," they chimed in together.

"Hey, girls."

"Will you light the pile soon?"

"Yes, ma'am, that's what we're getting ready to do right now. You ladies want to help?"

They looked at each other and back at Bobby. "Yes!"

"Okay. Dani, go up and ask Tripp for a couple of torches and bring them down to the pile," Bobby instructed and turned to the other two. "Kylie and Amy, you two go with her and each get a torch."

They got back to Bobby and stood patiently, waiting for further instructions. Most of the adults had finished up in the food tent and had found their seats around the pile. Lou came up behind Dani and put her arms on her shoulders. "Hey, sweetie."

"Hi, Mom," she said and smiled up at her. "This is very cool. I can't wait to see this go up in flames. It'll look like daylight by the time the whole thing catches."

"It sure will. What's that?" Lou pointed at the torch in Dani's hand.

"It's a torch. We're going to help light the fire."

Lou stepped back from her daughter, horror written all over her face. "I don't know if I want you guys messing with the fire."

"Relax, Mom, Bobby and the guys will help us. It's not like we're going to torch ourselves."

"That's not what I meant. I just don't like the idea of you being involved with the lighting part of this." She pointed at the pile that was well above their heads.

"It'll be fine, Lou," Jake said as he came up behind her and put his arms around her waist.

"I don't think Bobby would have ever let them have those torches if he didn't plan to supervise."

"What's wrong?" Kylie asked when she walked over.

"Mom's freaking out," Dani said, shaking her head.

"I'm not freaking out," Lou snapped. "I'm just worried somebody might get hurt."

"It'll be fine, Mrs. Croft," Amy assured her. "I've been to burns at Echo Ranch tons of times. These guys have it down. They're totally safe. Honest."

Lou looked at Amy and her girls and back to Jake, obviously hoping for some allegiance. "It's not that I don't trust you girls. It's just—"

"You guys ready?" Bobby asked, interrupting Lou.

"Yeah!"

223

They ignored their mother's insistence and walked away with Bobby.

41

Lou could feel the anxiety rising inside her and grabbed Jake's hands that were still around her waist.

"I don't know about this, Jake. They're—"

"Fine, Lou," he assured her. "We have that water truck," he nodded to the truck that had been pulled closer to the pile. "It probably has an amount of water in it equivalent to a swimming pool. Those two guys over there"—he nodded toward the two men standing by the truck—"have been dousing a ring around the pile ever since we got here. See?" He pointed to the wet perimeter as further assurance. "And all we need to do now is have a little faith that it's going to be fine."

Once everyone gathered, Zack stood up between them and the burn pile.

"Okay, everybody, listen up for a minute," Zack said. "Before we light this up, I want to go over a few rules." Satisfied he had everyone's attention, he continued. "There's a lot of really dry wood and scrub in there." He pointed over his shoulder to the pile behind him. "What that means is when it gets going initially, a fair number of sparks will start flying. I want everyone to pay attention to what's going on around them and make sure if you're hit with a spark to slap it off right away and make sure you stomp it out if it's still burning when it hits the ground. We've been doing this a lot of years. The reason we've never had a tragedy is because we respect the fact that fire is a hell of a lot more powerful than we are. Pay attention to what's going on around you. One last thing, I want you all to grab those chairs and pull them back another ten feet or so. The good news is there isn't any wind tonight, so it'll be a real manageable burn." He stepped back, looked at Bobby and his other guys, and gave them a nod.

Bobby positioned the girls at arm's length away from each other and explained what they needed to do once their torches were lit. Lou stood back with Jake, intently watching every move her children made. She was mentally reciting every prayer she knew, so much so she was beginning to get a headache. Dani's torch was the first to light. Once lit, she turned to Kylie with Bobby's guidance and lit her sister's torch. After Kylie's torch was ignited, she reached out to Amy's. In a domino fashion, once all the torches were lit, they turned back to the pile. One by one they

225

knelt and slid their lit torches up underneath the bottom. Then each person took his or her foot and kicked it securely under the pile before stepping back to the other side of the soak ring.

As soon as Lou could see her girls no longer had fire in their hands, she let out a deep sigh of relief.

"C'mon, girls, come stand back here by Daddy and me," she said.

The group stood back and watched the once-dormant pile of debris come to life. At first, a large billow of smoke curled out from the underbelly around the entire perimeter. Within minutes, a symphony of crackles, pops, hisses, and spits sounded. The flames gained momentum as they made their way to the top through the center of the pile. They pierced through from the bowels of the pile and reached high into the night sky like a series of willowy fingers and hands reaching for salvation from their inner depths of the darkness. Lou looked at her girls and was touched by their expressions. They were mesmerized. Their mouths gaped open, and their faces held expressions of wonder. They looked as if they had just caught Santa placing that last package under the tree. She turned and looked up at Jake. He was just as captivated.

The fire reached the height of its capacity about an hour into the burn. Bobby and the other ranch hands monitored the progress to be sure each time there was a shift or a change of direction in the intermittent breeze, they were on guard and ready to move should they need to do something immediately. Zack and the rest of the riders had formed a big circle, and Tripp had grabbed his guitar. He played random riffs, and every now and then he strummed out a full song. Lou was right back to her younger days when she had been a working hand at the ranch. The bonfires had come a long way since then. It was still bittersweet for her to be a part of something that; for many years, she thought she would never experience again. She relaxed further into her husband's arms and enjoyed the buzz of conversation.

"What are you thinking about?" Jake whispered into her ear.

"I don't know. Just stuff," she said with a sigh.

"What kind of stuff?"

"I was thinking about how crazy everything was a few months ago and how very different it is now. Look," she said and nodded toward the girls. "Did you ever think you'd see such harmony?"

226

"Yeah, Lou, I did."

She smiled up at him and said, "Yeah right." She sat back and shook her head.

"What's that supposed to mean?"

"What it means is we've been through quite the rough patch these past couple of years. There is no way you weren't lying awake right beside me on those sleepless nights."

"Maybe a few," he admitted with a grin.

"I don't know, Jake, I look at Dani now, and part of me is so proud of the progress she's made this summer. The attitude has improved immensely, and there's calmness in her that I've never seen before."

"But?"

"But a tiny part of me is scared to death to go home because I wonder if what we're seeing now is the eye of the storm and the rest of the hurricane will hit when she starts school again."

"Ever the pessimist," he teased.

"That's not fair," Lou said, sitting up. "I don't want to think like that, but that's who I am as a mother. I worry about our girls and them finding their way in life."

"I know you do." He pulled her back. "If it's any consolation, so do I. The one thing you seem to forget, Lou, is that we're in this together, no matter what. You must stop worrying about everything and let some of this stuff take its course. Hell, if parents could put their daughters in a vault from the ages of eleven until twenty-one, don't you think somebody would have invented something like that by now?"

"Now you're mocking me," she complained.

"No, I'm not. I'm just trying to get you to see the incredible job you've done with our daughter this summer. You need to start recognizing the baby steps you've achieved. Jesus, Lou, I seem to recall a child a couple month back whose only word was *whatever*. If, for no other reason, be proud that she's speaking in full sentences now." He nudged her.

"Okay, I get it. No more worrying. I'm so glad you came with Kylie," she said, changing the subject.

"Me too," he agreed. "It's been real nice to have nothing more to do than relax these past couple of days."

227

The fire had burned down considerably, and, although there was still a mound of molten embers, it was time to think about heading back to the barn. It was nearly eleven, and Jake had an early flight out the next morning. They had the better part of an hour's ride back to the barn. They started to pack things up and made their way back to the corral to get their horses ready for the ride.

"I sure am glad we got to do this before you head back, Jake." Zack said when he met them on the way to the corral.

"It was fantastic," Jake said. "The food was great, the company phenomenal, and you've made memories for both my girls that they'll cherish for a lifetime. Thanks so much for all you've done—not just tonight, for everything." Jake held his hand out.

Zack took a firm hold. "I'd do it again in a heartbeat. I can't tell you what a joy it's been to have Lou and Dani here all summer. It's been a real pleasure to meet you and Kylie too. I'm glad Tessa and I could be a part of making some lasting memories for your family. The girls are already up by the horses. They're nearly ready to go. The ride back under this moon will be a beauty."

The three-quarter moon was shining its perfect golden beams down on them in anticipation of guiding them home safely.

"I need to check in with Bobby. I'll meet you two up there in a few minutes, and we'll get underway soon."

Part III

42

At dinner that night, Lou knew it was time to make her announcement. Zack looked across the table at her and she could tell by the expression on his face he had braced himself for what she had to say.

"Girls," she said, "I was thinking we should get on the road the end of this week."

Dani set her fork down and looked at her mother and asked, "Why so soon?"

"Honey, we've got to get home. We need to get you ready for school, and Kylie heads back to school in a couple of weeks. I'd like to have some time to get her ready too. Besides, I'd like to spend time with all of us together before she has to leave."

"We just were together. Besides, we'll be together for four days in the car, Mom," she whined.

"I know that, silly. It's just that Daddy hasn't had much time with you girls either. I thought maybe we could all get at least one day of sailing in before Kylie has to leave," Lou suggested.

"That'd be cool. I haven't been sailing since last summer," Kylie said.

"I know, but how come we have to leave the end of this week? Can't we leave next week?" Dani persisted.

Zack and Tessa looked at each other and back at Lou. Lou couldn't look at them. She knew if she did, she would start to cry.

"Punk, don't you think it would be nice for us to go sailing together at least once?"

Dani didn't look up from her plate. Lou knew exactly what she was thinking, and he had four legs.

"Hey, Dani?" Zack intervened.

"Yeah?"

"I was talking to Bobby after you had your lesson with Poet this afternoon. He wants to take him out on the trail before you guys left. He thinks he's ready and—"

"Really?" Dani said, interrupting.

"He was telling me he thought that because you've made such progress with him this summer, you could probably handle him if you guys took him on some of the flats down in the south fields."

"Oh my gosh, Zack, really?"

"Good." He looked at Lou. "Because your momma promised me she was going to take a trail ride with me—just the two of us—and I figured we could do that tomorrow."

"Oh, Zack, I should start getting our stuff—"

"Nope," he said, cutting her off. "If you recall the conversation we had earlier this summer, you promised me you would give me one day when just the two of us could take a ride up to Final Fall. You do remember that conversation. Don't you?"

"I know, Zack. It's—"

"Then it's settled," he said then turned to Tessa. "Honey, why don't you go with the girls tomorrow? It'll give you a chance to see Dani's progress too."

"I'd love to," Tessa said and smiled at the girls.

Lou looked at Zack. "Well I guess it's settled then." She took her fork and stabbed the piece of pie on her plate.

Tessa got up and began to clear the dishes. Lou looked at Dani and Kylie. "Girls, why don't you help Tessa in the kitchen?"

"C'mon, Dani, grab that bowl, and I'll get these dishes over here," Kylie directed.

Once they were alone, Lou set her fork down, folded her hands, and looked at Zack. "I don't know that I want to ride up to Final Fall, Zack."

"Why the hell not?"

"Because it's going to be hard enough to leave here as it is. I just don't know if I can bear to go up there knowing I'm leaving again." Her eyes filled with tears.

Zack let her have her moment. "Now c'mon, Lou, I thought you'd want to see it once more. Hell, it's not like it's going anywhere. Besides, you, Jake, and the kids will be back again next summer. I thought it'd be a nice send off. That's all."

Lou reached up and wiped a tear from her eye. She looked at the man sitting across the table from her, and her heart skipped a beat. For the first time, she realized he wasn't getting any younger. He looked old. She wondered why she hadn't seen this before.

"Okay," she whispered.

"What's that?" he asked, cupping his hand to his ear.

The corners of her mouth turned up slightly. "Fine. Let's do it," she said.

"That's my girl. Let's plan to head out before ten tomorrow. We'll make a day of it."

"Why not," she said, grinned, and picked up the remaining dishes and walked away to the kitchen.

They got down to the barn early the next morning. Bobby had already gotten Lucy on the cross ties. Jasper was on his ties in front of her. Every time Lou saw Jasper, she was reminded of Eagle. Zack treated him just like Eagle. There was that unspoken rule on the ranch: that nobody was permitted to ride him but Zack.

Zack situated the saddle pad on Jasper's back, and Jasper let out a soft nicker.

"Yeah, I know, boy. We're going on a ride."

He grabbed the saddle and placed it on top of the pad, finished tacking him, and led him out of the barn. Lou was right behind him. They rode down around the paddock and up the hill toward the brood mare pasture. The foals and mares were already out, and no matter how many times Lou saw those babies, she still loved watching them interact with their mommas. How they had grown this summer.

They rode in silence for a while because it wasn't necessary to speak. She thought about the life Zack had built here for Tessa and himself. There was no question in her mind that if she were a horse, this would be the only place she would ever want to live. After spending the summer with them, it was abundantly clear that God's plan for Zack was to make a great life, not only for him and Tessa, but for all his four-legged creatures as well. This was the life they were all meant to live, and no better place than Echo Ranch existed for them.

The trail opened to the large meadow at the base of the western slope of the Rockies. The summer grass was tall and swayed in the gentle summer breeze. Wild flowers and undergrowth covered the ground. Jasper and Lucy both knew what was coming. They stopped for a moment to take in the scenery, then Zack smiled and looked at Lou.

"You still have it in you?" he asked.

"You bet I do," she said. "Is this a fair match, Zack?" she asked as she motioned to Jasper and looked back at Lucy.

"Hell yeah, it is. Don't let Miss Lucy fool you. She may be a sweetheart, but she's a right bitch when it comes to somebody trying to outrun her." And with that, he gave Jasper a kick, and they were off. They started out with a smooth canter that didn't take long to transition into a gallop. Lucy and Jasper's ears pinned back. They knew the race was on, and whoever got to the finish line first would surely win the prize of an endless supply of carrots. They were running side by side, gulping the freedom of wind in their faces and wide-open land around them. The thrill of the ride didn't leave much room for Lou to wonder about life and its many challenges.

In that place in time she just had to be—nothing more, nothing less. She was free and wasn't allowed to think about what the next school year would be like for Dani or how Kylie would adjust to her second year of college. There was no time to think about the next chapter in life. She needed to focus on Lucy the locomotive, who was wide open, and Lou's job was to hold on to the reins, maintain her seat, and steer. Each time Lucy's hooves left the earth, in that euphoric moment when all four were separated from ground, Lou felt like she was flying. The hillside neared with each transition; like a macro camera lens, they were zooming in on it with each pounding of the ground. The panorama of the meadow shrank as they zoomed in.

Zack began to pour it on just as Lou knew he would. He propelled Jasper forward, a little in the lead at first, but gaining lengths with each stride. Jasper outranked Lucy all the way around. Zack had the advantage of experience and familiarity with his horse, even if the horses themselves had equal strength. It had been far too many years since Lou had ridden on a regular basis, but she gave it her best effort and truly threw all caution to the wind trying to overtake Zack and Jasper on in their race to the hills.

"Some match." She laughed as she guided Lucy up next to Zack and Jasper. "Don't think I didn't know for a second how this race would end."

Zack grinned and said, "Well, Lou, this here boy"—he patted Jasper on his neck— "has a propensity for being first. I just didn't have the heart to hold him back. It would have wrecked his day."

"You are such a liar," she said, laughing.

She looked down at Jasper, and he turned and looked up at her.

"Yeah, that's right," Lou said to Jasper. "Zack is a poker player, and he knew exactly what he was doing with the first kick to your side." She looked back at Zack. "What are we waiting for?" She motioned to the trailhead. "Final Fall isn't going to wait forever for us."

"That's what I'm talking about." He gave Jasper a little kick and walked on.

They took their time winding their way up the mountainside. They couldn't have hoped for a more stunning day. The sky was its signature blue with a few passing cottony clouds. The summer breeze was warm, but Lou could feel a hint of fall. They passed by a few groves of aspens clinging to the outside trail. Lou knew that if the trees' roots gave in, the plunge to the bottom would be something from which there would be no recovery. The higher they climbed, the sparser the vegetation grew. Gradually it took a backseat to the rocky cliffs and sheer walls that eventually opened and leveled off to the tabletop at the crest of the mountain.

They came around the last switchback on the trail and took the final length of the path to the top. They led their horses around the lonely pine tree at the summit, and the land before them leveled off and gave way to a vast opening of a long flat tabletop of rock. At the far end, there was a small grove of trees and grass. Lou and Zack dismounted and led their horses to the grassy area. They took the tack off the horses and rested the saddles up against the trees, leaving Lucy and Jasper to tend to what they did best: grazing.

"This was a great idea, Zack," she sighed. "No matter how long it's been or how old I get, I have to say that this"—she waved her arms— "is the most majestic place on the planet. Do you know how many times over the years I've dreamt about this place?" she asked.

Zack smiled and said, "I know, darlin'. I love every inch of this land my daddy gave me, but I'd have to agree, this place is special. It always has been."

They sat near the edge of the rocks and looked out across to the mountains separated by the ravine below. A hawk circled the peak.

Lou watched him and asked, "What do you suppose it would be like to be that hawk for just one day?"

Zack pondered the notion. "Lou, I think in a lot of respects I've been as carefree and peaceful as that bird has been. Look around. We're in God's yard right now."

They spent the better part of the afternoon making small talk or just being alone together. Words didn't have much of a place in their day. They took the ride so they could remember the years and the times of their lives. The mother inside of Lou imposed subtle boundaries and kept contradicting her efforts to "go for it" with "don't be reckless." And Lou refused to consider her caution a bad thing; it was who she had become. Gone were the days of jumping off a cliff into the waters below without a care of whether she would land in two feet of water or an endless abyss with no bottom at all. Her brain wasn't wired like that anymore. Back when it had been, all that mattered was the invitation to jump and the adventure it would be; her innocence and youth had made her invincible and assured her before she landed that everything would be fine at the bottom. Motherhood and time had slowly whittled away at spontaneity. Lou told herself that whittling away was what happened with maturity. She had no regrets. She just needed to keep believing her life was good.

As for Dani, Lou knew her daughter would have plenty of bumps and turns ahead, but those roads weren't here yet. Besides, she didn't want to try to predict the future. This summer had taught her patience. She learned that it was never too late to be the person she was meant to become. She finally recognized that she didn't have to keep chasing after Dani to find her. Zack and Tessa opened their hearts and their home to Dani and Lou because that had been what they believed was the right thing to do, and Lou understood that. There were not expectations or stipulations tied to the situation. All Lou had to do was get there, and she had. The rest was up to God, and it had been.

"I can't believe we're leaving the day after tomorrow," Lou sighed.

"Now let's not go down that road just yet."

"I know."

"Yeah," he sighed, "I can't believe it's come and gone so fast. You know, I'm going to miss you two. I think about that daughter of yours—both daughters, actually—and it just warms my heart to see the next generation of you growing up. The world is a better place because of it, Lou."

She could feel the tears in her eyes. "Don't, Zack," she whispered.

"Don't what? Tell you that I think if Tessa and I could have, we would have ordered up one of you for a daughter of our own?"

That was all she needed to hear. She didn't care that the tears were falling down her cheeks. "Zack, we're going to see you both again over the holidays. It's not like we're saying good-bye for another twenty years," she assured him.

"Hell, I know that. I just wish time wouldn't go by so damn fast. Have you noticed the older you get, the shorter the years get?"

She reached up and wiped her tears. "Yes, I have. My god, I look at Kylie and Dani—especially Dani—and there are times when I feel like I'm having a panic attack they've grown so quickly. I think one of the most important things I've learned by coming out here this summer is that my girls aren't babies anymore." She sighed. "Dani has been the best teacher for that. I spent so much time trying to keep her locked up in my arms that I wonder sometimes if I wasn't the instigator in some of her shenanigans."

She looked at Zack and smiled. "I'm actually looking forward to her starting school. Last year, I was scared shitless around this time."

"Yeah, well, I'm glad Tessa and I were part of that village it takes to raise your kid." He pushed himself up and stretched.

The sun was making its way across the sky, setting the stage for another day's end. Zack looked up toward the peak where the hawk had been circling most of the day.

"Looks like Henry must have gone home for dinner."

"Hmmm?" She was confused. "Who's Henry?"

He grinned. "That hawk who was banking up there most of the afternoon."

"Oh." She smiled.

"C'mon, Lou, we should think about heading out. The days aren't quite as long as they were a few weeks ago. I don't want to be on the trail

236

once it's dark. Besides, there's a new moon tonight, which means we won't have much light."

43

Later that night after everyone had gone to bed, Lou lay awake in her bed tossing and turning. She reached over and turned on the light and looked at the clock.

"Great," she mumbled. "One o'clock."

She turned the light back off, fluffed her pillow, and scooted a little farther down under the covers as she pulled them up close under her chin. After another ten minutes, she threw the covers back and climbed out of bed. She quietly walked downstairs and out onto the porch. The night was cold and clear. The sky was swept with stars. She sat down on the swing at the end of the porch and spread a throw blanket over her lap. She reached out with one of her legs to the railing, gave herself a gentle push, and tucked her legs up underneath her. She laid her head against the back of the swing and relaxed into the gentle motion. Except for the endless dusting of stars in the heavens, the night was dark as coal. She heard a noise coming from the front paddock and squinted. Once her eyes adjusted to the absence of light, she could see a faint outline of Pearl standing by the fence. She listened a little closer and could hear her sweet and periodic nickers and ruffles.

"Sorry, girl," she whispered. "I don't have any treats."

Pearl stood quietly by the fence for another moment in hopes that Lou would change her mind and conjure up some treats. After a little while longer, the horse realized that wasn't going to happen, turned slowly, and sauntered away toward the far end of the paddock.

The swing had stopped. She untucked one of her legs and gave herself another push. She settled back under the blanket and let out another long breath. She rested her head back and closed her eyes. As soon as she was settled, her mind began to race. She went back to the first day they arrived at the ranch and remembered her extremely angry child. She chuckled at the memory.

"Lord, it's amazing we made it here," she whispered into the night.

The screen door creaked, which startled her. She couldn't make out who had just come out.

"Mom?" Dani whispered.

"Hey, Punk, what are you doing up so late?"

"I don't know. I guess I couldn't sleep. Kylie went to bed a while ago. I was reading, and I thought I heard something, but was afraid to get out of bed."

She walked over to her mom and climbed up onto the swing next to her.

Lou scooted over and opened the blanket.

"Come snuggle up next to me, and I'll cover you up," she offered.

Dani tucked herself in next to Lou and rested her head on her shoulder. Lou wrapped her arm around her daughter and pulled the cover back over the two of them with her free hand. She reached up and smoothed the hair back off Dani's forehead, and Dani flinched a little.

"Sorry." Lou quickly took her hand away. "I forgot I wasn't supposed to touch your hair."

"It's okay," she sighed. "I don't care if you do that."

"What's up?"

"I already told you. I thought I heard something, and when I heard the door open down here, I thought maybe it was you or Zack or somebody. I got out of bed and went down to your room, and when I saw you weren't there, I figured it was you. I came out here to see what you were doing," Dani explained.

"I couldn't sleep either." Lou sighed. "Look at the sky."

"It's so dark tonight. The stars look cool."

"Yes, they do, sweetheart."

"It'll be weird when we get back home."

"How so?"

"I don't know. It's just that I like it here."

"I do too."

Lou slid her leg out from underneath her and gave another push off the rail to move the swing.

"I mean, I'm totally excited to see all my friends, but I'm sad we're leaving here."

"Yeah?" Lou thought about this. "Well you know we're all going to come out again next summer."

"But for how long?"

"Oh, I suppose we could stay for a couple of weeks, maybe three."

239

"That just seems like it's so far away from now. I mean, school hasn't even started, and then we have to go through winter and spring before we even get to summer again."

"I know it seems like a long time, but think about it as something to look forward to, Punk. You'll have all kinds of things to keep you busy through the school year. Once that's over, we can head out here right after you get out of school if you want. Kylie will already be home from college, and Daddy can probably set things up in advance with the business so we can all come out together."

"Maybe."

"Dani?" Lou hesitated.

"Yeah?"

"I'm glad we came here this summer. I know I haven't—"

"Me too, Mom."

"What I was trying to say is I know I haven't told you this enough this summer, but I'm so proud of you for what you've done." She stroked her daughter's head. "I mean it. You've really made some great strides toward improving your attitude and—"

"Mom, I don't want a lecture," Dani warned.

"I'm not going to lecture you. I promise. I just want you to know that when I dropped your dad off at the airport the other day, he even said he sees a wonderful improvement in how you're behaving. We're proud of you Dani, very proud."

Lou laid her head back against the swing and listened to the night bugs. Dani let out a deep sigh and relaxed into her mom's shoulder. The porch door creaked again, which caused them to jump. Kylie came tiptoeing toward them and climbed into the chair next to the swing.

"What are you guys doing out here? It's freezing," she said and shivered.

Lou giggled and said, "At this point, if we hang out a little longer, I'm sure Tessa and Zack will be down shortly to join us."

Kylie ignored her comment. "Is there another blanket?"

Lou sat up, slipped her bathrobe off, and handed it to her.

"Here. Put this on."

She sat back and pulled the blanket back up over her and Dani.

"Thanks, Mom. It's still warm from you."

She wrapped the robe around her a little tighter.

"I thought you were sleeping," Dani said.

"I was. I got up to use the bathroom, and I thought I heard something. I went down to your room, and your light was on, but you weren't there. I went back to Mom's room, and when I saw she wasn't in her room either, I thought maybe you guys were down in the kitchen or something." Kylie looked up at the sky. "A million stars are out tonight," she exclaimed.

"Right," Dani agreed. "I was telling Mom it would be weird to go back home. The sky doesn't look like this there."

"No kidding. I think the brightest lights you see in the sky by our house are the ones coming from the mall," Kylie said, laughing. "Zack and Tessa are so lucky. This place is amazing."

"I was telling Dani it's going to be fun for all of us to come back out together next summer. You know, Zack was being sincere when he made the offer for you to come out and work here for the summer if you decide not to go back up to New York," Lou reminded her.

"Yeah, I know. It's cool to have this place as an option. I mean, it's a lot different because it definitely isn't set up like the Center, but it does have horses," she said, considering her options out loud. "Besides, maybe I could learn a lot of stuff from Zack about how he runs his business." She reached her leg out to Dani and nudged her with her toes. "Hey, Dani, how cool would it be to have a place like this to run our lesson programs some day?"

"Oh my god, it would be awesome. We'll probably get lost when we take the kids on trail rides." She giggled.

"Totally," Kylie agreed.

Lou sat quietly and listened to her girls discuss the future. They talked about where they would hold lessons and who would direct and what trails they would take the children on. She thought about a time long ago when she was young and had her whole life ahead of her. She remembered the first time she had ventured away from her own home. Life had been so simple. Taking risks had been easy. She shifted gears and thought about the births of her girls and the many sleepless nights she and Jake endured. She savored her here and now of the moment and secured it safely in her memory, not just for the drive back to Virginia,

241

but forever. Her girls were growing up, and after this summer, she would leave Echo Ranch, knowing she'd completed a very important circle in life. The greater gift for Lou, however, was belief that Dani had managed a big step in one of her own life circles. Lou had faith Dani was now equipped to take on the tenth grade.

Lou slipped her arm out from around Dani and sat forward.

"Okay, you two, I think we should all go back to bed and see if we can get some sleep." She stood and stretched.

Dani let out a big yawn and stood.

"Yeah, I'm pretty tired." She turned to Kylie. "Hey. Do you want to sleep over in my room tonight?"

Kylie thought about this and smiled. "Sure! Let's go."

They walked to the door, and Kylie turned back to Lou.

"Are you coming, Mom?"

"Yeah. You two go on. I'll be up in a minute."

"See you inside."

Lou watched her girls disappear back into the house, and she walked over to the porch rail. She leaned on it and looked up to the sky.

"Like I was saying, Lord," she said. "Thank you. Thank you for saving our family this summer."

She blew a kiss toward the sky, turned, and walked back to the door. It wasn't going to be easy to say good-bye to Echo Ranch. The big difference between then and now was the peace she had knowing another twenty years wouldn't pass before she'd be back.

44

The final days flew by. As much as Lou wanted to prolong their departure, the reality was that time refused to stand still. She found herself spending more time down at the barns with Zack and the girls. When Dani was working Poet, Lou liked to watch for a little while then take the Gator back up to the house while Dani and Kylie squared him away so she could help Tessa with dinner. Thursday night, just like the anticipation of the day she pulled in under the archway, she felt a familiar tug deep down inside, a tie to Echo Ranch that she couldn't explain with words, but felt nonetheless. They would be leaving in the morning, which made her heart heavy. She followed the girls upstairs after dinner to begin the process of packing up their things.

Lou headed for her room and grabbed the suitcases out of her closet. She set them on the bed, opened them up, and began to pack her clothes from the dresser. She continued with the items in the closet. She was concentrating on packing because she didn't want to think about the next day. Zack had gone back down to the barn after dinner. She had noticed he had done that the night before as well and hadn't come back up to the house until after they had all gone to bed. She knew he was having a tough time coming to terms with the fact that they were leaving in the morning, and he never had been one to show much emotion, especially sadness.

Tessa, on the other hand, had no problem sharing just how very much she was going to miss them. They had cried together over the past couple days, and, in a way, the tears seemed to wash away some of the sadness and leave room for the beautiful memories they had all shared that summer at Echo Ranch.

Friday morning, they got up early and went down to the barn. Lou, Tessa, and Zack stood in the barn doorway and watched the girls run across the paddock. Lucy and Bull trotted behind them as if they were playing a game of follow-the-leader.

"Look at those two." Zack shook his head. "I sure will miss you guys."

"Zack, please don't start," Lou said. "It's already bad enough. I'll probably cry the whole way to the Kansas border. I just want to savor this moment without tears."

She looked up at him and could already feel the tears stinging her eyes. Tessa reached her arm around Lou's waist, and Lou put hers around Tessa's shoulder. They watched Dani lead Poet back toward them. Kylie followed on his other side. They wore bright smiles, and Dani's ponytail swished back and forth behind her. Lou remembered the first night they had gotten to the ranch and Zack informed her that her baby girl was going to train a three-year-old horse. Watching her two teenagers coming toward her now made her feel like her heart might burst with pride.

Poet started out as a wild child, and he had gladly welcomed his rebellious teenager counterpart in Dani, Lou thought. Together, they had forged through their adolescent behaviors and secured a bond that no matter how much time or distance passed, no force would ever break it. Sadness washed over Lou when she thought about the moment when her daughter would have to say good-bye and hand the lead line over to Zack.

"He looks good, Dani," Zack said, praising her.

The girls led Poet to the gate and walked him through to the barn doorway.

"Zack, do you think it would be okay if Kylie and I groom him down before we leave?" Dani asked.

Lou saw the look in Zack's eye; his heart was aching, both with love for the girls and with sadness for their departure.

"I think that's a great idea. Why don't you take him in and put him on the cross ties? I've got something to take care of in the office with your momma." He turned to Tessa, "Honey, why don't you go with the girls?"

"Okay, dear." She turned to the girls and said, "C'mon, girls, I'll help you."

Lou followed Zack back to his office and sat in the chair across from his desk. "What's up?" she asked.

He sat down at his desk, reached into the drawer, and took the envelope out. He handed it across the desk to her.

"I want you to take this with you, but don't open it until I say you can," he said.

Lou took the envelope. Zack had written specific instructions on the outside: "Don't open until I tell you to."

She looked back at him and nervously asked, "What is this?"

244

"It's a letter."

"I know that, but what kind of letter?"

"The kind you read." He leaned back in his chair and crossed his arms.

"Zack, you're not making any sense. Is everything all right?"

"Of course it is, woman," he said sharply. "It's just a little something I wrote, and I don't want you reading it until I say you can read it. Now just put that in your purse and forget about it for now. When Tessa and I come out for Christmas, maybe I'll let you read it then."

Lou searched his face for a sign—any sign of what was contained in the letter—but couldn't get a read. "You're sure everything is all right?" she asked again.

"Yes, now just put the damn thing in your purse and forget about it for now."

"All right, you don't have to get huffy." She shook her head and stuffed the envelope in her purse.

They sat in awkward silence for a moment, and Zack said, "Lou, don't go getting yourself all worked up about nothing. It's just a letter," he said, softening the tone of his voice.

"Okay, Zack, if you say so."

Kylie and Tessa came into the office.

"Hey, Zack," Kylie said. "Dani wants to know if we should turn Poet back out."

"Yeah, she can do that." He stood and came around his desk. "Hold on a second, I'm coming right behind you." He turned back to Lou. She was still sitting in her chair looking down at her purse. "Are you coming, Lou?"

She looked up at him. "Yes."

45

They walked back to Dani. She had released Poet from the cross ties and was holding on to his lead line. She stood close to him and gently stroked his neck. She was whispering instructions to him. Periodically, he'd lower his head to her shoulder.

"Remember," Dani said. "I'm coming back next summer, and you have to promise to be a good boy so Zack doesn't call you a knothead anymore."

Poet bobbed his head up and down and pawed at the ground.

"That'll be the day," Zack said, chuckling.

Dani smiled at Zack and turned to lead Poet out of the barn. Zack walked up alongside her, and together they continued toward the pasture beyond the round pen. Lou took Kylie's hand, and they followed behind. They stopped by the round pen with Tessa and watched Zack and Dani walk on toward the pasture.

When they got into the pasture, Zack put his hand on Dani's shoulders.

"Now listen to me, Dani. This boy will miss you just as much as you miss him. You're in each other's blood now," he said, "and I'd venture to guess that's been just about how it's been since the first day you two met. I want you to say a proper good-bye to him and not get all weepy-eyed on him. Do you think you can do that?"

Dani looked up at Zack and tried to put on a brave face. Lou could see that Dani was fighting back her tears because it was important to her to make Zack proud. She reached up to her eyes and brushed her forearm across them.

She swallowed hard and said, "I can do this, Zack." She took a deep breath and turned to Poet. "Okay, boy. I have to go now," she said, her voice cracking as she began to cry, "but I want you to know I love you very much. I had the best summer ever with you, and I can't wait to come back and see you. I want you to work real hard for Bobby." She reached up and tickled Poet's nose. "And be good."

She reached her arms around Poet's neck and squeezed hard. She held on for a few moments more and slowly let go. She took a couple of steps back, and Poet let out a deep sigh. He looked down at her and then popped his head up and cocked it slightly to the right, pitching his ears forward. He looked back down at her, and she smiled.

"It's okay," she whispered. "I'll think about you every day until I come back. Now go on. It's time to go."

Poet bent his head down to her and tried to nibble her shirt. She giggled and pulled back. "I told you, don't eat my clothes."

She gently pushed his head away and took another step back. She clucked and clapped her hands, and Poet took a couple of steps back. He turned and began to walk away slowly. He eased into a trot and stopped. He looked back at Dani, lifted his head high, let out a long whinny, and pawed at the ground. He trotted a few more steps and broke into a faster pace, then, with graceful ease, he transitioned into a beautiful canter and moments later into a gallop. He kicked out a few times gaining momentum the further down the south pasture he traveled. He didn't look back.

Dani held her breath and watched her boy grow smaller on the horizon. She could feel the tears running down her face and didn't care. She was watching a part of her leave, and the thought of waking up tomorrow and the next day, knowing he wasn't going to be with her, was something she didn't want to think about right then. She just wanted to watch him, remember every day of the summer, and look forward to the next time they'd be together.

Zack put his arm around her shoulder, and they walked back to the barn.

"C'mon, Dani, there's something I left in the office that I want you to have."

They all walked back into the barn and stopped in the office. Zack picked a package up off his desk and handed it to her. She looked up at him.

"Well go on, open it up," he said, smiling.

Dani tore the brown wrapping off the package. Inside was a photo of Poet and Dani. She looked at it, spun around, and looked at her sister. "No way!" she exclaimed. "This is from the other day when we went on the trail ride."

Dani looked back down at the picture in her hands. She was sitting proud and tall on Poet. Kylie had taken the picture of the two of them.

247

Dani remembered the exact moment. She had just finished cantering him for the first time outside the ring, and he responded perfectly to her every command. She remembered being scared when they first started out because a part of her had been apprehensive as to what she would do if he took off with her. There were no fences to stop him from going, and she remembered deciding that she didn't care because she trusted him. When they stopped, Dani spun around, and in that flash of a second, Kylie snapped the photo. Poet looked as though he had posed for the picture, grand and erect with his head slightly cocked to the right and ears pitched perfectly forward. Dani had a beautiful smile, reflecting her feelings of love for Poet that resonated through the photo.

She walked over to her sister and threw her arms around her. "Thanks, Kylie, this is great. I'll put this on my desk when we get home."

"I'm glad you like it. I thought it was an awesome shot of you guys," Kylie said.

Lou cleared her throat and the girls looked at her. "C'mon, girls, it's time to hit the road. We've got a long drive ahead of us."

She turned to Tessa and wrapped her arms around her then buried her head in Tessa's shoulder and in a muffled voice said, "Words escape me for the millions of ways I want to thank you for what you've done this summer, Tessa."

"I know, dear, I know," Tessa said through tears as she comforted Lou. "Promise me you'll be safe, and don't push the drive. Call me when you stop tonight to let us know you're all right."

Next, Lou walked over to Zack, folded her arms around him, and began to cry. "I'm going to miss you so much, Zack."

"Me too." He gently released her and turned to Kylie. He held his arms out.

Kylie gave him a big hug. He reminded her about next summer: "Now remember, you have a place to come if you decide you don't want to go back to New York next year. I mean it."

"Thanks, Zack, I'll definitely consider it."

He let her go and looked over at Dani. She was looking down and kicking at the dirt with the toe of her boot.

"Well you better come over here and give me a hug," he demanded.

She looked up, ran to him and threw her arms around his neck and buried her head into his chest. Zack squeezed her and told her to remember the ranch and all the good times, but most of all, remember Poet. She promised she would. She held onto him tightly, and after another moment, Zack gently pulled her arms away. She reached up on tiptoe and gave him a kiss on his cheek. She backed away and headed out of the barn toward the car. Lou and Kylie followed.

46

Once they were situated in the car, Lou looked back at Zack, and Tessa and thought, not for the first or last time, that they were two of the most beautiful and important people in her life. They had been a huge part of her younger life, and she was having trouble accepting the fact she was saying good-bye again. She put her hand to her mouth and blew them a kiss. She settled her hands on the steering wheel as she turned to look over her shoulder to back the car around. She put the car in gear, looked in her rearview mirror, and slowly started to pull away. Zack and Tessa were standing in the doorway arm in arm, waving.

She vowed to hold this image close to her heart as she extended her arm out the window and waved back. She gave the horn a toot, and they began their last climb back up the road to the house. They followed the curve around the final bend beyond the house and drove down the straightaway to that magnificent entry arch, the last piece of Echo Ranch ground they would cross before leaving.

She couldn't bear to look back and felt deeply sad to look forward. She let the tears roll down her face. When she got to the main gate, she stopped to read the welcome message below the proud words: Echo Ranch, Jeremiah 29:11 "For I know the plans I have for you," declares the Lord, "plans to prosper you and not to harm you, plans to give you hope and a future…"

She remembered the moment when she and Jake had decided she would bring Dani here. She thought about the beginning of summer and passing beneath the arch then. Although at that time she had believed she was headed in the direction of hope, she hadn't known if she would find it. As she turned onto the highway, she had the comfort of knowing they had all found their gift of hope at Echo Ranch that summer.

She settled into her seat and smiled because she was leaving with many treasured memories of the strength she had developed over the summer. Most importantly, Lou had discovered hope, and she knew that it would stay with them forever.

47

Four days later, they pulled into the driveway of their Northern Virginia home. In the final days before school began, Lou busied herself with getting the house back in order. She plunged herself into countless hours of cleaning to avoid thinking about Echo Ranch. She took the girls shopping as she prepared them for school. The weekend before college classes started for Kylie, the whole family followed her down to South Carolina. They spent some time getting her settled into the dorm, had dinners, and toured the campus. The following Tuesday, Dani began her tenth-grade year. Surprisingly, Lou and Jake were looking forward to her year ahead.

Lou had noticed since they had returned that Chelsea hadn't been around much. She wanted to ask Dani why this was the case, but instinct told her to leave it alone. She secretly embraced the notion that perhaps Dani had begun to distance herself from Chelsea, and if this was the case, the last thing Lou wanted to do was encourage a rekindling of that relationship. She simply didn't trust Chelsea. Too many incidents over the past years had made the likelihood of that changing very slim.

Dani was different. She had developed an element of maturity that had not been there before the summer. Granted, she still managed an occasional spiral into a vortex of anger when she was told no, but she was learning to accept it without digging in and declaring full-fledged war with her parents. Once-familiar faces had started coming back to the Croft house, girls Lou hadn't seen since Dani had been in middle school. Lou could see the subtleties of fall in and around the neighborhood. The leaves on the trees had already begun their color change, and others had already fallen to the ground.

School was officially back in session, and with it came the hustle and bustle of the constant demands of transporting Dani from one activity to the next and frequent trips to the post office to send care packages to Kylie. The house became quiet on the weekends with Dani either at a sleepover or cheer practice. The difference between the ninth-grade Dani and this tenth-grade Dani was more than remarkable Thanksgiving came, and a light dusting of snow accompanied it. Lou always welcomed the first snow of the year. It breathed beauty onto the stark and naked trees and set the stage for the excitement and anticipation of the holidays.

48

Kylie had gone back to school shortly after Thanksgiving for exams and, with the full load she was taking, she would need every available moment to study and prepare. In a few short weeks, she would be back for Christmas and winter break. Christmas that year promised to be particularly special because Zack and Tessa would be with them. Dani and Zack had become faithful pen pals. He was religious in sending Dani current photos of and updates on Poet.

The Saturday evening after Thanksgiving, Lou and Jake had come back from the movies around ten o'clock. Dani was spending the night at a friend's house. It had been a long day, and after the buzz of the holiday, they decided to call it a night. They were lying in bed, reading, when the phone rang. Lou shot Jake a worried look for fear something had happened with one of the girls.

He picked up the phone. "Hello?" He listened for a moment and looked over at Lou. "Sure, Tessa. She's right here."

"It's Tessa," he whispered and handed Lou the phone.

Lou took the phone and placed it against her ear, "Tessa? How are you? Is everything—"

She gasped and put her hand to her heart. Jake snapped his book closed and reached for her.

"No," she moaned.

Jake grabbed for his wife and, at the same time, reached to pick up the phone up.

"Tessa? Tessa, this is Jake. What's the matter?"

After listening to Tessa, Jake handed the phone back to Lou, who took it. Tessa told Lou, again, that Zack was gone. Lou listened in disbelief and tried to focus on what she was hearing. Tessa said that Zack had been late coming up to the house for dinner, and after nearly an hour, she had decided to go down to the barn to see if everything was all right. When she had parked the Gator, and walked into the barn, she knew something was wrong because Bobby was standing in the doorway to the office. Bobby had tried to stop her from going into the office. She pushed past him and could see her husband slumped in his chair, his head down on the desk. Once Tessa had realized Zack wasn't moving, Bobby told her he had just found him and had already called 911.

Lou could imagine Tessa running to her husband's limp body and shaking him, calling his name over and over. After several failed attempts to revive him, she would have turned to Bobby and crumpled into his arms and wept.

Lou finished the call and promised to call Tessa back in the morning to discuss arrangements.

"Oh, Lou, I'm so sorry," Jake said, comforting her. "I don't know what else to say, honey. I don't know there's anything I can say."

Lou pushed away and sat up. She smoothed the bed covers around her and wiped at the tears that refused to stop falling. "Oh, Jake," she cried. "What's going to happen now? How are we going to tell the girls? What is—"

She stopped and looked at Jake.

"What are we going to tell Dani?" she said, her lip quivering, and she started to cry harder.

They sat in their bed, holding each other without speaking. Lou thought about the glorious summer they had experienced and how blessed the reunion had been.

"Oh, my God, the letter," Lou whispered. "The letter, Jake. Zack gave me a letter right before we left. He told me I couldn't open it. He told me—" She broke down and began crying again. She sat down at the foot of the bed and wept.

She went down to the office in the basement and pulled the top drawer of her desk out. Resting on top of a couple of folders was the letter. She picked it up and read the message on its outside: "Don't open until I tell you to." She placed it against her heart and looked up at the ceiling. She knew now was the time to read it. She turned it over and tore the seal open. She sat down in her chair and unfolded its pages. When she read the first line, she had to take a moment because the reality was sinking in that Zack was gone. She dabbed at the tears in her eyes and read.

49

Dear Lou,

Well I suppose you've opened this letter because it's the right time to do so. I'm sitting in my office down at the barn, and I just finished turning Jasper out. You and my girls haven't even left yet, but I know that time is coming soon enough. I feel like I've earned the right to call them my girls because they stole a good portion of my heart, and I know they're going to take some of it back home with them once they've gone.

Anyway, as cornball as this may sound, the place just isn't going to be the same for Tessa and me in the days to come. See, Tessa and I talked about having kids on a lot of occasions over the years, and we'd always come back to the same conclusion. How in the world would we possibly be able to give them the time and attention they would require? How could we juggle the devotion we have toward our four-legged kids and this ranch if we added real kids to the mix?

We'd think about that for a couple of months, and I'd go to an auction, sometimes alone, and other times with Tessa. Invariably, I'd end up coming home with at least one new horse, but usually more than one. And then the months would trickle into another year, and the notion of kids would go on the back burner until we finally arrived at that fork in the road. We knew we weren't going to have kids, but we were complete and at peace with our decision and happy with what we already had.

I'm going to take a ride up to Final Fall after you leave. Jasper and I are going to hang out on the tabletop for a while. I can already feel the change of seasons but like to feel it from up there. Remember those times? I always liked this time of the year the best—summer to fall. I'll sit up there for a while and think about the amazing gifts I've had in my lifetime, both spiritually as well as human interactions. And then I'll feel a tear or two in my eyes when I think about you guys. I'll think about that first day you and Dani got to the ranch and saw you standing in the doorway of the barn while Buster tried to shoe that knothead Jasper.

Lou chuckled. There was no way Zack thought that horse was a knothead. *He loved him too much to really believe that,* Lou thought to herself. She looked back down at the letter and continued to read.

Seeing you again after so many years was one of the gifts in my life that makes a lot of the rest of them pale in comparison. Now, Lou, there's something I've got to tell you, and it's real important that you pay attention. See, I think my beautiful Tessa is still here because she's most likely the one who told you to read this. Pay attention because everything will be all right.

About a month after you and Dani got to the ranch, I went into town to meet with my attorneys to take care of some important business. Tessa and I had talked a lot about this over the years. In a divine sort of way, however, when you called with your rescue mission for Dani and eventually got here, we knew that's what we wanted to do for sure. Since we don't have kids, we started thinking a lot about what would happen to Echo Ranch once we'd gone.

God truly is almighty and powerful, Lou. I believe he sent you and Dani to us. And what's more, I believe he painted your future destiny to be with horses and wide-open spaces by giving you the blessings of your two beautiful girls.

I had my attorneys draw up some real specific plans for Echo Ranch once I was gone. Like I said, no matter if Tessa is still there or not is how the rest plays out. The key to the entire plan is you, Jake, and the girls. I'm giving you my version, which isn't spelled out over a ridiculous number of pages. That's what I pay the attorneys for, so you're going to be getting a lot of pages from them. The simple version is that it's yours now.

She gasped and dropped the letter. Her mind was reeling over what she'd just read. She started rocking back and forth in her chair and was trying to process what the letter meant. She took a deep breath, trying to compose herself. Her hands shook as she reached for the letter, picked it up, and continued to read.

There's a but, and it's real important. It has to do with Tessa. If my lady is still alive, she's still the boss of everything at Echo Ranch, but she's going to need your help and your family's help as well. I don't expect you to finish reading this letter and get on the next plane to Colorado, but what I do expect is that you get your affairs in order and get here soon. She needs a sense of family around her. You'll never know just how very much you and your family gave that to her this summer.

She set the letter in her lap. Chills were running up and down her spine. She looked to the ceiling, and somehow, she felt he was there with her. She looked back down at the letter and continued to read.

I have faith everything will work out as it should.

Now I know this is a lot to digest in one sitting. Spend some time talking about it with your family and make your decision together. I just want you to know that Tessa and I put a lot of thought into how this day was going to play out. Remember, if she's still down there and I'm not, the most important thing I wanted for her was to make sure she'd be taken care of the way she was meant to before it's her time to come with me. Once she's here, I got that covered.

There's one last thing you need to know because I think you still question it. You're a good mom, Lou. Actually, you're a great mom, and as for those girls of yours, well words just cannot find their way from this pen to paper to describe just how fantastic I think they are. They're great kids, and while Kylie is well on her way, Dani isn't all too far behind in her footsteps. I think you know that now, but I just wanted you to hear it from me as an added assurance.

So dry your eyes. It's getting late, and I've got work to do. Just because I'm not there anymore doesn't mean there's still not a lot of work to be done. I love you more than the mountains and streams I wandered or the fields and horses I tended to throughout my days. Don't you worry, Lou, our paths will cross again, of this I'm certain. That's God's plan, darling, simple as that. Take good care of you and your family and make sure my precious Tessa is part of that plan.

A big hug and lots of love,
Zachariah Samuel Calhoun...Zack

She leaned forward in her chair and gently placed the letter down on her desk. She breathed in deeply and let her breath out slowly. She ran her fingers through her hair and sat back in her chair and closed her eyes. She thought about Zack and Echo Ranch and how difficult the memories would be now that he was gone. She was afraid to open her eyes for fear her tears would fall harder and faster and longer, and she wouldn't know how to stop them once they got started. She thought about the entrance to the ranch and Jeremiah 29:11 and how everything beyond that gate was now at the hands of the Croft family. She shuddered and wondered how they would ever carry on the legacy.

"Lou?" Jake was standing in the doorway.

Lou jumped out of her chair and ran into his arms. Sobs shook her body, and Jake quietly held her. He didn't say a word, which was exactly what she wanted. He knew she was strong enough to handle the challenges ahead. She was the glue that kept their family together, and this current turn in their road was something she would manage to navigate, and, in the end, she would come out stronger.

He gently unfolded his arms, placed his hands on her shoulders, and looked into her eyes. "Come sit down." he said, guiding her back to her chair. He looked down at the letter and back at Lou.

"Is that the letter you were talking about?" he asked.

Words wouldn't come. Lou nodded her head. She reached for the letter and, without looking at him, held it out to him.

He took it, sat down in the chair next to her, and read it. Lou knew he had gotten to the part about the ranch being theirs when he caught his breath. He looked at his wife, and a whole new round of tears came spilling down her cheeks. He finished the letter and set it back on the desk. He scooted his chair closer to her and picked up her hand and squeezed it. They sat side by side in the quiet confines of the office well into the early hours of morning. The talked about how they would break the news to the girls and decided they would wait until Kylie finished her exams before they told her.

****

Lou flew out to Colorado for the funeral. They decided she would go by herself. They didn't want to expose the girls to such sadness right before Christmas. It was heartbreaking enough to explain why Zack and Tessa wouldn't be joining them for the holidays.

The service was tender and beautiful. Tessa gave the eulogy for her beloved Zack. Her sweet voice drifted across the quiet winter day in the valley where the Calhoun family plot had been established many years before. Bobby had ridden Jasper out to the memorial site, and

257

quietly they stood side by side as the many friends and neighbors passed by Zack's grave.

Lou spent a few more days beyond the service with Tessa. They talked about Zack's letter and the early days on the ranch.

The night before she left to return to Virginia, Lou could feel the presence of an ominous quiet in the house. Once the memorial and constant stream of well-wishers had subsided, Lou finally had her coveted time to visit alone with Tessa. Later that evening, Lou lit a fire and selected a bottle of wine and joined Tessa in the living room.

"How I love the quiet," Lou sighed and poured a glass of red wine for each of them.

"Thank you, dear." Tessa took a sip and set her glass on the coffee table.

They sat quietly, and when the periodic creaks and moans of a house that had stood strong through so many times insisted on breaking the silence, Lou turned to Tessa. "I think the story I loved the most that Zack often told was how Echo Ranch got its name."

Tessa looked at Lou and could see the glimmer of tears in her eyes.

"Would you tell me the story again?" Lou asked. "I think Zack would want you to."

Tessa smiled and leaned her head back against the sofa. She closed her eyes and the words soon followed.

"When I met Zack, I knew he was the one for me from the get-go. He was such a proud and strong man, but his softness contradicted that macho far more often than I think he cared to admit." Tessa chuckled and shook her head. "He courted me for a long time, and I remember the first time I met his parents. Samuel could be quite cantankerous, but he never fooled me. I believe he was a teddy bear deep down inside, too. I remember finishing dinner with Zack and his family one night years ago and we all retired to this very room.

Tessa looked toward the fire. "I seem to recall it was late fall. There was the feel of the first snow in the air. Zack and his dad were chit-chatting over some nonsense or another and the next think I knew, they were talking about how Samuel had almost lost the ranch. He leveraged everything he'd ever owned to save it. He said that was why the place was aptly name 'Echo Ranch'— "Tessa smiled over the memory. "—and he got this real serious look on his face when he said that. He said, 'this place is *Echo* Ranch because the precise meaning of an *echo* is something that is thrown out there, but no matter what, it always comes back to the person or thing who threw it out there.'

As Tessa's voice trailed off, she reached into the cuff of her blouse and took the tissue out and dabbed at the tears in her eyes. She looked at Lou and held her arms open to her.

Lou got up and walked over to Tessa. She curled up next to her and rest her head on her shoulder. They sat in each other's arms and listened to the intermittent hiss and simmer from the logs on the fire well into the night until there was nothing more than embers. Lou would be leaving in the morning, but had been waiting for this moment to tell Tessa something very important before she went up to bed.

She looked at Tessa and whispered, "I want you to know the Croft family would be honored to carry on the legacy of Echo Ranch."

Epilogue

One morning in early spring, Lou rose and pulled the bedroom curtains back. She folded her arms and looked to the sky to assess the day. The sun was already up, and the icicles hanging from the roof gutter above the window steadily dripped. She let out a deep sigh as she watched little pools form on the windowsill from the melting ice. She turned back to the bed and began to make it. She fluffed the pillows and tossed them up against the headboard. Dani came into the doorway.

"Hey, Mom, I'm leaving to catch my bus. Don't forget I have practice tonight."

"Okay, Punk."

She went back to the window when she heard the front door close and watched her daughter cut across the front lawn toward her bus stop. Dani paused and turned when she reached the sidewalk as if she knew her mom would be watching her. She saw her and gave her a brief wave and continued her trek to the bus. Lou smiled and waved back. There was a stunning cardinal perched on one of the branches of the old pine tree.

She picked up her coffee and walked to the window for a closer look. She watched him preen, then pause and start preening again. He stopped periodically, looked to his left and back to the right in jerky movements, then went *peck, peck, peck* back at his handsome body. He ruffled his feathers a few times and settled back into the solitude of his branch. The moment reminded her of the last ride she and Zack took up to Final Fall. A hawk was ever-present, circling the peaks. She smiled thinking about the moment when Zack informed her he had named the hawk Henry. She looked back at the cardinal and whispered, "I've met some of your distant relatives."

As though the bird heard her, he looked toward the window.

"They're quite handsome too. Maybe not as handsome as you, but they have their own special beauty." She sighed.

Without warning, he spread his wings and took off in flight. Lou held her breath as she watched him until he was no more than a speck in the sky. It was a sign. Lou was convinced that there were lots of signs, but this one seemed like a message from Zack. He was reminding her that he was true to his word: he was there. He needed her to know he would always be there for her.